A 500 YEAR LOVE

TK Cassidy

JSNM Ink Publishing

ISBN: 978-0-9660152-9-4

Contents

Acknowledgements

Special thanks to:

- Linda Merrick Williams for her help and memories of her beloved Panama – any mistakes are mine, but the story is much stronger with her insights
- My long time supporters, Barbara Treasure and Jennifer Rush
- My friend and additional fresh eyes, Rayda Reed • my beta readers.... the amazing Lisa Musil
- And as always, my abiding love for MSB (Dale Fleming). You are – and always will be – the best part of my life!

For more information,
Visit the author's Amazon page:
TK Cassidy Amazon Author Page

For even more information,
Visit the author's website:
TKCassidyWrites.com

When you meet your soul mate, remember that meeting was 500 years in the making. Always appreciate and be kind to one another.
The corollary – when you meet a true friend, you will be bound together through space and time for 500 years.
-Buddhist saying

2022

Bridgette Katherine Deane, Bridey to her friends and Bridey-Kate to her family, looked at the elegant business card in her hand. The warm off-white linen paper, the gold embossed lettering and, under her name, the long-coveted words "executive photographer" stared back at her. The hours she'd spent learning about the advertising business from the ground up, honing those photographic skills that made her work so identifiable, the friendships and family obligations she'd missed along the way were all reflected in those warm confident letters. She traced the elegant font one more time before leaning the card against the bottom of her bedside lamp and turning out her light to sleep.

Still smiling, she closed her eyes and tried to shake off the afterglow of the party that had celebrated her all evening. So many well-wishers, so many hugs and claps on the back for her accomplishment. The huge offices were filled with a diversity of people, only found in the advertising business. Brooks Brothers suits stood shoulder to hip with hippie wannabees and nerds of all description. This was truly an industry that needed every subset of society to create a perfect product. As usual in such a situation, Bridey wished she could be alone in the corner with her camera, unnoticed but seeing all the colors and shapes that mingled and reformed over and again. She was always far more comfortable behind the camera lens than being the center of attention.

Finally, hours later alone in her apartment, she settled down under the duvet hoping for a deep satisfying sleep. She sighed as she drifted off. But refreshing sleep didn't come as quickly as she thought. She tried to drift off but her mind wouldn't stop in one place. Just as so many nights before this one, she was led down a path of fleeting figures, of a strange yet familiar place, scents and sounds she knew but were still oddly foreign to her. For a while, she was back in the elegant ballroom from earlier that evening being greeted by smiling but disembodied faces of people, strong arms with sleeves rolled halfway up reaching for her and hands trying to capture her hands.

Then, she felt her body leap and she ended up in a lush green field, knee deep grasses waving in the breeze, the scent of fresh mown hay rippling through the air. She looked to her left and saw the familiar broad road leading out of the yard she'd dreamt of so many times. The sound of horse hooves and jingling tack filled her ears as she watched the stiffly starched backs of military men riding off to some unknown encounter with destiny. She squinted in her sleep trying to place any of them with no luck and yet she always felt she had been right here before. Then she felt a familiar shiver of fear as the leader of the parade shifted in his saddle and looked back. Even at that distance she saw his dark eyes glaring at her as if in warning and her body shuddered involuntarily again.

Then just as abruptly as she'd been pulled there, the scene changed. The smell of sea air filled her lungs mixed with the sour odor of unwashed men working on a creaking old ship and the acrid scent of pine tar used to keep the leaks closed in the multi-patched wooden hull. She felt a familiar urge to run to the edge of the ship and hang over adding to the waste being thrown overboard. She heard the wind howl through the snapping sails and felt the high waves pitch the ship sideways. She fell against the wooden mast and cried out. Fear filled her entire body as she prayed for a miracle to help her survive the storm.

Suddenly she felt strong arms, bare except for the sleeves that were rolled to the elbow, wrapped around her as someone came up behind her and pressed her tightly to the wood. She knew he whispered but his words were lost in the wind's moans. She simply sighed with relief knowing she would be safe now despite the waves that were washing over the deck.

As she was enjoying the feeling of safety, the mountains of waves were replaced by a vast jungle filled horizon. She was still soaking wet, but now the air was heavy and indolent. She could barely breathe as she walked down a long, cobbled corridor. The sounds of mosquitos and bugs filled her ears. The smell of illness reached her nose before she got to the door. She stopped and pressed her hands to her weakening stomach. Willing herself under control, she stretched out her hand toward the knob. She had to go in. There was no one else to do the job.

The door gave under her grasp and she stepped into a garden. Huge trees dripping with Spanish moss stood guard around the edge of the meadow. She listened to a child – her child – playing nearby and saw the nanny bringing in a tray of cool drinks. She felt safe in this little glen but who knew what waited for her ... just beyond.

Then finally, just as sleep overtook her, she saw the face that was in every dream, in every crowd. Silverwhite hair. Shockingly blue eyes. Deeply tanned skin. Strong arms with sleeves rolled halfway up. The man she searched for in all her pictures. The face she knew so well and didn't know at all.

He stretched out a gloved hand and breathed her name ... and she slept!

"Dear love,
What is taking you so long? I'm really looking
forward to meeting you soon. I hope I can
find you before my heart explodes from all the
heartbreaks I've experienced.
I wonder what you look like. I wonder if
we've met before. I have so many things to
say to you.
Please hurry.
Love, Me" — Anon

Two

"Look! I get it!" The exasperation in her boss's voice was clear. Bridey kept her back to him and stared out the massive twentieth floor window. Below her was everything she loved; everything she worked for. In the city, she felt alive.

The streets bustled and pulsated at any hour of the day. There was never a time when the energy was limp. All you had to do was open up and let the feeling flow over you. The hundreds of boring hours she'd spent growing up in the small rural village where the weekly changing of the church signs was the biggest regular event were far behind her here. She never wanted to go back there... ever ... for any reason.

She felt her boss's hand on her tight shoulder. "I know how much you hate leaving the city and ..." He dropped his hand with a grunt. "... I even remember once telling you I'd never send you out to the sticks again once you made management." He took a few steps away and whipped around.

"But, Bridey. It's the Markham account." His voice dropped to a whisper with a pleading note

Bridey bent her head and twisted her body around until she was looking at him like a silly dodo bird on a limb. She raised the eyebrow closest to him and said, "And....."

He threw his hands into the air and let them fall to his side. "You know she's my cornerstone. She was my first major client and seems to think she is as responsible for this firm's success as I am." He shrugged deeply and grimaced. "She's kinda right."

Bridey shook her head and stepped toward him. "Tell me."

With a visible sag of his shoulders, the man returned to the massive oak desk and seated himself. "She was in Montana or Wyoming or somewhere at some fundraising thing for wild horses when she saw this guy. According to her, he is perfect for the new cologne line she wants to put out. She wants him. She wants you to get him and shoot the project."

Bridey felt a surge of pride that this powerful woman would demand her services.

"Ok, so why do I have to go out there? Why don't we bring him here?" Bridey shook her head. "I mean, call him up, offer him loads of money and get him on a plane." "Tried that. Apparently, she and her minions tried to find him when they were there. It's a small tight-lipped community. No one would give out any info. I called all over that place looking for him. No one could tell me. He apparently has a ranch way out in the sticks."

"So let me get this straight. She tried to find him ... with no luck." Bridey lowered herself in the armless chair across the desk and placed her hands about a foot apart as if bracketing an idea on her lap. "And you tried without any luck..." She slid her hands to the left a bit and looked askance at him. He nodded in chagrin. She moved her hands to the right and continued, "And you think I can just show up out there, saunter into town and they'll throw the city keys at me?" She shook her head and threw her own hands up. As they dropped in her lap, she all but screamed, "What in the name of God's little green apples would make you think that?"

The man almost leapt across the desk! He shook his finger in her furious face. "THAT! That right there!" Bridey pressed herself into the wooden back of the chair at his surprise attack. "No big city slicker like us would ever invoke God's little green apples!"

He raced around the desk and took Bridey's hands in his. "Face it, Kid! You'll always be a small-town girl deep down inside."

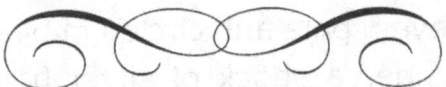

Bridey grumbled. She groused out the door all the way to her own office. She muttered and cursed under her breath for the rest of the afternoon as she made arrangements to fly out West. The secretaries and clerks parted ways for her as she left for the day. She had heard her own assistant explaining why her normally open door was closed … to everyone.

The cabbie kept glancing at her in the rearview mirror as she complained and groused under her breath. The porter who took her bags just tugged his cap instead of sticking out a hand for a tip. Even the stewardesses stepped aside as she strode down the gangway. When she found her first class seat on the only nonstop flight, the entire flight crew fawned all over her until her glares gained her the solitude she wanted. Five hours later, she was still grousing.

Then, halfway across the country, she stopped complaining. Her insides felt like she had been beaten. She shook herself all around and decided enough was enough. She could spend her days sulking and whining, or she could suck it up and get over it. She looked out the window and saw the green fields of farming country slowly slipping into miles and miles of brown sand. She snuffed and turned away from the window. The only thing she hated more than farm country was the desert.

She opened the file in her lap and gasped. The deepest blue eyes, pale and circled in black, stared out at her from under a shock of silver hair. Her insides gave a quiver as she stared at the intense eyes. Somewhere on the back of her mind she felt like she knew him. There was something about that line of his jaw and the set of his shoulders. The chest was broad tapering down to narrow hips and long legs. Then there were those muscular arms crossed over his chest; sleeves rolled up to just below the elbow. The sight of arms half exposed always sent a shiver through her. She had never heard another else mention that particular aspect of a man as being a huge turn on. Butts? Yes. Eyes? Of course. But no one had ever mentioned half naked arms as a sign of sensuality and yet her heart leapt every time. She shook her head to clear the reverie.

Come on Bridey. It's just a dream. Just your imagination.

She flipped the picture and checked the man's age. He was the same age as she was. Cord Grant. *Hmm, good name.* Her eyebrows flickered as she looked back at the picture. Handsome man. Her eyes lit on the arms again for one brief second. No wonder the wealthy Lana Markham wanted him to be the face of her product. Bridey sniffed and thought, *hell, I'd buy anything from this one myself.* ANYTHING!

The moment the plane touched down; Bridey walked down the gangway to the terminal with a renewed sense of purpose. This didn't have to take that much time. She'd simply drive to this little town, sweet talk the natives, find the man, offer him an obscene amount of money, get him to sign the contract and be back on the plane before the sun set tomorrow. She snickered under her breath and thought her boss was right – *big city folks would have no idea where to start*... but she knew exactly where to go.

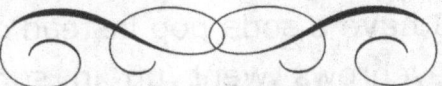

The dingy cafe was the same as any other diner in a thousand small towns. The combined smell of greasy fries burnt coffee and fermented apple pie smashed into her and memories flooded in behind. She hated that smell and breathed in through her nose in an effort to keep the gag reflex from engaging. Throwing up at the front door wouldn't endear her to the locals. She pasted her million-watt, work-the-room smile on her face and strode over the black and white checkerboard floor, nodding to anyone who looked up, and was rewarded with several cautious smiles in return. She slid into an empty fake red vinyl bench, brushing the seat off first, and grabbed a sticky menu from the metal frame under the window.

The heavy-set waitress appeared beside her with a pot of coffee in her hand. The glossy white name tag with Peggy engraved below a big red *Hello* rode above a massive décolletage. Peggy smiled as she reached for the overturned coffee cup on the table.

"Honey, you're in luck. I just made a fresh pot." She hesitated for a moment. "Unless you'd prefer something else." She regarding Bridey's clothes and hair. "Maybe you want one of those fancy lattes or expresso thingies. We don't do those here."

Bridey would have killed for a venti green tea frappe, but she waved a hand and laughed. "I got no use for that yuppie stuff either, but it's so warm out there. Could I have a soda pop instead of coffee?"

Peggy's eyebrows went up in surprise. "Sure? What kind?"

"I'm thinking something clear." Peggy nodded and left.

Soda pop, Bridey sniffed. Nobody called a soda by that unless they'd grown up in a small town. Breaking that habit had taken her months when she moved to the city. But the ruse had obviously not been wasted on the waitress. Bridey was counting on the waitress being a well-spring of information. With any luck, Peggy would be able to tell her what she needed to know.

At that moment, the tiny bell over the door tingled. All eyes turned toward the door. Bridey almost gasped as the very man she needed to find sauntered in. Like Norm from *Cheers*, he was greeted by shouts of his name.

"Cord!"

"Cord! How ya doin'?"

"Hey Cord?"

He smiled and answered each person on his way to a stool at the end of the counter. He swung a leg over the stool and casually rolled the sleeves of his shirt up to the elbows while he surveyed the row of booths. Bridey nearly choked on her soda when he rolled up those sleeves. She steadied internal roiling as his hooded eyes skimmed over her. She smiled over the edge of the icy drink Peggy'd delivered. His eyes narrowed further before he turned his attention back to Peggy.

"Hey darlin'," Peggy leaned against the counter. "What is it you're craving today?"

He reached out and took her work-worn hand in his. Lifting her fingers to his lips, he crooned, "My darling, you know what I want. You're just being cruel to me. When will you give in and leave old Charlie back there? We can run away to..."

Peggy jerked her hand away, blushing like a schoolgirl. "Now you just quit." She looked over her shoulder at the scrawny old man cooking behind the window. "One of these times he might hear you and Charlie might not think you're fooling."

"But Peggy, my love ..."

"Adam and Eve on a raft, Charlie. For my boyfriend." Charlie looked up and waved. Cord smiled and waved back. The snickering cook immediately turned back to his grill.

"See," Peggy quipped. "I told you! Insanely jealous!" Both Cord and Peggy laughed softly as the waitress turned back to her other customers.

Bridey smiled at the exchange. That was one of the few things she missed about small towns. The easy flow between people who genuinely liked each other. You just don't see much of that in the city.

Cord's gaze caught her eye. He gave a subtle shrug and turned to the local newspaper. He shook the pages out and used them as a shield to stave off any more attention. Bridey took the hint and turned her attention to the farmer's breakfast Peggy brought to her. The sunny side up eggs swam in enough grease to fry the hash browns again. Two scrawny wrinkled sausage links lay under toast that had been barely warmed in the grill. She picked up her fork and let the utensil hover over the food.

"Hard to decide where to start, isn't it?" The voice came over the top of the newsprint. "Took me a while too. I suggest that you cut off a bit of the egg and a bit of the sausage. Then add some hash browns. Pile the mess on your fork. If you chew the concoction up and then add a bite of the toast, the bread will soak up a lot of the grease and the soda will wash everything down quicker."

Bridey grimaced and proceeded to follow his instructions. As she lifted the glass to her lips and washed the food down, she saw him lift his cup to her in salute. "Well done." he stage whispered. "Couple more bites ought to get you off the hook."

"Thanks." she acknowledged. She diligently turned her attention back to the plate as Peggy set Cord's order down in front of him. Cord bestowed a brilliant smile on the waitress. "Ahhh Peggy! You outdid yourself. This looks wonderful."

Bridey peeked at his plate which looked identical to the mess on her plate only more of everything. Amazingly, he dug into the mountain of food like he hadn't eaten in a week. Peggy cleaned up the newspaper and sniffed as she walked away, smiling. Cord looked over at Bridey and waggled his eyebrows.

Bridey found herself smiling. This was one charismatic guy who knew how to work a room. A guy like him would own New York in a heartbeat. Schmoozing the right people and stroking the little people would come naturally to him. She couldn't help wondering why he'd turned Lana down, but she was going to have to find out.

Peggy appeared at her side. "Well, you didn't eat much, but you gave it a good try." She reached across and picked up the plate Bridey had pushed away. "You in town for the rodeo?"

Cord slipped off his stool and walked by. He stopped and planted a loud buzz on Peggy's cheek. "You going already, Cord?"

"Yup, I have a few errands in town. I gotta get back. Jezebel's about to drop her foal. I don't want her to be alone with her first. Add this to my tab, OK?"

"Sure, honey. Keep us posted." Cord made a grunting sound, walked down the aisle and out the door. Bridey struggled to control the urge to rush after him. With Peggy standing between her and the door, that wasn't really an option anyway. From the corner of her eye, she watched him climb into an old green pickup.

"So, what were you saying?" Peggy pulled her attention back.

Bridey started to say no but then … "Yes. I'm living in NYC now, but I haven't had a chance to see a real rodeo in a long time. I was nearby and saw a flyer at a gas station. I'm ahead of schedule so I thought I'd swing over."

"What is it you do for a livin,' Sweetie?"

Bridey smiled at the term of endearment. She was gaining ground. "I take pictures for magazines and ad agencies. Usually, I photograph scrawny models and pampered pets, but the chance to shoot some real people doing real work was just too much for me to pass up."

Peggy's grin broadened. "So, you aren't one of those city born people who just comes out here to make fun of the underprivileged folk then?"

With a wave of her hand, Bridey scoffed, "Heavens no. I was born on a chicken farm in Alabama. I'm no city kid ... besides, I clean up right good, doncha think?"

"I told Charlie not to worry. I could tell by the way you wolfed down his good cooking – even if not much, that you weren't no slicker." She turned and yelled, "You owe me ten bucks, Charlie!" Charlie waved without looking up.

"That Charlie," Peggy smiled affectionately. "Such a way with words." She started to walk away and then turned back. "Oh, and Honey, don't get any ideas about that one. No women in his life. He stays on that ranch and only comes in when he has to ... maybe once a month."

"Why?"

Peggy's eyebrows flew up. "Huh, never really thought about it. You know small towns. Everybody knows everybody's business but, if someone wants to be secretive, we try to protect them. Cord's a good one. Not a soul in town he hasn't helped or been kind too. No one will do him dirty."

"Well, I'm only here a day or two." Bridey brushed imaginary crumbs off her designer knock-off skirt. "He's cute and he does have a way about him but, believe me, he's safe from me."

"Death cannot stop true love.
All it can do is delay it for a while."
— William Goldman,
The Princess Bride (1973)

Three

Thick dust rose up from the tree-lined dirt road in front of Bridey. Following the old green truck far enough back not to be seen wasn't as easy in the country as tailing someone in the city. Hopefully, she wouldn't come on the old truck before she was ready. She suddenly broke out of the whirling dust and stopped. When she looked into her rearview mirror, she realized the grey cloud had turned to the left. She backed up and turned down the side road, driving slowly until she came out of the trees.

A breathtaking expanse laid out before her. She could see the truck rolling down the last few feet of the road into a well-manicured yard. The outbuildings and rail fences surrounded by open meadows of lush grass had been well cared for by the owner. Brown and white animal figures dotted the grassy areas. Backing up a few feet to be sure she was under cover of the trees, she maintained a clear view of the yard and watched as Cord left the vehicle. The echo of a slammed door radiated across the still valley as he walked inside.

Bridey surveyed the road once more. If she drove slowly, she'd be able to get very close to the house without being seen ... maybe even up next to the truck. Just as she was about to slip the car into gear, the door opened and Cord stepped out. Without looking up, he strode across the yard and entered the barn. A few moments later, the most beautiful horse she had ever seen burst into the corral behind the barn, followed by Cord.

The colt was clearly young and full of himself. She smiled as she watched the horse race around the circular corral, stopping only to dip his head down and kick his heels high in the air or rear up as if being attacked by an invisible enemy. The photographer in her knew she'd have to have pictures of the incredible animal.

She watched as Cord, rope coiled over his shoulder and whip in hand, calmly stood in the middle of the dirt rolling his sleeves up – those cursed sleeves again — and smiled as he watched the playing horse. Occasionally, a laugh rang out as he enjoyed the animal's antics.

With his attention riveted on the horse, Bridey slipped gears and let the car roll down the long lane, through the gate that had been left open. She rolled to a stop beside the truck, slid out and immediately stepped on a rock and twisted her ankle. She fell against the car with a hardy curse and leaned down to rub the ache. Bridey wished briefly she'd bought the great looking boots she'd seen in a shop window that morning. She glared at the stylish half boots she wore with their too-narrow-to-be-sensible heels.

"No time to worry 'bout that now," she whispered to the big red and white chicken that stood at the front of the truck pecking the ground. "These'll have to do."

She closed the front door softly and stepped to the back door. The door opened silently and she pulled the case holding her cameras. The zipper gave easily. She pulled out a large camera with a powerful lens and slipped several rolls of film into her pocket. Electronics had taken over the rest of the world but a good, highspeed camera with quality film still gave her the effect and product she knew would sell her work.

She hooked the long mesh strap over her shoulder and inspected the camera as she walked toward the barn. A few surreptitious pictures from the barn, then she'd slip into the sunlight and make herself known. Halfway down the aisle, the passage was blocked by a sturdy gate. Bridey climbed up on the lowest rail and focused her camera on the sunlight area beyond the door. Cord had lassoed the colt and was focused on trying to fit a halter over his long nose.

Every time she tried to snap a few pictures, the duo moved out of the doorway and she would have to reposition herself to see them. *This is not working,* she thought after the fourth time she shifted. *I have to get out there with them.*

She walked back to the front of the barn and stepped out into the heat. Staying as close to the wall as she could, Bridey climbed the corral fence and dropped quietly into the enclosure where she was hidden by the barn. Step by silent step, she eased to the edge of the wall and peeked around.

There in the middle of the paddock stood Cord. The big stallion stood in front of him, a rope draped loosely over his neck. Cord held the jaws of the still animal and stared into its eyes. The horse returned that gaze. The pair looked like they were carved in some sort of basalt stone. Slowly, she lifted the camera to her eye, adjusted the lens and snapped a couple of pictures. The normally quiet click of the camera echoed in the silence. Instantly, the horse pulled back as if he'd been bitten and raced off around the paddock, bucking and kicking. Cord held a rope slack rope in his hands as he whipped around and saw the woman from the diner perched on the top rail of the corral.

"What the hell are you doing?" he yelled.

"I just wanted a picture." The camera whirred as she snapped a few more shots. The horse immediately went into a more frantic panic mode.

"Get out!" He swore as he gathered up the rope. "Easy, Son. Easy!" He called across the field, but the horse wouldn't be calmed.

Oblivious of the danger and enthralled by the beauty of the animal, Bridey continued snapping shots. Each whir of the advancing film further unnerved the horse as he raced around the paddock, kicking his heels at the invisible enemy.

"Get down!" Cord screamed and raced toward Bridey. "Get down!" He reached out a gloved hand to help her off the fence and get her into a position where he could protect her from the colt.

Bridey dropped the camera from her eyes in time to realize the horse was racing around the fence in her direction. She saw Cord running toward her with his hand stretched out – the bare sinewy arms, his gloved hand – the same ones she'd seen in her dream so many times. Unnerved by the sight, she leaned back instinctively, unbalanced and fell to the hard packed dirt below, scarcely missing being kicked by the frightened animal she found so intriguing.

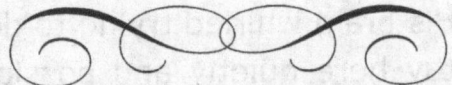

"Oh my God! NO!" Cord threw himself over the fence and knelt beside the woman. She was so still. He gathered her up in his arms and staggered to the house. Inside, he put her on the couch and went to the kitchen for a first aid kit, water and cloths to bathe her wounds.

On his way back, he realized he hadn't checked for a pulse. Seeing the woman from the diner laying in the dirt brought back the horrible memories of the day he'd found Deborah dead on the floor of his stepfather's study. This time, instead of cold flesh, his fingers met warmth, a strong pulse just below the surface. She was alive.

Cord placed a cool cloth across her forehead and checked for bleeding or broken bones. There were none. A ragged sigh of relief escaped him as Cord sank to a nearby chair and stared at her. What was he going to do now? She appeared to have fainted not just fallen from the fence. Briefly, he remembered the look of fear in her eyes as she stared at the hand he'd offered her. He looked down at his gloved hands. They were a bit dirty, but certainly not worth fainting about. He slumped back into a soft chair nearby and rubbed his forehead. Who was this person? Why was she here? This was the stuff of romance novels, or maybe in his case, horror novels. He couldn't leave her alone, but, if Edson had sent her, he couldn't risk being found either. Cord felt trapped like a wolf caught in a heavy steel clamp. His brain whirled trying to decide what to do. Did he stay here quietly and possibly die at the hands of the person who had set the trap or try to escape the metal jaws and maim himself in the process? If she was one of Edson's minions, he'd be better off to cut his losses and run.

Dammit! I'm not giving this up. I worked too hard for it. He sprang up out of the chair and paced the length of the room. He stopped next to the sofa and looked down at her once more. Cursing himself for a fool, he turned the cool cloth over on her forehead. He really had no choice but to stick around at least until she came to. Then, he'd very clearly point her to where he'd sent the rest of her kind and got back to the colt.

24

God knows how long the colt would take to settle back down.

Cord eased himself down on the other end of the overstuffed sofa. Part of him marveled at how little space she seemed to take up. He noticed the soft flame of her reddish hair, the pale white of her skin, the long slender neck, narrow shoulders, and the gentle rise of her breast. His own body responded to her fragile beauty.

Stop! His mind demanded he turn his attention away from such thoughts. He couldn't let this woman get to him. He'd sworn off women after Deborah. He never wanted to be in such a vulnerable position again. The pain was too great. He ran a nervous hand through his hair. He didn't need this. He let memories drift into his mind unchecked.

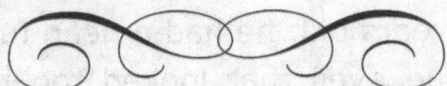

Cord was four when his loud, angry father, who had the grand illusion of being race car driver, was killed at an illegal drag race on some country back road. He wasn't even driving that day. He was just there, standing on the sidelines to watch the competition. Cord couldn't remember his mother ever crying, though he knew she must have, after his father died. He did remember mornings when her eyes were red and swollen from lack of sleep before the accident. To Cord, they seemed to have loud fights with much yelling and screaming almost every night. Cord remembered waking in the night to muffled cries coming through his closed door.

He also remembered moving into the mansion a year later. His five-year-old mind took in the flowing driveway lined with huge trees and paved with cobblestones swept clean of debris. The front of the house with enormous double doors still awed him. His mother held his hand tightly, nearly dragging him behind her to a side door, a much smaller, more ordinary opening. A warm, cozy kitchen lay just beyond the door. Cord felt at home immediately. Inside, his mother stood with her hands on her hips and surveyed the area.

"Momma?" He looked up at her in question and concern. "Momma, is this the place?"

She turned and looked down at her too-serious child. At five years old, he had a head full of pale hair and silver, blue eyes that looked too much like his father's. He was going to be a definite lady-killer when he grew up. That such a beautiful gentle child came from the hurricane relationship between his parents never failed to amaze her. She vowed again to nurture the gentleness in him and make sure he never grew up to follow the violent footsteps of his father.

Her eyes softened as she knelt in front of him. "This is where we're going to live now. I'll show you our rooms in just a moment." She stood and walked over to a chair. When she sat, she pulled him into her lap. For a moment, she cuddled him and loved him like she hadn't done in a very long time. Cord sat very still, soaking up the rare moment. He knew, without a doubt, his mother loved him. She just wasn't given to words or excessive displays of emotion. He listened to the faint rumble of her words in her chest, as his head lay pillowed on her bosom.

"Cord, I know things have been scary since your daddy died, but now I'm going to work here. A very important man has hired me to cook for him and agreed to let you stay with me." She dropped her hands to Cord's slender shoulders and gently pushed him away from her, tipping his face up. He looked up into her eyes.

"You're going to have to be a big boy now and help me."

"I promise I will, Momma." He tipped his head sideways in askance. "Do I have to sweep and make beds and take the garbage out?"

Staring into her son's solemn silver-blue eyes, his mother pulled him back into her arms. She hated adding this extra burden to him. He'd gone through so much already. Some days he seemed the adult in their little family. He was growing up so fast. Much too fast. "No, Cord. You have to do something a lot harder than that. You have to be very good, and very quiet and try very hard to stay out of Mr. Stanton's way. This is his house. He has a son about your age, but the boy goes to boarding school. Mr. Stanton is very nice, but I don't want you bothering him."

Cord nodded his head in a silent promise to be the best little boy in the world. If that would make his momma happy, he'd do anything.

"There now! Enough!" His no-nonsense mother put him back on the floor. The tender moment was gone and she led Cord down a short hall to explore their new home.

A whole new world opened to Cord after that day. His mother was busy from sunup to sundown cooking and preparing meals for the sixteen men who worked the ranch. She showed Cord a small grassy area outside the kitchen away from the front of the house where he could play and warned him strongly about never going to the front of the house.

He was six when he discovered the horses. He'd always known they were nearby. Occasionally, he heard one whinny or saw one trot by the house, but he never ventured out of the side yard to look at them. The peaceful garden area was a perfect playground for the quiet, inventive little boy. A large lilac bush became a pirate ship, a train or a robber's hide out – whatever he decided the little stage should be.

He was in the middle of drawing a picture for his mother in the shade of the lilac bush on a soft summer afternoon when the stillness was broken by the sound of pounding hooves. The sound seemed to be coming in his direction, closer and closer, louder and louder. Instinct made him sit still as he listened. Just as he thought he'd be run over by the loud noise, he looked up and saw the underside of a horse sail over his head.

The huge animal landed with a thud and a grunt, cantered a few paces and then circled to a prancing stop. The rider reached down to pat the sweating animal. The black stallion arched its neck in pride. The sweat on its coat glistened in the sun. Cord had never seen anything so beautiful in his life. Cautiously, he stood up and walked a pace or two toward the dancing animal. The coal black king of the wind threw up his head and stepped sideways, snorting at the small human coming his way. The man vaulted from the saddle, never loosening his hold on the reins.

"Stand still!" the rider commanded the boy. "Stay right where you are."

The man calmed the nervous horse, stroking its neck and head until the animal stood quivering at his side. The man's eyes never left the big stallion. His voice, just above a whisper barely loud enough for Cord to hear, calmly asked.

"Who are you, Son? Why are you on my property? Why were you in the bushes?" The horse threw its head up again as another man dressed in dirty jeans with a rope in his hands. Cord's mother, apron flapping, came running around different corners of the yard at the same moment.

"Cord!" screamed his mother.

"I'll get him, Sir," cried the man with the rope.

The horse reared, thrashing its legs out blindly, unnerved by the commotion. The man stood his ground and demanded, "Stand still all of you! No one move."

The voice struck just the right chord of respect into everyone. They watched as the man calmed the thrashing animal, slowly with hand and voice. When the sweating animal was calmer, the man called softly, "Will. Walk slowly over here and take the bridle. You two stand perfectly still. Don't move."

The man in the dirty jeans glided without a sound over to the horse and raised his hand slowly. Cord heard the snap of metal on metal. Both men walked the slightly dancing horse to the edge of the yard.

"Rub him down good. He worked hard today," the rider commanded.

As the glistening haunches of the big horse disappeared through the bushes, Cord let out air that had been trapped in his chest. His mother flew to him checking him for damage and, at the same time, apologizing over and over to the man who stood behind them, hands on hips and an odd look on his face.

"I'm sorry, Mr. Stanton. I thought he'd be out of the way here. I'm so sorry."

Stanton raised a hand to her nervous chatter. He stepped closer to the pair. Cord looked into the tall man's eyes without fear. He, after all, had done nothing wrong. The man looked down at the calm slender child.

"Are you OK?" Cord nodded.

"Did the horse frighten you?"

Cord shook his head. "He's beautiful. I was sitting in the bushes. I heard a horse running. When I looked up, I thought I saw an angel fly right over my head. It was wonderful."

His mother gasped. The man's smile broadened. His mother stood and began to apologize again. Once more, Stanton silenced her.

"You're not in trouble, Mrs. Grant. Neither is this brave little guy. The horse was acting up and I decided to let him run. I don't make a habit of jumping into the yard but, normally, no one is here. When The Devil decided to jump, I let him. I'm sorry I frightened you, but your son seems quite all right. You are, aren't you, Son?"

Cord shook himself free of his mother's hand that rested on his shoulder and walked up to Stanton. He stuck his hand out just as his father had taught him and said, "I'm Cord, sir. Cordry Grant. I'm pleased to meet you."

A smile played around Stanton's lips as he looked at the serious child. He took the proffered hand and shook it firmly in response. He looked at Cord's mother.

"So, this is your boy, Mrs. Grant?" She nodded at her employer.

"Well, to be honest," he said with a smile, "I was beginning to suspect that you'd lied about having a child with you. I believe this is the first time we've seen each other." He looked back at the little boy. "How old are you?"

"I'll be seven soon, sir."

"Why aren't you in school?"

31

"I don't know."

Both of them looked at Mrs. Grant. She shrugged and said, "I just hadn't even thought about it, sir."

"Well, think about it now. This is a fine brave young man you have here. He deserves a good education. There is a fine school in the village. You take him in tomorrow and make arrangements. I'll be gone for the next few days. You'll have plenty of time to take care of it."

The man turned to walk away. He stopped at the edge of the opening where the horse had disappeared a few moments earlier. He regarded the boy's awed face.

"You really liked the horse, didn't you?"

Cord's heart skipped a beat or two. "Yes sir. That was the most beautiful thing I've ever seen."

"You weren't even a little bit afraid?"

Cord smiled and shook his head vigorously.

"Do you think you'd like to learn to ride?"

The thought of being on top of that beautiful animal was frightening and exciting at the same time. Cord didn't trust himself to answer. He simply nodded his head.

"Good. You go to school and do well. Learn to read and write. If it's OK with your mother, I'll arrange for Will to take you down to the barns. You can earn your keep down there, helping to take care of the horses. Will can teach you to ride."

Cord looked at the man with eagerness shining in his eyes. "I can ride the black horse?"

Stanton threw his head back and laughed. "You like to start at the top, do you? No, you cannot ride The Devil. Not until you learn from the ground up. One day, Son. One day you'll be ready for him and then you can. Go with your mother now."

Stanton disappeared into the brush. Cord turned to look at his astonished mother. Deep inside, he knew she was going to let him do it!

Over the next few years, Cord learned and excelled at both his studies and the horses. Will praised him for his calm patience and strong hand while his teachers rewarded him for his intelligence and hard work. He taught him how to roll the sleeves on his shirt high enough for the horses to smell who he was.

"Horses know their friend by smell ... and their enemies. You need to give then skin to smell."

Life was good. Cord was happy and so was his mother.

The only thorn in his perfect rose patch of a life was Stanton's son, Edson Lawrence Stanton the Fifth, three years older than Cord. A scrawny, spoiled, showoff with none of his father's soft-spoken manner or regard for others. From the moment they met, Edson's animosity for Cord flourished.

Edson only came home from boarding school every year for Christmas vacation and a small part of summer holidays. Most of his out-of-school time was spent on holiday trips with other families. When he was forced to be at home, he made his feelings clear from the moment he stepped out of the limo. He hated the country life, hated the horses and wanted to be away as quickly as possible. He was rude to his father and downright mean to the staff.

Cord met Edson for the first time when he was ten. Edson stormed into the kitchen the morning after his arrival, berating Mrs. Grant for not cooking his eggs properly. Cord stood quietly and watched until the boy began to poke his mother in the chest. He calmly walked over and put his hand on the bigger boy's arm, stopping the next poke.

"Don't," he demanded quietly.

Edson shook his arm free and turned his full fury on the smaller boy. "Who the hell are you? You have no right to touch me. I own this place. I can do anything I want to anyone or anything in this place. You are nothing!" He drew his arm back to throw a punch. Cord stood still waiting for the pain to start.

Just then, the elder Stanton came around the corner. "Edson!"

The boy froze, arm still cocked.

"Stop it this instant."

The arm stayed for a moment and then slowly dropped down. Edson glared at Cord. Cord stood his ground.

"What's this all about?"

Both Mrs. Grant and Edson began to speak, one apologizing and the other demanding retribution.

Stanton put his hands up to ward off the noise. He looked at Cord who still said nothing.

"Cord? What happened?"

Cord calmly explained how he and his mother were discussing the day's events when Edson had burst into the room. "I couldn't just let him poke her, sir. I saw her flinch. He was hurting her."

Stanton turned to his son. "Is that true?"

Edson's face turned red and the fury began to rise in him. "Who cares what really happened? That bitch tried to kill me with a badly cooked egg, but you don't care. You always take anyone else's side. I hate you." He stormed out of the room. The three were left in the wake of all that anger, listening to the sound of footsteps and slamming doors until the house was ominously quiet.

Shamefaced, Stanton turned to Mrs. Grant. "Perhaps now you see why I'm so impressed with your son and his good manners. I can't apologize enough for my son. I don't know what to say. His mother died when he was very young. He's always been an angry, vicious child. I'll never forget how he wandered from room to room for months looking for his mother, furiously fighting anyone who tried to stop him. He never gave up trying to find her. The harder he looked the angrier he got. I finally sent him to boarding schools hoping that the change would help him accept her death. Nothing seemed to help him. I've tried doctors and medicines and therapy. Other people say he is a delight to have around, open, friendly, and funny. But the moment he gets here, he . . ."

Stanton suddenly realized who he was talking to. "Well, suffice it to say, he seems to think I'm responsible for his mother leaving him in some way. I'm sorry. I shouldn't be telling you these things. I'll do my best to keep my son out of this area. He'll only be here for a few days. He never stays long."

He began to walk out of the room, shoulders bent with the weight of the world. Just before going out the door, he turned back to Cord. "And, Son? You did the right thing. No one should ever be allowed to mistreat any living creature if you can stop it. Edson ..." The man looked at the ground and appeared to be thinking over his thoughts. "... well, he has always had a mean streak. I don't know where that comes from. We just keep a close eye on him while he is here."

The house was eerily silent for the rest of the morning. Cord spent the afternoon in the barn. He helped Will groom the horses. Then, perched on the fence, he watched the older man schooling the jumpers in the covered area. Soon he'd be on top of one of those beauties jumping over the low fences. Cord lowered himself to the ground and drifted away to check the other horses.

Wandering from stall to stall giving a pat here and a treat there, Cord made sure all his charges were in good shape. He'd just patted an old bay mare that was due to foal in a few weeks when he heard a terrified snort and a human cry from the nearby stallion barn.

Racing to see what was wrong, Cord rounded the corner just in time to see Edson running from the shadows of the barn. Cord heard the horse Stanton called The Devil – the same one he'd been riding that first day – raising a fuss in the stall. He ran to the stallion's pen. On the floor just inside the stall was a buggy whip and a short lead rope. Edson had been trying to take the animal out of the stall. There were strict rules that no one handled The Devil, but Mr. Stanton or Will.

Cord climbed to the top rail of the pen and whispered quietly to the upset horse like Will had taught him. He put the soft musical sound in his voice, the one that horses listened to. Cord spoke to the nervous horse. "Easy, Son. Easy. It's OK now. I won't hurt you. I just want to see if you're OK."

The Devil's ears flicked back and forth, catching the sound of the soft voice. He pawed the straw on the floor and shivered, ready to fight if he had to. Cord continued to murmur softly. The horse stood still, tense but calmer. Slowly, Cord slipped off the rail into the stall and held out a steady hand toward the horse. The giant stretched his neck out and snuffled the hand and bare forearms. Cord carefully looked the horse over, checking for scrapes or scratches. He found none. He reassured the horse once more and stepped back to leave.

A quiet voice met his ears. "Is he OK, Cord?"

Without turning, Cord nodded assuring Stanton there was nothing wrong with the horse. He continued to move slowly so as not to frighten the huge animal again. On his way out of the stall, he stopped to pick up the rope and whip. The horse snorted, but Cord continued to soothe the horse with his voice. Tossing the offending items over the fence, he slipped the latch and squeezed out. Once outside the pen, Cord sagged against the wooden post, his knees turning to water. He looked at Stanton who watched him from across the aisle.

"I heard the noise and came running, but you beat me to it. I never saw that horse let anyone but Will or I touch him. You surely have the gift, Cord. How did those things get in there?"

Before Cord could answer, Edson and Will came running around the other end of the barn. Edson stopped suddenly. He saw his father, Cord and the rope and whip lying on the ground in front of them.

"Father!" he gasped. "I was just coming to find you. I found Will instead. I came down to check the horses and found this urchin in the stall with The Devil. He was trying to get a rope on him. When the horse wouldn't let him, he got the whip. That's when I left to find you. He ought to be fired. Him and his mother. I know you hate to see animals abused. Fire him!" The boy's voice rose to a crescendo, almost a shriek that had all the horses shifting nervously in their stalls. He paused for breath, chest heaving. Stanton turned to his head horseman.

"Will? Is all this true?"

Edson glared at Will who shifted uneasily from one foot to the other and said, "I ... I, uhm ... I'm not sure. I heard the stallion scream. By the time, I dismounted, tied up the horse I was working with and got outside the arena, I saw Edson running out. I called to him and he stopped. Then he came to me and said I had to get to the barn right away. Something was wrong with The Devil."

Edson stepped forward between his father and the hired man. "Yeah! Yeah! That's exactly what happened. I was trying to find someone to help."

Stanton drew a deep breath and sighed. "Will, go back to your work. We'll talk later. Cord. You do the same."

Edson watched the hired man leave. As Cord began to walk away, Edson shouted at his father. "You can't be serious. That bastard tried to hurt your pride and joy. You can't let him stay. You have to fire him! You have to! Now!!!"

Cord froze in his tracks. Stanton roared. "Stop it! I don't know what happened before I got here, but I saw Cord in that stall with that animal. The Devil wasn't frightened by him nor was he trying to hurt the horse. I don't know what happened in the stall, but I do know you, Edson. You've been caught mistreating animals and people who won't answer to your whims so many times. Because you're my son, I hoped you'd one day grow out of your love for causing trouble. I have obviously let my love for you blind me for too long." He signed and looked his furious son right in the eye. "I think its best you pack up now."

Fury shook Edson. For a brief moment, Cord thought he'd strike the older man, but Edson suddenly dropped his shoulders and smiled. "Well, hell Pop! I should've known you'd side with the hired help. You always do. You're right, just like you always think you are. I'll go now. It's what I wanted anyway. I hate you and I hate this place."

He thrust his hands deep into his pockets and sauntered away. He passed Cord. Without stopping, he hissed, "You'll pay for this, Grant. I'll make sure if it takes my whole life."

The heart that is meant to love you will fight for you when you want to give up, pick you up when you're feeling down, and will give you their smile when It's hard to find your own. – Trent Shelton

1543 – Great Britain

She struggled to stay focused on the droning of the old priest in front of her and to forget the pain of the stone floor where she knelt. The heavy weight of the dress she was sewn into and the deep black emotional stabs she felt driving over and over into her heart made her want to run from this cold place. A cold rivulet of sweat seeped from under the towering, itchy wig that precariously balanced on her piously bowed head. She shivered as she felt the sweat run the full length of her spine. Dizziness flowed over her so fiercely that only her white knuckled hand on the worn railing kept her from overbalancing.

Behind her, she heard the great wooden doors creak open. She tensed at the sound of heavy breathing and grunting along with the sounds of a pair of wooden crutches clattering against the ancient stones in the aisle that led to where she knelt. She could almost see the tottering old man dressed in glorious robes that would have looked elegant on a younger man, but only served to pull him further into a hunched shape. She heard the sickening low moaning grunt that accompanied every footstep that brought the disgusting human being that would soon be her husband closer.

Gasping for air, he finally reached the railing and dropped the crutches as the two ever present squires grabbed his elbows to lower him to the floor. From the corner of her eye, she saw him look over at her. His leering face never reached her eyes. She could smell the distinctive, almost rotting odor of the aged man her father had brought home two weeks ago. He was four times her fifteen years, but that wasn't uncommon in the social circles of her family. She heard him groan and his joints crackle as he knelt down beside her despite the help of the two young squires. She flinched slightly as his dry, rough hand pressed down on top of her soft hand.

She quietly stiffened her spine. This was her destiny. Her children would be able to live a much finer life than she had, even if her family fell from grace with the king. Her parents had told her how proud they were of her for bringing such wealth to their family. When she realized what they intended to do, her cries of anguish fell on deaf ears. In private, she cried until there were no more tears to be had. In public, she was the dutiful daughter. At the memory of her parents' indifference, a single tear slipped down her cheek and splashed on the worn wooden rail.

The heedless priest droned his Latin phrases tying her to the horrible man for all time. The cloying scent of the burning incense nearly lulled her to insensibility. In her quiet mind, she summoned the fantasy she'd seen so many times in her dreams. The man she knew she was truly destined to love. She conjured up the elusive image of the cloaked man who she had prayed would ride into the cathedral at any moment and sweep her up as he had done many times in her dreams. Another spasm of pain bruised her heart as she silently prayed for anyone to save her.

From all her dreams, she knew the sight of the huge black stallion he rode, muscled and fierce, fiery and full of temper. If smoke had suddenly began coming out of his nostrils as he pranced and fidgeted under the knight, no one would've been surprised. The two, rider and animal, seemed joined at the spine. As everyone in the church stepped aside, she watched the image of the pair as they moved with no fear or concern toward her ... completely riveted on her.

She knew exactly how the huge animal would burst through the doors of the church and dance up the aisle, sparks flashing from his hooves as the metal shoes met worn stone. She'd seen the very move in her dreams so many sad long nights. As she struggled to stand, the animal would stop in front of her and bow to dip a knee. From his back, a black glove leading up to bared forearms, sinewy and strong, would come into her view, hand out, palm up. Without hesitation, her own hand would quickly be lost in his strong fingers as they wrapped around her trembling ones.

She knew when she looked up, the unnerving silver gray, almost blue eyes would be staring at her, shining brilliantly. So much love would flow out of those eyes that she'd be lifted on pure emotion to her feet. Then, with the ease of picking up a child's toy, he'd pull her into the saddle in front of him.

"Katherine!" he'd whisper and speak the words she longed to hear just before they rode off. "It's time!"

She shook her head to clear the overpowering images. She had no idea who this Katherine was or why he called her that, but she knew she would go willingly if he'd just appear. On that thought, the priest snatched her hands off the railing before him.

"Lucinda Dianna Margaret Marie, daughter of Sir John the lesser of Middleborough, arise and become Lady Katherine Jane Victoria, wife of …."

Instantly, her head swam and her knees turned to water. She felt faint. She was now Katherine. Her name was the name her hero had whispered. *Come to me, dark knight. Save me before it is too late*, she prayed silently.

She turned her head slightly toward the massive wooden doors, straining to hear the sounds of dancing hoof beats and the snort of the steed. But no wild-eyed stallion burst through the cathedral doors. No silver eyed knight would rescue her today. The priest yanked her to her feet and she heard the man next to her struggle to his. The final words drifted over her ears. "I now pronounce you..."

Too late, she cried silently. *Too late ... again.*

⤜⤛⤜⤛

Nine months later

She struggled to see the child. *Please God, make it a son.*

The horrid old man had made the fact that she was there to breed him a son abundantly clear from the moment she'd walked into the cold, dank castle. He struggled through the halls, screaming demands in every direction. Poorly clothed servants timidly scurried away to fulfill every wish. He bellowed at her to follow him as both his squires, one half husband's age and the other barely a boy, shoved her along behind him. When he reached the last door in the dark stone hallway, he threw the door open, grabbed her arm and shoved her inside. She was barely in the room before he bellowed at his squires.

"Strip her!"

The older squire leered at her and leapt in to grab her around the waist. The younger more cautiously began taking her clothes. She begged but nothing would stop them. She cried. She pled to no avail.

"Come on," screamed the old man. "Get 'em off her!" The older squire slapped at the younger and shoved her into his arms. With ruthless glee, he began tearing her clothes away from her body. The younger one held her arms tightly as ordered but looked away from her nakedness.

The old man laughed a nasty mean laugh. "There ya go, Danno. Teach that young 'un how it's done." The older squire snickered and tore at her clothes with even more gusto. When she was naked, he stepped back. She stood there as the two older men stared at her. Then the older lord and master grunted, waved his gnarled hand and the older squire picked her up and threw her onto a pile of furs. Trembling, she wondered what would happen now. She'd been raised gently and had no knowledge of what went on between men and women but, from the look in her husband's eye, she was sure he was going to kill her. Then she watched horrified as he untied the rope at his waist, dropped his pants and tottered toward her.

"Hold her down!" The squires grabbed her arms and stretched them out until she lay exposed to them all. She closed her eyes and tried to think herself away from the room. The stinky old goat struggled to climb on to the bed and grunted as he worked his way over top of her. He put his hard, rough hands on her breasts and smiled devilishly as she screamed in pain. Bright red bruises appeared on the pale skin. Smiling with delight at his handiwork, he let his hands move down her body. She pulled her legs together and struggled to avoid his touch.

"Get her legs! Dammit!"

She felt hands grab her knees and wrench them to the side. Crying out, she begged the squires to help her. Neither responded. She thought she heard the older one snicker under his breath and turned her face away from him and his master. The younger squire was looking at the ground. His face was red and damp with tears. She closed her eyes and let herself go limp.

From that moment, the only sounds in the room was the old man's grunting and groaning as he slid his hands down to the part of her that had never been touched. Once more she cried out and bucked to get away when his rough hands pushed and pressed into the place between her legs but he fell heavily on her and fumbled around with his clothes. Then she felt something else enter her. In shock and fear, she screamed and thrashed with all her might to get him off her. He reached up, slapped her hard across the face and then dipped his greasy head down to bite her tender skin. She screamed again.

"Shut her up!" The old man gasped. The older squire took a hand off her arm long enough to stuff a rag into her mouth. Barely able to get air, she had no choice, but to lie still.

"That's it, girlie," the fetid breath wisped across her face. "Get used to it. We're gonna do this until I get what I want." He began bucking and pounding her tender flesh until she thought she'd faint and then, suddenly with a loud groan from him, he lay heavily on her panting loudly. Slowly, the red-hot flush of humiliation engulfed her.

With a satisfied grunt, he rolled off her. The squires let her arms go to assist their master. She curled into a tight ball as far from them as she could get. Every muscle and bone in her body hurt. She felt the lumpy, stinking bed move as the squires helped the old man off the edge. He turned, slapped her on her backside and guffawed. She flopped over and glared at him, hating him with every inch of her being. While the squires pulled his britches up from the floor, he smiled smugly down at her in a way that made her soul shrivel slightly.

"You did good, girl. One of these days you'll get to enjoy this just like the other whores." He batted the squires' hands away, knocked one of them to the floor and yelled. He grabbed his canes and started for the door. "Get the maids up here. Clean her up. Make sure she is here and ready next time."

As they stumbled out the door, the younger squire with the red handprint on his cheek looked back at her huddled on the bed and gave her a weak smile. The door closed. The horrific abuse went on for another six long, horrible months until she told him she was pregnant.

Now, she hoped those horrible days were over. The nurse cautiously whispered that she'd birthed a son and then slinked away from the bed. He'd be pleased. She prayed he'd let her raise her son without any more humiliation. She held her beautiful son and gazed at him in wonder. She could hear the nurses whispering in the corner. They wouldn't look at her. She could tell that something was wrong, but she just wanted to be alone with her son.

The door burst open and in stumbled the drunken man she was married to.

"So, it's over, I hear." His words slurred. Even from across the room, she could smell alcohol on his breath. "Yes, milord." she said. "We have a son."

"I!" he screamed, "I have a son!" He strode to the side of the bed and glared down at her. Unconsciously, her hold on the baby tightened. As she glared at him, one of the nurses sidled up beside the man. She whispered in his ear. His face shriveled, reddened and a raging howl roared from his mouth.

"A cowl! He was born with a cowl? You witch!" He grabbed for the baby and tried to tear him from her arms. Instinctively, she curled around the crying infant to protect him.

The old nurse who'd been with the man since childhood slipped up to his side. "Surely she's a witch, lord, and the child is of Satan. That's what the birth cowl means. The Dark Lord tries to hide the evilness with a veil of skin over the child's eyes!"

"You witch. I'll have none of that foolishness in this place." He cuffed the nurse. "Go get the priest." He turned back to the bed. The nurse whispered again. Instantly, the man threw his hands up and backed away as if he'd been bitten by a snake. "You are an abomination! You and that thing you birthed will be destroyed immediately!"

"Help me!" She called out to the others in the room, but the nurse and the squires stayed cowering in the dark corner. No one moved. The old man backed away from the bed and beckoned to his squires. "Kill them. Kill them both."

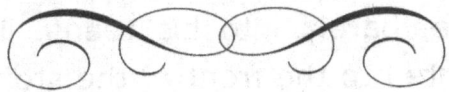

Six months later

The stallion was getting fractious. He hadn't let the horse run free for many days. This peace wasn't something either of them liked. Travelling through the countryside looking for some small fiefdom that needed his warring skills suited neither his temperament nor the horse's.

They crested a small hill and looked down on a deep green valley below. *Maybe she is here*. The errant thought traveled with a trill of hope through his mind. He shook the idea off quickly. He'd been dreaming of the red-haired woman since childhood, but he'd given up on the idea that she existed. The one woman he'd be willing to give up this life for was just a dream. The woman who cried out for him to come and help her over and over in his night terrors. The horse, perhaps sensing his sorrow, shifted under him.

"We might as well go see what can be found here, Son." He nudged the horse forward. At the bottom of the hill lay a lovely glen with a small pool surrounded by trees that swayed in the light breeze. A teen knelt beside a newly covered grave. When he heard the horse snuffle, the young man jumped to his feet and started to run off.

"Hold, young squire!" He raised a gloved hand in peace. "I mean you no harm." He stepped off the horse, pulled off the gloves, rolled up his sleeves and walked toward the trembling young man. "Who lies here?"

The squire, barely into his teens, lifted a shaky hand and pointed to the front of the stone. Brow knit, the man moved to where he could see the name on the stone. He reached his hand toward the stone and breathed the beloved name, "Katherine."

He barely stifled his gasp. Without knowing how, he knew this was her. He was too late to save her. He'd heard her desperate cries and hadn't come soon enough. His jaw tensed as he ground his teeth into each other, rage seeping out every pore.

"Tell me what happened."

The nervous young man explained as the knight knelt by the stone and grew angrier with every word. *Six months. He had just missed saving her.*

He turned to the boy and growled, "Who did this?

The boy pointed to the rundown castle at the other end of the glen. Without another word, the man remounted and drove the horse into a frenzy as he raced toward the doomed castle.

Five

When Edson came home again, Cord had grown and filled out into a fine young man. Cord topped well over six feet tall. His pale white hair had lightened to an interesting silvery gray. The serious eyes, prematurely gray hair and height lent an air of maturity that made most people think he was much older than his years. The kids at school called him 'grampa' in good-natured fun. When he drove his mother to town for supplies, girls of all ages watching him as he walked by, bur he remained unaware of the effect he had on them. Cord became the favored protégé of horsemaster, Will, when he proved he could handle any horse on the ranch, but girls remained a mystery to him. Stanton followed Cord's progress, envying Mrs. Grant her son and Will's easy friendship with Cord.

In early spring of his sixteenth year, Cord received two gifts he'd never even let himself dream of owning. The first came at breakfast on a day that promised to be a perfect late spring day – cool crisp morning, a warm afternoon. *Great horse working weather,* he thought.

Watching the sunrise glow light up the soft velvet sky, Cord sipped his coffee and looked forward to the day's work for more than one reason. He and Will had a field full of young fillies and colts to begin working with, looking for the next champion among Stanton's stock. Cord gazed out the window at a distant group of mares and their young grazing on the dew-sprinkled grass, wondering if life could get any better.

As had become his habit, Will joined Cord and his mother for breakfast. At first, the meal had been a good time for Will and Cord to plan their day, talk over any ideas they had and decide who was handling which horses that day. Lately, after their meal, Will spent a bit of extra time lingering over his coffee, chatting with Cord's mother. Some days, Cord went on to the barns without the older man, but not today. He heard the clatter of dishes being cleared from the table and waited for Will to start for the door. Instead, he heard his mother sit back down at the table and Will clear his throat. Cord turned to see them both staring at him. His mother was sitting next to Will, blushing like a schoolgirl, nervously twisting a towel in her hands just below the edge of the table. Cord's eyebrows knit. His mother was never nervous. Something was wrong. He was just about to ask when Will cleared his throat again.

"Cord, we have, I mean, I have something to tell you. Or, rather, ask you. Come back and sit down for a minute or two." He looked at Cord's mother who blushed furiously and looked down at her work worn hands. He waited as Cord came back to the table and sat in his usual place.

"Me and your mom. Well, we got to know each other pretty good lately and, well, I think ... no, I'm sure, we're in love. We wanna get married. Mary, here wanted to see how you felt about the idea first."

Surprise clutched at his heart. Cord had never considered his mother as a love interest. His mother and Will. But then 50 wasn't that old, he mused. The surprise gave way to a golden glow of happiness. The day just got better after all. He kept his face still and grim as he looked from one to the other.

"You? You want to marry *my* mother?" He paused as Will cleared his throat again, swallowed visibly and nodded.

"And you? You want to marry him?" He asked his mother.

"Now, Cord!" she began, but he stopped her.

"Just how long has this been going on behind my back?" Cord stood up, arms akimbo and glared at them. He let them shift uncomfortably for a brief second and then broke into a broad smile. "It should've been going on in front of me!"

His mother jumped up with a gasp of relief to hug him. Will reached out to shake Cord's hand. Cord ignored it and gruffly pulled the older man into his arms. "I couldn't be happier. Congratulations – Dad." This time Will blushed furiously and pulled Mary into his arms. Cord wrapped them both up in his long arms and they stood for a few blissful moments.

"Ahem. Am I interrupting something?" Stanton stood in the doorway surveying the loving scene.

"Oh! Oh. Mr. Stanton, sir." Cord's mother stuttered, stepping out of the embrace.

"Good morning, sir." Will nearly snapped a salute.

Stanton stood looking at the speechless, embarrassed pair. He looked at the unruffled Cord. "Well, it looks like I have to turn to you for an explanation."

Cord smiled wider. "Will just asked my permission to marry my mother – and I gave it."

"Well, Glory be!!! I couldn't be happier. Well done, Will, old man. Tell you what – we'll build you a little cottage between here and the barns. Much better than the rooms you have now, Mrs. Grant, don't you think? After all, a married couple must have their privacy." He laughed out loud as the two blushed. He took Will's hand in a firm grasp and clapped his shoulder. He looked over at Mrs. Grant. "So, it's to be Mrs. Delaney now, is it? I do hope you'll consider having your wedding in the side garden. After all, that's where you two first met."

Mary Grant, soon-to-be Delaney, did something Cord had never seen her do before. All three men stood in uncomfortable shock as Mrs. Grant lifted the tortured towel she still held in her hands and wept loud drenching tears. They stared at the weeping woman and at each other, none of them sure what to do. After a few long moments, she looked up, smiled weakly and shooed them out of the kitchen with claims of how much work there was to be done. Relieved, the men stepped outside. Halfway across the meadow to the barns, Cord asked, "So, when's the big day?"

Will stopped short. Surprise registered on his face. He lifted his beat-up old hat off his head to run a hand through his thinning hair. "I don't know." He laughed. "In all the excitement, I forgot to ask."

Both Stanton and Cord roared as Will turned back to the kitchen. Stanton threw an arm over Cord's shoulder and turned him back down the pathway. Still laughing, he pointed to a lilac bush. "Do you remember the day we first met? You were so little sitting under that bush. I was trying to control The Devil when I saw this little scrap of a kid step out of the bushes. Your eyes were bigger than your face. I saw the wonder in them and the joy. I knew from that moment you would be good with the horses. Will tells me how well you're doing.

I'm proud of you and I want you to know that." Cord took the man's hand as he offered it.

"I also want you to know I never forget a promise. I'm going to make a promise today and try to fulfill one I made long ago. First, I want you to know that you'll always have a place to live here. Never doubt that. As long as I'm alive, this is your home. Second, I promised you that one day you could ride the Devil. Well, the fool animal died before I lived up to the promise I gave you. So. Here's the next best thing."

They rounded the bush and there staked in the yard was a colt, a yearling, glistening black, the spitting image of his father, the horse called The Devil.

Cord looked at Stanton in confusion. Stanton never looked at Cord. He just continued talking. "I remember the day The Devil died. I was sorry to lose that creature. He was special to me but you, well, you seemed more upset than I. You had a special rapport with him that I – no one – ever had. Remember?" Cord nodded.

"The day after we buried him, this youngster was born. You were the first one to touch him. I saw the glow in your eyes when you announced we had a colt. I decided yesterday, watching you work the young colts, that you deserve one of your own. This is your colt. All yours, to do with as you please." Stanton turned to the stupefied Cord. A smile spread across his face. "Well? Are you going to leave your colt staked out all day? Go take care of him."

Cord didn't know what to say. He couldn't talk. He simply did what he was told. He walked toward the colt that sniffed the air suspiciously for a moment. When he recognized the boy's scent, the colt dipped his head and nickered. Cord ran his hands over the silky neck, overcome with emotion. The colt laid his heavy head on Cord's shoulder. If there'd been any horse in the world Cord wanted, this colt was this one. Cord turned around to thank Stanton, but he was gone.

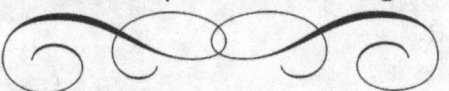

The next morning 19-year-old Edson came back.

Cord was out in the field, working Devil's Son on a long line. The colt showed promise of growing into a magnificent beast as big and strong as his sire and with the same flighty edginess. But he and Cord understood each other. Cord knew most of the colt's posturing was just show and the colt knew just how much he could get away with. Cord gave the command to stop and the colt turned to face him. As Cord took a step toward him, the colt snorted and reared to his full height. Cord stood his ground. The colt walked a step or two forward on his hind legs and then dropped back to the ground, landing dangerously close to Cord's boots.

"You old fraud," Cord scoffed as he scratched the horse's ears. "Like, anyone would be scared of you."

The loud, sharp sound of hands clapping made the colt throw his head and back to the end of the rope, tossing his head nervously. Cord turned to see Edson lounging on the gate, a cigarette carelessly dangling from his lips. Cord turned his attention back to the colt. His jaw clenched in anger at the idea of Edson being back on the property.

"Isn't that just sweet. Still got a thing for dumb animals, I see." Edson flicked his cigarette into the straw in the middle of the enclosure. The dried grass fueled a small flame. The colt smelled the smoke and shied away. Edson watched in amusement as Cord tried to stamp out the little blaze and control the horse at the same time.

Cord kicked the sand over the flames and led the excited colt to a gate on the opposite side of the corral that led into a broad open meadow. Cord kept his back to Edson. Letting him see the anger in Cord's eyes would only fuel Edson's meanness. He turned the colt loose and watched him run and jump with the pure joy of freedom for a moment or two, fists clenching and unclenching at his side. Once he had his anger under control, he turned back to Edson.

Striding over to the fence, Cord noticed that he was now a good head taller than Edson. Where Cord had filled out, gotten taller and stronger with the hard work on the ranch, Edson was shorter, skinny and almost frail looking.

"What are you doing here?" Cord demanded.

"Why, haven't you heard?" Edson waved a hand magnanimously. "I'm back for good. I've been summoned to the home to learn how to run this place so I can take over when the time comes. Dear, dear Daddy isn't feeling so well it seems."

Cord's brows knit. He hadn't noticed anything different with the older Stanton except that he traveled more than he used to. Of course, Stanton had been on an extended vacation for the past six months. He hadn't seen him recently. Cord stepped past Edson on his way to verify the information.

Edson grabbed his arm. "Not too long now, Plow Boy. When I do take over, you and your dear momma will be out on your asses." Cord stood his ground. Every fiber in his being wanted to knock the impudent Edson into the dirt. Edson sneered up at Cord. "I'll make sure you are and I'll make sure you never work around here again. You've mooched off us long enough, ruining my life and my relationship with my father. I warned you that you'd pay for it. And soon, you will. Gawd, how much I'll enjoy watching you slink away with nothing. Not much longer now." Edson's sadistic smile chilled Cord's blood. He tore his arm from the bony fingers digging into his skin and walked as casually as he could to the house. His mother would know if this was true.

Once inside, he closed the door softly and watched his mother puttering at the sink. Suddenly, she seemed much older to Cord. How old was she? He knew she'd been near 35 when he was born. He leaned softly against the door and looked at the gray in her hair. She'd been so happy since she and Will had married he hadn't even realized that she must be nearing 60. Both Will and Stanton were at least ten years older than she. She turned around to see her son leaning against the door.

"Hello, my Son. What brings you to the kitchen at this time of day?" Her sunny smile warmed his heart. "I suppose you smelled these rolls I just pulled out of the oven. You men amaze me. You always seem to know when the sweets are ready. Will should be back in a minute. I'm making him wait until they're cool. You'll have to do the same. Go wash up and give me about half an hour." Cord stood still and watched his mother flitting around the kitchen like a woman half her age. He wondered what they would do if Edson kept his promise. Suddenly, she stopped puttering around and looked at her son who hadn't moved or spoken. Wiping her floury hands on the front of her apron, she asked quizzically, "Cord? Is something wrong?"

Cord stepped across the floor and wrapped her in his arms. "No, I was just looking at you and wondering what I'd done to deserve such a great mother."

"Oh, you fool! You're as much a romantic as your stepfather!" she said, pushing away from him, an embarrassed but pleased grin on her face. "You must be learning those things from Will. He's got the Irish gift for blarney, that one, and he's giving it to you."

Cord put his hand on his mother's shoulder. "Mom, can we talk for a minute?"

Mary Delaney stared into her son's unnerving gray eyes. Something must be wrong to make him leave the horses in the middle of the day.

"Sit down," she said as she poured two glasses of fresh lemonade. She slid into a chair opposite him and took a deep drink. "Now! What's going on?"

"Edson's back." He took a deep drink of the sweetsour liquid. His mother nodded.

"I thought I heard him outside, calling poor Carl names. He makes Carl so nervous. As much as Carl loves being a chauffeur, he hates driving Edson anywhere. On the way from the airport, he even made Carl get in the back and drove that huge car like he was in a race. Almost wrecked it, he did. When the police stopped them, he climbed into the back seat and blamed it all on Carl. That boy is pure evil."

Cord stopped her. "Momma? Where is Mr. Stanton?"

"Why, he's on a cruise. He said he's always wanted to go on one and now he is. He called just the other day and said he was coming home with important news. Why? Is there something I should know?"

Cord shook his head. "I don't know. Edson came out to the corral while I was working Devil's Son. He made some typical Edson comments, something about being called home to learn to run the place since his father isn't well. I just wondered if you knew anything about it."

Mary stood up. "He's always made himself clear how he feels about us. Oh, Cord, when he finds out Will married me, he'll kick him off the place too. What if Mr. Stanton is ill? I have to talk to Will. We can't stay here if that wicked boy's in charge.

Cord looked at his mother, eyebrows raised. He'd never told his mother most of the things Edson did to cause him trouble. She read his eyes as if trying to read the thoughts behind the troubled eyes.

"Cord!" she continued, "Don't be so foolish. You don't think he confined his nasty behavior to the barns, do you? I cleaned up enough of that boy's messes and listened to enough of his foolishness to be certain of how he feels about us. I know the minute Mr. Stanton is gone so are we." She tore off her apron and started for the door. "I have to talk to Will."

Cord reached the door first. "Mom, wait! We don't know for sure anything is wrong with Mr. Stanton. You know how Edson lies. He might be doing this just to make us panic. By the looks of things, his plan's working on you already." He gently escorted his mother back to the table and settled back down across from her. "Let's just wait to see what happens. OK?"

Mary's sad features looked across the table at her son. "It's just been so good here. I was hoping this job would never end."

"Me, too, Mom. Me, too."

That's how Will found them a few moments later. His happy, roaring laugh filled the kitchen as he burnt his fingers trying to snatch one of the still hot cinnamon rolls. Dancing around the kitchen in faked agony, Will ran to the table and plunged the singed fingers deep into Cord's drink to cool. Cord complained goodnaturedly and threw an ice cube in Will's general direction. Ducking just in time, Will grabbed his wife into a quick whirling jig around the kitchen, ending in a loving embrace. The man had certainly changed since he'd married Mary Grant Delaney. Both of them were so much happier, so much quicker to laugh and play like a much younger married couple. Cord saw his mother look at him over Will's shoulder. They silently agreed to say nothing – yet.

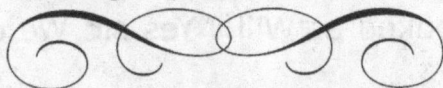

Stanton returned a week later. Much to the relief of everyone, he was fine. Edson played Lord and Master all week, demanding they wait on him hand and foot. His heavy-handed behavior might have been funny if he hadn't been so mean and crass. Edson had no idea how ridiculous he looked in the long purple velvet lounging robe he wore every day with a large Cuban cigar that he never lit, dangling from his mouth. He looked like a little boy playing grown up. He made their lives miserable in the house, but he stayed away from the barns. Cord took over most of Will's duties just so Will could stay near the house in case his wife needed him.

When Carl was summoned to meet Stanton at the airport, no one let Edson know his days of kingship were over. The look on his face when he came storming down the stairs in that dressing gown at 2:30 in the afternoon to see why no one had answered his bell was priceless. He almost fell down the stairs as he stopped short. In the foyer stood his father, looking healthier and more relaxed than ever. Cord shot a look at Edson who lifted an eyebrow in amusement.

"Well, if it isn't dear Daddy come home."

"Edson? Just getting up?" Sarcasm laced the older man's words.

Deviously, Edson thought up an excuse. "Yes, I am. We had a birth early this morning. I was up all night helping. Just got to bed a few hours ago."

Stanton looked at Will. "Yes sir. We did get a new foal last night."

Stanton harrumphed when he heard Will omit his son's role in the arrival.

"Well, we'll go the barn later to see the youngster. Right now, I have a new arrival of my own to introduce you to." He walked back to the door and opened the exit with a flourish. "Everyone, meet Mrs. Edson Lawrence Stanton the Fourth. Deborah to her friends and my wife of three weeks."

The silence was thick enough to cut as into the room stepped the most stunning woman Cord had ever seen. She was much younger than Stanton, hardly older than Cord. Her coal black hair gleamed even in the dull light of the foyer. Her skin was snow white against the deep black of her hair. From under delicate eyebrows, unexpected ice blue eyes surveyed the group. Her perfect rose red lips smiled slightly. Waiting for someone to say something, she reached out and touched her husband's arm. Stanton smiled and patted the small hand that slipped through the crook of his elbow. His eyes never left his son's face. Wave after dark emotional wave washed over Edson's face. Anger. Fear. Rejection. Hurt. As everyone who knew him watched with bated breath as the well-known sullen look settled in Edson's eyes at last. He began clapping his hands, slowly and deliberately, as he finished coming down the staircase.

"Oh, this is rich. This is so rich. This is what you called me back for? To show off the trollop that snared you? You senile old jackass! If you think for one moment I'll stand still for this, you're out of your mind." He strode across the marble floor in a rage to confront the woman.

For a moment, they all thought he would strike her.

Cord's mother gasped. Both Will and Cord tried to step in front of him, but they weren't quick enough.

Stanton was. He stepped between his wife and his son, stopping his son by jamming his open hand into Edson's throat just above his Adam's apple. He squeezed just tight enough to turn Edson's face bright red. In measured tones, he issued a warning.

"You're my son. I have no wish to have you permanently removed from this place, but you will respect my wishes and my wife or you will be removed – for good from here and from the will. Do you understand?"

He loosened his grasp just enough to allow air back into Edson's lungs. In all the time they'd been there, none of the group had ever seen Stanton actually touch his son. Obviously, Edson was shocked as well by his father's swift reaction and threat. He looked at his father, at the woman, and then at the others. Without another word, he spun on his heel and ran up the steps two at a time. Once again, the house echoed with the sound of the doors slamming in his wake.

Mary Delaney cleared her throat and walked over to the shaken woman. "Hello. I'm Mary. I've been cooking for Mr. Stanton for a long time. This is my husband Will. He cares for the horses and this is my son Cord. He helps Will."

Stanton looked gratefully at Mary. He patted his wife's slender hand again and looked into her brilliant eyes. "Please don't judge everyone by my son. He's, well, I should have warned you but ... well . . . ."

Deborah smiled at her husband and placed her other hand on his cheek. A sweet soothing voice came from the slightly parted lips. Cord felt his own soul melt as the dulcet tones softly washed over his ears.

"Don't worry, Larry. I'm much stronger than I look." She looked at Cord and winked slightly.

Edson left a few hours later without a word to anyone and the whole house breathed a sigh of relief.

"It's like that at moment the whole universe existed just to bring us together."
– Jonathan Trager, Serendipity (2001)

Six

As happy as he acted, Stanton seemed to age quickly in the following year. He went to parties and on short business trips as he'd always done, but they seemed to tire him rather than invigorate him as they had in the past. Introducing Deborah to all his friends kept him at a run. The more exhausted he became, the more concerned Deborah was, but no one could convince him to slow down. He was determined to keep up a killer pace even if Deborah didn't want to.

Cord, who found himself tongue-tied whenever she was around, tried not to be in Deborah's presence. His experience with women was limited to quickly stolen kisses in the back of the school bus with local cheerleaders. Horses had always been his prime interest. He wasn't sure how to deal with the emotions and the unexpected physical reaction the beautiful woman stirred in him. A romantic at heart, he spent long nights in the old tack room he'd converted shortly after his mother married – and dreamt of Deborah. He lay trying to sleep, trying not to think about the earthbound goddess who was now his boss's wife. He tried to be polite and calm when she was around, careful not to let his interest show. Despite his best intentions, he found himself watching the way her mouth moved when she spoke and the graceful, dancer-like way she walked. The sound of her voice was the sweetest melody he'd ever heard.

She made him sweat on the coldest of days. Her face turned up in his dreams. He tossed and turned all night long, unable to sleep for seeing her incredible eyes and hearing that sweet silken voice. He dreamt of the feel of that face under his hand, the kiss from those lips and a touch from those slender hands racing over his skin.

When Stanton finally decided Deborah had been introduced to enough people, he called a stop to their whirlwind social life. Stanton suggested Deborah learn to ride. Since Will was too busy getting ready for an upcoming horse sale, the job fell to Cord. Day after day, he taught her what to do. His fingers burned when he touched her leg to adjust a stirrup. He held his breath while he helped her up into the saddle and watched her beautiful form as she sat on the horse, straight and tall. His dreams became more and more fanciful after he watched her canter the horse around the arena for the first time. Her laughter filled the arena, making everyone smile. If she wore a bra, the thin cloth did no good. If she didn't, good lord ... if she didn't ... Cord nearly lost control of himself just thinking about it.

How many times did he curse himself for being in lust with another man's wife? How many times did he pray he could be that other man just for one night?

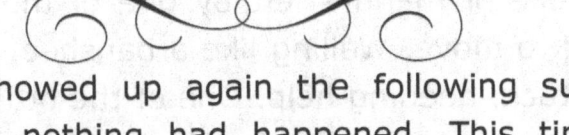

Edson showed up again the following summer acting as if nothing had happened. This time he brought reinforcements with him. Five college buddies and six barely legal young women descended on the ranch without a word of warning.

Edson smiled magnanimously at his friends as he introduced them to his father. Pointedly ignoring everyone else, he announced, "We decided we're tired of Europe and the Continent. My friends wanted a taste of ranch life so I invited them here for a few weeks." Stanton had little choice but to graciously agree.

Life quickly became a nightmare for everyone but the guests. No one knew who was sleeping in which room but, from the sound of it, there wasn't much sleeping going on. Music and talking all night. Loud laughter. Breaking glass. Cars arriving and leaving at all hours. Just about the time everyone who worked on the ranch was getting up, the city kids were turning in, leaving huge messes to be taken care of in the morning.

More than once, Cord had to dampen the hormones of one of the girls who threw themselves at him openly. The girls seemed to think he was there to be another sexual conquest. They put themselves into stupid, sometimes dangerous, predicaments just so he'd have to *rescue* them. One of them walked up the aisle of the foaling barn in foolishly high-heeled boots no sensible person would wear to a barn. She stepped into a pile of manure left by one of the horses and refused to move. Wailing like a banshee, she claimed to be stuck, needing help. One of the other wranglers walked over and offered a hand. She slapped the offending glove away, loudly demanding that Cord rescue her.

Disgusted, Cord strode over to the girl who threw herself into his arms, acting as if he had just saved her from near death. The mares needed their peace and quiet. Cord left his arms hanging at his side and walked a few steps while the girl hung from his neck, trying to reach his face with kisses. He forced her hands apart and dropped her outside the door, slamming the wood shut. The others who saw the scene snickered until they saw the look in Cord's eyes. They quickly went back to work. Cord made his feelings as obvious as possible, without being downright rude. He wasn't interested. But nothing deterred the girls from their foolishness.

Within a week, Stanton was fed up. He ordered all of Edson's friends off the property. All except Edson, who raged and stormed as the others left. A heavy but grateful silence fell over the house again. Edson was livid. Everyone who knew Edson watched him carefully. The feeling that something was about to happen weighed heavily on all of them.

Six nights after the group had left, the underlying currents finally reached the boiling point. Edson received a package in the afternoon post that sent him cackling like a maniac to his room. He didn't come down to dinner that night. The next morning, he appeared at breakfast and announced he'd like to make amends for his bad behavior. He insisted Cord and the Delaney's join them for dinner. Suspicious, they looked at the elder Stanton who nodded his approval. They nervously agreed. After the dessert was served, Edson stood to make an announcement with a too bright gleam in his eye. Cord felt his mother's hand reach under the table for his. He knew she was holding Will's as well.

"My friends had such a good time here." Edson gestured magnanimously. "They wanted to do something to show how sorry they were for disrupting everything. I took some pictures while they were here. They developed them and had them put into a video montage for me. If you'll join me in the den, I think you'll enjoy this." Reluctantly, they followed Edson to the den.

The pictures were surprisingly good. Shots of the horses and people working. Beautiful landscapes and sunsets. Shots of the guests having a good time. Subtly, the pictures began to shift toward a darker mood. Inserted here and there were brief flashes of Cord carrying one of the girls. He recognized one or two of the occasions depicted in the photos.

One idiot girl had gotten *trapped* in a stall by a mare too old to care whether the girl was there or not. The girl claimed to be too terrified to move. With a disgusted sigh, Cord went in and pulled her out. She had jumped up into his arms, calling him her hero and then refused to be let down. She'd draped her barely clad body all over him trying to kiss him. When that didn't work, she'd pretended to faint. He had no choice but to close his arms tighter around her. He heard his mother make a disgusted noise from the other end of the sofa.

More scenery flashed by. There was Cord again, carrying a dark-haired girl in his arms. Her shirt was open and the very short shorts she wore did little to hide her body. Cord bit back a gasp. He remembered that day as well. He'd been embarrassed but, in the picture, they looked like the cover of a romance novel, like he had just ravished her or something. The face wasn't clear, but the dark hair looked familiar. His eyes flew open as he realized she looked like Deborah. His guilt over his fantasies raging, Cord glanced over at Stanton to see if he'd seen the resemblance.

More shots of the horses and then the other steel toed boot they'd been waiting for fell. On the screen was a picture of three completely naked people. An out-of-focus woman with black hair lay spread eagle on the floor, her blurry face distorted with either pain or pleasure, her back arched. One of the young men had his mouth poised over her breast, tongue curled around the nipple. Another young man lay at her other side, his face leering at the camera as he ran his hand over the woman's belly. The arms of another unidentified person reached in from the bottom of the picture to touch the woman's most intimate area. The picture left nothing to the imagination at all.

"My goodness," Edson said in mock horror. "Seems to be a little out of focus." He adjusted the picture and Deborah's face appeared clearly. Mary and Will Delaney turned away in disgust. Cord's tortured dreams leapt out of the screen at him. He looked at Edson who leered at his father and Deborah.

"Oh, my, what have we here?"

Deborah cried out. She leapt to her feet and faced Edson, screaming "You bastard!" She looked at the others, shadows of the picture dancing over her features. "I want you to know that this is a lie. Edson tried to force himself on me one night. When I refused, he swore he'd get even. This is the way he is trying to do it. That's not me!"

A strangled sound came from beside her. She looked down at her husband. His stricken face stared up at her. The blood vessel in his temple throbbed, dangerously enlarged.

"Darling? Larry?" She dropped to her knees beside him. "You have to believe me. It isn't me."

"I know," he gasped. "I know." He looked up at his grinning son, hatred in his pain-ridden eyes. "Get ... get ow, ow . . ." Before he could finish his command, his head fell back against the chair. Edson calmly sauntered out of the room, laughing.

Will and Mary scrambled into action. Will pulled Deborah away and instructed his wife to call an ambulance. Deborah wept over her husband's too-still body and prayed he was still alive. Cord stayed with the little group and did his best to comfort his mother while Will and Deborah made Stanton as comfortable as they could.

Badly shaken, Cord stormed out of the house in a blaze of fury as soon as the ambulance raced down the dirt, sirens blaring. He went to the barn. Someone had to be sure the stock was cared for and make sure the wranglers knew what to do before he could go to the hospital himself. How could anyone be this cruel? How could anyone hate this much? How could anyone stand there smiling, knowing he was killing his own father?

The more he thought about the situation, the angrier he got. When his fury and anger rose up over his shock, he ran back to the house, intent on taking Edson outside to beat him into the ground. But he rounded the corner of the house just as Edson's Corvette screamed out of the driveway. Rocks and dust flew. Cord thought he could hear the laugh of a madman carried back to him on the wind stirred by the sleek car.

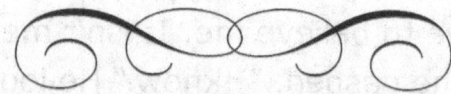

Stanton was confined to the hospital for two weeks. The first few days in intensive care kept everyone on edge. They took turns staying close by in case they were needed. Deborah refused to leave even long enough to eat or sleep. Any doubts anyone may have had about her love for Stanton fled during those few days of anguish. On the third day, he seemed to spring back. By the end of the week, he was demanding the doctors let him go home. Deborah convinced them she and the Delaney's would add private nurses to care for him. The doctors agreed reluctantly.

Deborah doted on her husband day and night. No one doubted her denial about the pictures. They all knew Edson too well. As soon as he felt well enough, Stanton called them all together to clear the air.

"I want you to know that I've known all along that wasn't Deborah in the picture. Deborah has a very distinctive birthmark on her abdomen that would have appeared clearly long before her face came into focus. I'm grateful to you all for showing your loyalty and supporting her through this."

Murmurs went around the room. Mary stood and said, "I think you know us well enough to know we'd never believe anything Edson said until there was proof positive." Deborah slipped an arm around Mary's shoulders and hugged her in gratitude.

"One more thing," Stanton paused for a moment. "I'm going to change my will as soon as I'm a bit stronger. I'm cutting Edson out completely. I'm leaving the ranch to Deborah and Cord jointly. Either one can buy the other one out. Neither has to stay but, since I doubt I'll have another legal heir in my condition, I want to make this clear. Edson will have to be told.

When I'm stronger, I'll call him. I want to tell him what I'm planning so there can be no mix up or confusion. Until that time, things will go on as always. Understood?"

Cord stood up, shaking his head. His hands were shaking at the prospect of the gift. He stammered, "Sir, I'm overwhelmed here. I guess stunned is a better word. I appreciate being considered for such an honor but I can't let you do this. Sell the ranch if you want to or leave everything to Deborah. I don't think I want to be involved with Edson any more than I am. And I certainly wouldn't look forward to a life of watching my back."

Stanton straightened up in bed. "Don't even start, Cord. You can't change my mind or make me change my plan. I know how much you love the place. You deserve a share and your parents with you. I also know how much you respect Deborah. I know you'll honor my wishes. Deborah will need someone behind her to keep Edson at bay."

He let his head fall back against the pillows, exhausted from the effort of making his mind known. The others stood to leave, bidding the sick man good night and walking out, stunned at his news. Deborah stood by the door as they filed out. As he stepped out, she touched Cord's arm lightly.

"It's what he wants, Cord. Don't worry. We'll work it out." She stepped back and closed the door.

Stanton didn't live long enough to change his will officially. He typed out his instructions on his laptop, printed the changes, signed the papers and meant to mail them to his lawyer. Two days after his announcement, he had a major heart attack in his sleep. No one was with him when he died. No one knew until they heard Deborah's scream.

Edson stayed away until the day of the funeral. While the Delaney's and Cord supported the griefstricken widow at the gravesite, Edson moved in. He didn't bother with the funeral. In fact, he didn't even let them know he was back. He just curled up like a snake under a rock and waited to strike.

When they came home, Deborah went quietly to her room and locked the door. The Delaney's went to their cottage and cried in each other's arms until they slept in the wee hours of the night. Cord went into town and got roaring drunk. He almost got into his car before a friend recognized him. He took Cord to his own home to sleep the drunk off.

Cord woke up very early the next morning with a vengeful headache. He slipped out just before dawn, found his truck parked outside the house, climbed in and drove home. Driving with the window open to try and clear his alcohol-fogged mind, Cord smelled the smoke before he saw anything. He knew the rank odor of fire. Fear cleared his mind faster than the fresh air could. He was about a mile from the house when he saw the clouds of smoke that confirmed his fears. But the fields weren't on fire. Part of the house and the stables were engulfed.

Billowing clouds of dark smoke, glowing red from the flames beneath, rose up before him. He stomped on the gas pedal and raced up the dirt road. Throwing gravel in every direction, the truck fishtailed before coming to an abrupt stop. Only two buildings were on fire – the stallion barn and the cottage. The cottage was totally engulfed. His heart clutched in fear that his parents might be inside.

The sound of a horse screaming in pain pulled his attention to the barn that was burning from the backside. The horse screamed again in pain and fury. His horse, Devil's Son, was the only stallion in the barn at the time. He ran toward the barn but the heat drove him back. The horse cried out seconds before the roof caved in, then only the sound of the raging flames filled the dawn.

Fear driving him on, Cord turned on his heels and raced to the cottage in time to see the walls collapse in on themselves. He stood paralyzed at the gruesome sight. Tears rolled down his face as Cord prayed again his parents weren't inside. At that moment, he noticed the car at the side of the house. Cord keeled over in agony. His parents went to bed early and that would have been hours ago. If the car was there, they were home. Sobs strangled in his throat as he struggled to his feet. The tiny hope that they were still in the big house glowed in his chest.

Cord pulled out his cell phone as he ran to the big house, calling out to them. He stopped outside long enough to give the information to the 911 responder and then hung up. Inside, Cord ran from room to room searching for his parents or Deborah. There was no sign of anyone. The house was ominously quiet.

The den door was slightly open. He raced to big oaken door praying he'd find them all inside the room. He tripped over a crumpled heap that lay on the floor. Deborah. Her shiny black hair spilled around her ashen face; a deep bruise darkened her cheek. The startling blue eyes stared blankly up at him. She wore a virginal white night gown. One shoulder strap was torn. A small dark hole spoiled the fresh whiteness of the gown and blood oozed over the front of the delicate gown.

Cord cried out and crawled back to her. His hand trembled as he touched the soft hair he'd dreamed about so many nights and reached up to close the sightless eyes. Tears flowed freely. He raced through the house calling for his mother. No one answered. At the base of the staircase, he sat back on his heels too stunned to think. In the space of 12 hours, he'd lost everything that meant anything to him. Everything. What happened? What?

"Well, isn't that just sweet?" Cord jumped at the sneering voice behind him. Edson sat in his father's chair, wrapped in the ridiculous velvet dressing gown. Cord fought the anger in him and stood to face Edson. "Why didn't you stop this? Have you called the fire department?"

Edson stood up and arrogantly walked to the marble fireplace. He struck a pose and said, "Stop it?

Stop it?! Why should I want to stop it when I started it?"

Cord's knees wavered. He'd started it. Blood rushed to his ears and began pounding as his mind struggled to understand what was going on.

He took a step toward Edson, rage mounting moment by moment. Edson smiled and waved a casual hand in Cord's direction. "I wouldn't entertain any nasty ideas if I were you."

Cord felt a hard round object press against the back of his head. Edson smiled again. "Kelleher there is very good with a gun and with a torch. He likes killing things, don't you, Kelleher?"

The huge man behind Cord cackled in a way that made Cord's stomach turn over.

"Maybe you'd like to have Kelleher tell you how he disabled that horse you were so proud of before he lit the barn afire? Hmm? Would you?" Kelleher snorted meanly under his breath. "Or maybe you'd like to know about how your parents screamed when they couldn't get out with all the windows and doors nailed shut?" Rage rose up in Cord's chest. He clenched his fists. Only the pressure of the gun kept him from leaping forward and grabbing Edson's throat.

If Edson noticed his rage building, he paid no mind and continued, "Now I, of course, am not even here so I wouldn't know but as you can see," He gestured toward the figure on the floor. "The bereaved widow seems to have ended her own life. Kelleher had to help a little, didn't you, Kelleher?" Edson smiled wickedly.

"Having good help is such a joy, don't you think, Grant?"

Edson paraded back and forth, laughing maniacally. Cord clenched and unclenched his fists, waiting for an opportunity to attack either man.

"Now here's how I see it." Edson flopped back into the chair. "You can leave now and everyone will assume you died in the fire. Or I can call the sheriff and say I found you trying to force yourself on the beautiful widow. Everyone has seen you mooning over her all this time. Plenty of witnesses to that. She must have drawn a gun to protect herself, but you took it away and shot her instead. Then you simply lost your mind and began to torch the place. I showed up just in time and stopped you from escaping with a bullet."

As the last word hung in the air, the sound of sirens coming up the drive rent the air. Cord stepped forward. "Your only flaw in that plan is that I already called the cops."

"Kelleher." Edson nodded toward Cord. The butt of the gun struck Cord in the back of the head. The last thing he heard before he blacked out was Kelleher's cackle and Edson's shrieking, "I'll be back... you can count on that."

True love stories never have endings.
Mark Bach

Seven

Bridey's eyes fluttered but stayed closed. *Where was she? What happened?*

She could feel a cool damp cloth on her forehead. The last thing she remembered was seeing that cowboy stretch his hand out to her. That hand! So very like the one in her dream. She must have fainted from the shock of it. Fainted! She never fainted! He must think she was a complete fool to have fallen at his feet.

As she started to raise her hand to move the cloth, she felt the sofa cushion beneath her tilt slightly sideways, as if someone had just sat down beside her. Bridey chose to lay still and focus on keeping her breath steady and even.

The cloth moved. A work-roughened hand stroked her cheek gently. She heard that voice murmur, "Wake up. Please just wake up and be OK." She barely opened her eyes to see the cowboy turn the cloth over to the cooler side and replace the pad gently on her forehead, higher this time. She felt him shift again as he stood up.

A nearby chair groaned softly.

Carefully, Bridey opened one eye further. There he was, sitting across from her, cradling his head in his hands, sleeves rolled to the elbow which were resting on his knees. For a moment, she felt guilty for deceiving him even this little bit. Obviously, he seemed more upset than right. She stared at his silver hair. The way he'd jumped the fence when the horse panicked belied the age a full head of gray hair suggested. Between his fingers, she could see a tan that stood out starkly against the lightness of his hair. She thought of the deep color of his eyes.

His body was long from DNA and lean from hours of hard work. Broad shoulders, muscular arms and legs showed he'd been doing ranch work most of his life. This was no movie star wannabee cowboy. He was the real thing. What was his story? Just as she was about to speak to him, the body she was admiring gave a shudder as if the pain he was feeling was too great to stay inside. For a brief moment, she thought he might be crying into his hands.

The eyes she'd thought about seconds before looked up and caught her staring at him. The icy blue, ringed with black, and, right now, bright with concern, orbs stared at her. When he saw that she was awake, the eyes instantly became distant and hard. He stood up. In one long stride, he towered over her, demanding,

"Who are you? Why are you here? What was that all about?"

Bridey lifted her hand to her aching forehead against the barge of question.

Cole reached out to her in concern. "Are you OK? Can you get up? Did you break anything?"

The questions came thick and fast. Bridey struggled to sit upright as he continued to barrage her with searching questions. Concern showed in every line of his angular, handsome face. Weakly, she held a hand up toward him, silently begging for a second to assess things. He waited impatiently, watching as she sat up and put a hand to her head.

No dizziness. No pain.

"Give me a second." She felt the back of her head where a nice goose egg of a bump was forming, tender but not painful. Briefly, she wondered if she'd have a bump on her backside as well. She refrained from checking.

"I seem to be OK." She smiled weakly at the glowering face above her.

Cord spun on his heel and disappeared through a nearby door. Bridey heard the sound of running water. The cowboy was gone for a few long minutes. When he returned with the glass of water, he'd steadied himself. Calm anger emanated from him like an icy wind over a winter landscape. He had to get rid of this woman. Now!

She was sitting on the sofa when he returned, rubbing the ankle that had failed her.

"Does that hurt bad?" He asked, handing her the glass of water.

"No, just a bit of an ache." She took the glass, careful not to touch those fingers or look into his disconcerting eyes. "I twisted my ankle a bit when I was getting out of the car. But I can walk fine. Thank you." "Good." He walked across the room to the massive wooden door and opened it. "I hate to be rude, but this isn't my house and you aren't welcome here. Get out!"

The glass nearly slipped from her hand. Bridey was prepared for a difficult conversation but not to be ordered out.

"Fine, but we need to talk first." She rooted herself to the sofa in case he came back to try to carry her out of door.

The door didn't close. "Talk about what? About the weeks you just set me back with that colt? Do you want me to pay for your fancy boot, broken by that ungrateful pebble on which you stepped? Do you want my name so you can sue me for whatever made you faint?"

Astonished, Bridey stared at the man. His glare demanded more answers. What in the hell was all this? She'd done nothing but say hello and accidentally upset his horse. Standing up to her full height, she said, "No, I have no intention of doing any of those things. That's not why I'm here."

"So? Just why are you here?"

"I was sent to find you."

The door slammed shut. Bridey dropped back to the sofa while long legs carried the furious cowboy back to her. He reached down and lifted her completely up easily. Seeking some kind of protection, Bridey dug her fingers into the cushion beneath her. The cushion offered no assistance as she carried the fabric with her, dangling in the air behind her.

"Who ... who sent you?"

Bridey paled as she felt her head begin to swirl again. Cord saw the wave of panic wash over her. Immediately sorry for his actions, his own eyes soften. He shook her slightly before setting her back on the sofa. "Sit down before you fall down," He demanded. "I don't need some city woman fainting on me again."

Cord pulled a chair close as Bridey tried to control her shaking. "Now tell me. Who sent you?"

Bridey looked around, "Where's my purse?"

"You don't need anything in that purse to tell me who sent you," he demanded.

"No," Bridey stared straight into the accusatory eyes. "But you may need to see my id to believe me."

An oath slipped out from between the angry lips as the cowboy pushed the chair back. He walked out the front door, leaving it open behind him. Bridey took a deep breath and tried to compose herself a little more. A moment later, the cowboy strode back into the room. In one hand, he carried her bag and the other carried her camera. She reached for both. He pulled back the camera and held out the bag.

She dug deep into the side pocket of the leather tote that carried her identification and pulled out a small gold case full of business cards. She slipped the clasp and took out a card printed on gold parchment. In elegant but simple script, the deep brown ink read simply "Bridey Deane, Managing Partner – New York" with her phone number beneath the letters. She handed him the card and leaned back, waiting for him to recognize her name.

The fingers dwarfed the elegant card. The eyes that read the words didn't react at all. The lips that should have smiled didn't. His dark eyebrows raised quizzically above the icy blue eyes that showed no change. "This is supposed to explain something?"

Bridey sat stunned. He didn't know who she was. If he didn't know her work, she was certain that fool Damian hadn't mentioned that she was coming. Bridey cursed under her breath. Even if he wasn't the cowboy she was sent to find, he was perfect. She'd have to do some fast-talking to get him to agree after all this drama.

"I'm a photographer hired by a company that sells men's colognes. Damian Montrose, friend of the owner's, said he told you I was coming to photograph you. You are Brock Delta, aren't you?" She spouted the first name she could make up in order to make him think she was here accidentally. Maybe that would temper his anger to some extent.

Cord snorted. He was right. She was a movie fool, a groupie of some sort. He snorted again and handed her the card. "No, I'm not Rock Dealer or whatever his name is. You're in the wrong place, Lady."

"Well, no matter Mr. -, Mr.?" She offered her hand.

"Grant." He stood tall, arms tightly crossed on his chest. He made no move to take her hand.

"Well," She stood up and dusted herself off a bit. "It seems as though I've bungled this from the beginning. I not only have the wrong person, but I've also done something to make you angry. Now I can't figure out what made me faint or why you reacted like you did. All I can do is offer my apologies for passing out and spooking the horse." She stood directly in front of him and offered her hand once more. "Can we please start over if I promise not to faint and not to ever go near another horse as long as I live?" She saw his hesitation and moved to capitalize on his hesitation. "And I'll make it a part of my will that none of my children or grandchildren will ever go near a horse as long as they live either. How's that?"

Cord struggled to keep his angry demeanor as the woman tried to patch things up. She stared at him until he couldn't hold out any longer. He stuck his hand out and took hers. Bridey's heart skipped a beat as she felt his strong fingers wrap around hers. There was something here, something she felt, like a half remembered dream. Her head swam lightly. She ordered herself to gain control.

"Thank you," she gasped and pulled her hand away from him. She turned her back and rummaged through the tote bag again.

Cord, his hand still in midair, stared at her back. The jolt of electricity he'd felt when she touched him rooted him to the ground. He felt shaken, unnerved, like nothing he'd ever felt before. His hand wanted to reach out and stroke her hair, to take her in his arms, to crush her to his chest. That one touch told him how she'd feel ... how she'd feel in his arms, her kiss, everything about her. She turned back to face him and he let the lingering hand fall to his side.

The coy smiling little woman was replaced almost instantly by a confident, no-nonsense businesswoman. Cord's eyebrows raised at the change in demeanor. "Now, Mr. Grant, here's the deal. I'm in a position to make us both a lot of money."

Cord kept his eyes and face still as the young woman's green eyes searched his. Bridey rolled on in her speech. "Not millions, mind you, but enough to make you feel a whole lot better about your future." No reaction.

"I'm talking about at least a couple hundred thousand dollars over the next few years."

Cord flinched. That was a lot of money and he could certainly use it.

"What would I have to do?" he asked suspiciously.

Bridey smiled. Experience had told her when they started asking questions she had them hooked. "Not much. Just let me take your picture."

"And?" Cord asked suspiciously, knowing there had to be more.

". . . And give me, or rather my client, permission to use your photo to sell her product. Here." She leaned over the leather tote again and rummaged around. Her hand held up a dark bottle shaped like a saddle horn.

"Try it."

Cord snorted in disgust and turned his back without taking the bottle. He walked over to a picture window. He stood for a moment letting the panoramic view soothe his shaky nerves. That was a lot of money. But was that enough to make coming out of hiding worth the sacrifice?

"Would I have to leave here?" He didn't face her to ask the question.

"Maybe not." She hesitated. "I'm sure the client would like to meet you and you'd have to come to New York to sign the contracts. Of course, if you want any say in the layouts, you'd have to come to the City." Bridey was so busy congratulating herself that she barely heard his simple answer.

"No." He wouldn't leave here to go to New York City. He couldn't be a part of an advertising campaign that would have his face plastered all over the country. Even after all these years, he knew Edson hadn't given up looking for him. Edson, the madman who now had no keeper, would keep trying to find him as long as he was alive and he had money to turn over every stone. Cord had some peace now. He'd buried himself far enough away that he was reasonably sure Edson couldn't find him. He couldn't risk exposure.

"No." Cord walked over to the door and held it open again. "Now it's time for you to leave."

Disbelief and more than a little anger filled Bridey. She turned and began to gather up her things. Here she offered this cowboy more money than he'd ever be able to earn as a ranch hand, the chance to be famous and the chance to visit a place most people only dreamed about and he was showing her the door.

Fine, she thought, *there are other cowboys out there. We can find another.*

"You can leave that." Cord spoke softly as Bridey lifted the camera. She clutched the machine to her chest, like a security blanket.

Leave her camera! Fat chance.

"Leave it or unload it. Whichever you prefer." The quiet threat in his voice stilled Bridey.

"I'm not leaving my camera. This is an expensive top-of-the-line piece of equipment I need to do my job."

"Then unload the film." Cord demanded, taking a step towards her.

"No. What's in here belongs to me. The film is mine and so are the shots. You have nothing to say about it. I promise not to use your photos for anything, but there are other pictures on this film that I do need."

"Tough. Unload it or I will." Cord stretched out his ungloved hand and stepped toward her, hoping she wouldn't faint at the site of his hand again.

Bridey clutched the camera to her chest. She wasn't giving the equipment up. Her other hand gripped the straps of the heavy leather tote. Without fully understanding what she meant to do, Bridey stood, trembling until he was within arm's reach.

With speed and strength multiplied by fear, she swung the heavy bag around and felt the leather connect with the side of his head. She watched with astonished eyes as he slowly sank to his knees onto the wooden floor beneath his feet. His eyes studied hers for a brief second before he fell face down onto the hooked rug in front of the sofa.

"Oh, God," she cried out. "Oh, God help me, I've killed him." For a moment, she stood over his body wondering what to do. She tentatively reached out to touch his neck and felt a shallow pulse. Breathing a heavy sigh of relief, she grabbed the leather tote holding the camera and ran out the door to her waiting vehicle. Without pausing to fasten the seat belts, she slammed the truck into gear and raced down the drive and back toward the City.

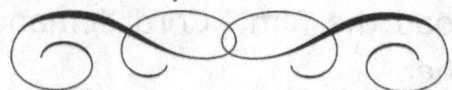

Cord's head spun in a deep dreamy state. He struggled to wake up, but his eyes wouldn't obey. Carefully, he tried moving his arms and legs. Each one responded like a limb was supposed to, but he felt like a heavy weight sat on his chest. With each breath, the weight settled a little more. Panic set in as he tried to sit up and remove the pressure before heaviness crushed him.

He thought he heard something move slightly above his head and reached out a hand. He stretched as far as he could. His cold fingers could feel the heat of a body just out of his reach. He called out as loudly as he could, "I need you to take my hand!"

The only name he could think of leaped to his lips, "Katherine ... please. I need you to take my hand." He could feel the warmth of a smaller hand hovering over his. His thoughts confused him.

Who was Katherine and why wouldn't she take his hand? What was happening to him?

A warm tongue licked his hand and he opened his eyes. The old collie looked at him in deep concern. Cord smiled at the idea that the dog might be named Katherine. The sound of a rooster crowing brought Cord further out of his daze. His jaws hurt where the bag had connected. His body ached from lying on the hardwood floor. If the rooster and the glow in the sky through the window were to be believed, he'd been on the hard cold floor all night.

Gingerly, he sat up and rubbed his jaw. He never would have expected that she'd hit him. What the hell was in that bag anyway? Bricks? Cord stood up slowly and stretched trying to get the kinks out of his neck and shoulders. There before him in the middle of the braided rug was the only real evidence besides his aching jaw that the woman had ever been there. He picked up the business card. Her name was Bridgette.

So, who the hell was Katherine? And why did he feel like he should recognize the woman?

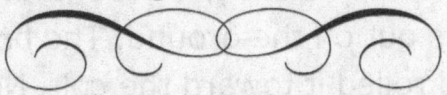

For days afterward, Cord carried the card in his pocket. Often his hand rubbed past the pocket that sheltered the stiff paper. Once in a while, he even pulled the card out to look and wondered if he had made a mistake sending her away.

Cord felt the strain of Stallings' time limit closing in. He had made enough progress to get the colt to let him groom the shiny black coat. The colt had finally accepted him, eating from his hand, allowing his feet to be picked up and wallowing in the pleasure of a good grooming. The stallion stood quietly and let Cord run his hands anywhere he wanted to, always wary but slowly becoming more trusting.

Once in a while, the stallion even showed signs of playfulness. Cord worked with the stallion on a cool summer's evening a couple days after Bridey's visit. The breeze, which had saved the day from being too hot, picked up as the sun went down. In one hand, Cord carried the bucket of feed and the other held grooming tools. The horse snorted and pranced in place as he watched Cord come through the gate.

"What's your problem, Kin?" Cord talked to the horse as he cavorted around. The horse nodded its head up and down, nostrils flaring as if trying to catch a scent. "What? Do you think I have suddenly become a wolf or something?" Cord snickered under his breath and put the bucket down. He heard the colt take a step or two toward him. Calmly, he bent over to lay the grooming tools out on the ground. The breeze knocked his hat off and rolled it toward the colt. Nostrils flaring, the colt reared up and ran at the hat. Just short of stomping on it, the huge beast stopped and delicately sniffed the beaten felt hat.

Cord watched the horse nose the hat and smiled. "That's right. It's mine. It's not going to hurt you." He stepped up to the horse and patted its neck. The horse's head stayed near the ground. As Cord reached down to pick up his hat, the horse snaked out his head and snatched up the battered felt between strong white teeth. He threw his head high and raced off to the other side of the corral.

"What the hell?" Cord walked over to where the colt had dropped the hat and now stood over it, watching him. Cord reached for the hat again, and the big animal grabbed the brim and whirled away.

Cord laughed softly and waited until the colt stopped on the other side of the corral. "So, you want to play, do you?" Cord spoke in his soothing tones. "Well, I don't want to. You want the hat, you keep it." He turned his back and walked to the bucket again. Watching out of the corner of his eye, he saw the horse nodding his head, hat dangling from its mouth. Step by cautious step, the colt walked forward, pausing between each delicate pace. Cord felt like the colt was sneaking up on him. He reached into the bucket and lifted a handful of grain, letting the golden seeds spill back into the bucket from between his splayed fingers. The colt's ears pricked forward. He let the grain drift through his fingers again and again until the colt stood beside him. The hat still dangled from the black lips, but the eyes were fastened on Cord's hands.

The colt dropped the hat and tried to push his way past Cord to the bucket. Cord was ready for him and moved the bucket until he was between the horse and grain. The horse snorted and tried to reach around the man. Cord moved the bucket further away. The horse looked at Cord and pinned his ears back.

"No, you don't!" The ears tipped forward again. "If you want to tease, you have to learn to take as well as give." The big horse lowered his head. Gently, the same way Devil's Son used to, he laid his head over Cord's shoulder and snuffled, sounding for all the world like a little kid apologizing.

Cord gave the horse's neck a pat and stepped away from the bucket. As the greedy horse ate, Cord walked over to the sodden hat on the ground. He was never going to get that cleaned up. But the horse's playfulness showed a new level of their relationship. Cord was pleased.

"Nice work." A voice came from over the corral bars. Cord looked to see his boss leaning on the top rail. "I never thought you'd get that close to him. I'm impressed. Can you ride him?"

Cord had been waiting for this moment. "Nope, threw a rope around him two days ago and he settled down nice, but the saddle was a whole different story."

"Your month is about up. What are you going to do?" Stallings shifted his weight to his other leg.

"I don't know. I can't afford to keep him if he won't be ridden, but I'd hate to see him end up dog meat or in a rodeo. He's a good horse with lots of potential." "As what?" asked the rancher.

"He's got good blood in him. Make an excellent stud."

"Got no papers on him though."

"Yeah, that's a problem. I guess I will give him to you and you decide what to do. After all, you are the one who's been feeding him."

"Hmmm," Stallings stepped away from the fence and walked to the gate. As soon as he lifted the latch, the stallion threw his head up. The horse watched Stallings step through the gate. Stallings took a step toward him. The horse reared to his full height and backed into a corner. Stallings sensibly backed out of the corral.

"Just what I thought. I can own his body, but you own his heart."

Cord stepped outside the corral and stood beside the older man. They watched the horse lipping hay for a few moments. Cord sighed. There was only one way he could think of to save the horse.

"I have a few days of vacation coming, don't I?"

"Yeah."

"Well, I need them. I have to go to New York. When I get back, I'll have enough money to pay for his board until I can get him to work. I know he'll be worth it."

Stallings looked at Cord. "New York, you say. Since you have been here you've hardly stepped off the place to go to town. Now you're telling me you're going to New York." He shook his head and looked back at the colt. "Much as I like horses, I ain't never met one I'd do that much for." He walked off toward the house.

As soon as Stallings left, Devil's Kin strolled over to the fence and snuffled Cord's shirt through the rails. Absently, Cord reached back and rubbed the satiny nose. "Like I said before, Horse. You better be worth this!"

"Love is the emblem of eternity;
It confounds the notion of time;
Effaces all memory of a beginning;
and all fear of an end."
Germaine de Stael

1686 – Central America

England – February 1681

Eighteen-year-old Tommy Gray rolled up his sleeves and sat on a bench outside the stable, chewing on a piece of straw he'd taken from the new bales he'd spent all day stacking. His arms and back ached from the strenuous work, but he felt the kind of good that came from a hard job done well. He smiled at the idea that any sane person would think stacking bales was a great way to spend the day, but he loved the hard work. Anything that got him into the paddocks with the horses was his idea of heaven.

"Gray!" He turned to see the man he'd worked beside all day, the one who groused about how tired he was, running to the stable. Aches and pains apparently forgotten, he was all cleaned up and ready for a night on the town. "Come on, Tommy-boyo! Pay day! Time to go spread some joy in town."

Gray laughed and waved the man on. He knew all the men who went into town would come back in the wee hours of the morning, trusting their mounts to find the way home and then spend the next day miserable as they did their chores. No such thing as a holiday on a working horse farm. "You go on," he called. "I'll keep watch on things here."

He watched as the three men rode out the main gate as fast as they could, laughing and baiting one another. No, he'd rather sit here, listen to the night and thinking about her.

Katherine.

He'd dreamt about her since childhood. He talked about her so much that his mother thought he had an imaginary friend. She was not an imaginary figment to him. The red hair that flowed down her back and glowed in the sunlight was real to him. He closed his eyes and imagined his fingers running through the silken locks. He knew the jade green eyes that smiled up at him as well as he knew his own face. He knew how the clear creamcolored skin as soft as a rose petal felt under his hand.

He also knew the terror and fear some of his dreams brought him. Whenever she came to him in a dream, the ending was always the same. One of them is in danger, unable to reach the other. So many times, he had stood in front of her with his hand outstretched, her hand just beyond his reach, calling her name, only to have her jerked away from him.

One of these days, he'd succeed. He'd do anything and go anywhere to find her.

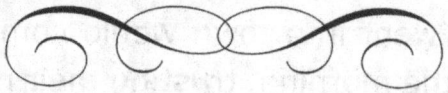

Scotland – June 1685

"But Father!" Anna-Kate drew herself to her full height and still had to stare up at her father. She refused to let his imperious glare dissuade her. "There is no reason why I shouldn't be allowed to go. Matthew is no more capable than I." She spun on her heel and stormed a few steps away. When she whipped around again, she continued, "I can shoot better than he can any day. I ride far better than he does."

Her father stared at his indignant child. He commanded hundreds of men who'd do exactly what he wanted the instant he asked without question. He rubbed his hand over his face and wondered why he couldn't control a small slip of a girl. She stood across the room, chest rising and falling, face flushed, hands on hips, defying him in every line of her body. This, he knew, was his fault. Without a woman in the house, Anna-Kate had grown up free of the usual feminine constraints. She didn't understand how much more danger she was under simply by virtue of her sex.

"I'll not be held captive, Father." She dropped her hands from her hips and walked back to where her exasperated father stood at attention. She put her hands on his chest and felt him relax slightly. "You yourself said this was a chance of a lifetime. Why is the chance available to Matthew and not to me?"

She turned again and sauntered to the sideboard where her father's favorite Scotch stood waiting. The crystal bulb came off the decanter with a satisfying pop. She poured a stout amount into a matching glass and turned. Warming the amber liquid slightly as she held the glass, she walked back to her father's favorite chair and indicated he might sit. She could see him arguing with himself for a few seconds but then he sighed and gave in.

Once he was seated and had taken the first stiff swallow, Anna-Kate settled on to the small, padded stool at his feet. She waited for the tell-tale second sigh, the one that told her he was softening.

"Poppa, I understand you're worried," she continued, keeping her voice honeyed and low. AnnaKate leaned her head against his arm, knowing he couldn't resist her when she acted demure. "But Uncle James has been down there for five years. His letters are full of the beauty of the country and the people. He has a big house, with maids and gardeners... just like here."

"Drat, Anna-Kate! Panama is not just like here. They're wild people. Your uncle may have befriended some of them as his company helps build roads across the country but there are other things. "My God child," He drained the glass and Anna-Kate leapt up to refill the empty crystal. His voice followed her as she retrieved the decanter and brought the whole bottle back. "His letters have also talked about jaguars that can be heard in the nearby jungles, snakes as big as a man's arm that can bite you and kill you within minutes! And crocodiles!
Do you hear me? Crocodiles!!!"

Anna-Kate quietly refilled the glass clenched in her father's fist, patted his arm, placing the decanter on the Asian carpet at her feet and then she sank back onto the wee stool. "But Papa, he also talked about the beautiful birds, the gorgeous water, and the deep green jungles. He said the compound around the house was kept clear of dangerous animals and guarded at all times. No one is allowed to leave the compound alone … so I'd always be safe."

Anna-Kate's father stood and walked to the long, heavily draped window and stared out onto the vast snow-covered land laying before him. "What about the journey there? The trip alone would take months. There are so many dangers to be considered."

"Matthew will be with me at all times. I'll stay below decks in my room and, if you want, you can send Thane with us." Her father scoffed loudly and lifted the nearly empty glass to his tight lips once again. He thought about the giant Scot who'd been his children's loyal guardian since birth. No one would cross the redheaded giant of a man. His children would definitely be safe with him, but how would the land-loving, kiltwearing Scot fare on a ship for so long? The idea of a seasick Thane made him both smile and sigh.

"Father, you have to give me this. Let me go with Matthew. We'll go for two years and then come back ready to do whatever you want. Matthew'll go into the military and I'll become the lady you've always wanted me to be and yes! I'll even seek out a proper husband."

"That, my beautiful young woman, would be a dream too difficult for me to hold onto until I see you actually walking down the aisle at my side."

Anna-Kate laughed gaily and wrapped her arms around her father's waist. He lifted the arm with the Scotch in his hand to be sure none of the precious liquid was spilled. He pulled this difficult, wonderful child to him and said gruffly, "Careful now, wee Anna ... we don't want to waste the Scotch."

Anna-Kate reached up, kissed her father's bristly cheek and ran to the door, "I'm going to tell Matthew and Thane. Then I'm going to write to Uncle James and tell him to be ready for us."

"Now, darlin,' you better let me tell Thane," he snickered. Anna-Kate giggled and waved as she scampered out the door, leaving a trail of joyful laughter in her wake.

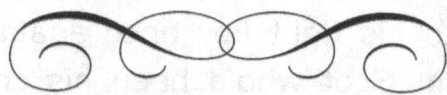

Panama—one year later

Anna-Kate stared at her father's letter in her hand like the paper was a foreign object from a different world. She had no idea what she was going to say to him. The months that had passed since she had stood on the rail of the great ship, happily waving good-bye to her father seemed centuries ago. So much had happened.

Thane, a man of the land and mountains, never took to the rolling of the ship. He spent most of the trip below decks, moaning on his bed. Any time he ventured up to the deck was spent hanging over the railing, losing food he didn't have in his belly to the sea. He'd lost so much weight that he barely looked like the mountain of a man sent to look after her and her brother. The day they'd buried him at sea was the worst day in her young life. Her mother had died when she was too young to understand. But losing Thane, the man who'd been the best uncle she had known, was her first experience of losing a loved one. She'd wept for days until Matthew had finally made her get out of her bed, eat something, and share her sorrow.

The eleven-month trip presented stunning sunsets and sunrises and amazing storms that threatened to sink the sturdy ship. She'd seen dolphins swimming in the wake of the ship and odd birds flying overhead. Every time they put into a port, she and Matthew had hired a burly sailor or two to wander through the streets with them and see them safely back to the ship. When they'd crossed into the tropics, the weather had turned wonderfully warm and they'd seen smooth sailing for weeks on end.

The captain apologized on the last day of the journey. She knew her father had had to pay a small fortune just to get her on board, the captain being a man who still believed that women on board a ship was bad luck. But there had been no unexpected problems other than the loss of Thane ... instead, he added, someone must be looking out for them as he'd rarely had such a smooth sail.

Anna-Kate accepted his apology as they stood together by the rail and sailed through the waters of the Caribbean Sea. The town of Colon sprawled off to the right. The jungle seemed to come right down to the water. Anna-Kate scanned the deep green expanse wondering where her uncle's compound might be. She gazed at the distant mountains and crisp blue skies while they waited for the small flotilla of boats to arrive to facilitate their anchoring.

The powerful memory of that pristine, fateful day flooded into Anna-Kate, forcing her to sit in the nearest chair. She dropped into the cane-bottomed seat and stared out the window at the deep cerulean sky. She closed her eyes and remembered the sound of the waves lapping against the wooden boats, the screeching birds rolling above and the slap of the oars as the men rowed closer.

That's when she saw him. Not all of him at first. But, in the sea of shorter men with dark skin and hair, his sheer height stood out. She stared at his back as he directed the men expertly. Uncovered in the tropic sun, his strong, tanned forearms guided the boats alongside the ship. Just before Matthew grabbed her arm to go below, the man turned and looked up. Anna-Kate gasped. Unable to tear her eyes away, she watched as he reached up and removed his hat to acknowledge her. A shock of white hair fell onto his forehead. His brilliant blue eyes took her breath away. The deep tan, white hair and blue eyes were so distinctive. *I know him,* she thought. But how was that possible? She knew no one here except her uncle.

As she packed, she tried to shake the vision of the man's face from her mind with no luck. She was sure she wouldn't have forgotten such a man.

"Matthew?" She called to her brother in the next berth.

"Yeah?" He popped his head out of the door like a rabbit sniffing the wind. "What? We gotta hurry! I want to get out there."

"Did you see that man on the boat?"

Matthew scoffed. "Anna, there were a lot of men out on those boats." He ducked back into the room.

"The big one. The boss. You had to see him. He had white hair. His sleeves were rolled up to his elbows and..."

Matthew had backed out of the room and was struggling to pull his steamer trunk to the end of the aisle. Huffing and puffing, he scraped the heavy wooden case along. "Is ... yours ... ready?" He stopped at the end, breathing heavily. "This is where I really miss Thane." He looked up to see Anna's downcast face. "Sorry, AnKa," using his childhood name for her for the first time in years. "I shouldn't have said that." He walked over to put his arm over her shoulder. "Let me get your trunk."

Anna-Kate wiped the mist from her eyes and watched her brother struggle. "I just wondered if you saw him."

"No, Anna ... I don't ... remember anyone ... like that." He tugged the trunk in beside his. "Now get your hat and let's get up top."

"Anna!" A weak cry from inside the room pulled her back from the memory of that time. She hadn't seen the man since that brief sighting but she still couldn't shake the feeling she knew him.

"Anna. Please."

She stood, picked up the letter that had fallen to the floor in front of her, and walked toward the closed door with the yellow quarantine sign taped to the crossbar near the top.

Pausing for a moment, she picked up a clean handkerchief from the sideboard, doused the linen liberally with lavender scent, placed the cloth under her nose, and drew in a deep breath. The heat from the stuffy room hit her as soon as the heavy ornate door opened, along with the smell of sickness. She waved her hand before her face to rid the air of the ever present mosquitos. She was getting used to the heavy humid air, but she still found breathing hard. She could hear cicadas and the croaking sound of the toco toucans in the jungle.

This wasn't the way she'd wanted her wild adventure to end. She'd never been trained to do any of this work. Thanks to Ezora, the native woman who ran her uncle's house, Anna-Kate had learned quickly. Her brother's cot lay on the far side of the room. Even in the dimness, she could see he was drenched with sweat.

"Matthew, I'm here." Anna-Kate dipped a cloth in the basin next to his bed and wiped the sheen of sweat from his forehead. Tears came to her eyes at the sight of her strong vital brother wasting away from the illness. The doctor'd given her a new medicine which was believed to cure the dreaded malaria. She mixed the whitish powder into a tin cup and knelt down beside his cot. "You need to drink this, Matthew."

Matthew had enough strength to wrinkle his nose, but he didn't fight her when she lifted his head and put the cup to his lips. He grimaced as the bitter liquid drizzled into his mouth and he swallowed weakly. If she could just get a few sips into him every day, he would have a chance to live. Matthew pulled away and laid back on the pillow.

"Go check Uncle James." Matthew urged. "I haven't heard him all day. I'm worried."

"Shhh," Anna comforted him as she stood. "I'm sure he's fine."

She turned toward her uncle's cot. His face was ashen and his eyes stared unseeing at the fan spinning slowly above his bed. Careful not to gasp out loud, Anna kissed him on the forehead and pulled the soaking wet linen over her uncle's face.

"Hello, Uncle James." she said, for Matthew's sake, barely controlling the tremor of tears in her voice. She backed away from the cot and pulled a room divider from the end of the bed, blocking Matthew's view. She walked back to her brother's cot.

"He's asleep, I checked and his breathing is steady. I think he's even cooler. I'm pretty sure he's turned the corner ... just like you will do any day now." She knelt down and wiped her brother's face again. "Tell you what. I'll talk to Ezora and see if she can take you and James out for fresh air today. Does that sound good?" Matthew made a slight groaning sound. "I'd love to see the sky," he whispered and dropped off to sleep.

Leaving the letter from her father to read to him later, Anna stepped into the hall and nearly ran into Ezora carrying fresh linen to the room. Seeing her stricken face, Ezora dropped the linen and rushed to take Anna-Kate into her arms. She let Anna sob for a few minutes and then whispered, "Which one?" Choking back her sobs, Anna-Kate pulled her weight off the much shorter, smaller woman and said, "James." Ezora put a hand to her mouth. "Shhhh! I didn't tell Matthew. Can you get Naoto and Idris? We need to try to get his body out of there while Matthew's asleep." Ezora nodded and bustled down the hallway in search of her husband and son.

Two days later, Matthew's fever broke and he immediately began to look better. Anna-Kate drew her first relieved breath in days. After telling Matthew about James, they decided that they needed to go back home. With James gone, there was no telling what would happen to the guards that kept them safe. No doubt Ezora and her men would stick by them, but they weren't equipped to keep James' business running. That was never part of the plan.

Late that evening, Anna-Kate sat in the parlor, listing what had to be done before they could return, when Ezora burst into the room. For the quiet little woman to cause any sort of commotion was so atypical that Anna knew immediately something was terribly wrong.

"Miss. Come with me. Hurry." Ezora's gnarled fingers wrapped around Anna-Kate's arm and she pulled her to her feet with surprising strength.

"Ezora! What's wrong? Is it Naoto?" Ezora went scampering down the hall only shaking her head in response to her question. Following Ezora through the kitchen and out the back door toward the stables, AnnaKate couldn't imagine what would make Ezora take her out into the mosquito-riddled night. Across the dark yard, she saw the small house where Ezora and her family lived beside the barn. The door was open. A light blazed from inside and several dirty men stood at the opening.

Ezora beckoned her to come in. Slipping between the men, she entered the small room. On a long wooden table lay a bruised, bloodied body of a large man.

"We were working in the channel under the bridge." Ezora's son whispered. "He always worked in the water with his men. No other boss worked like that with us."

Naoto's muddy face implored Anna-Kate, "Can you help him, Missy? He's a good boss." Naoto fidgeted at the brim of the hat in his hand, a once white hat. "One of the mules on the bridge above us spooked and fell off the bridge into the water. The wagon came down too. Boss, he pushed me away but couldn't get away himself." Naoto pleaded with her, tears rolling down his face. "Please, Missy. Ezora doesn't think she can save him. What will we do?"

Anna-Kate stepped toward the man on the table. His legs were bent at ridiculous angles where legs weren't supposed to bend. One of his shirt sleeves was empty, the sleeve still rolled up to where the elbow should have been. Bile rose up into her throat as she moved closer. When she saw the jagged spoke of a wagon wheel jutting out from his stomach, she knew no one here had the skills to save him. He moaned. She ran a hand down the bare forearm that remained to take his hand which still had a leather glove on it. She moved to his head and stroked his forehead like she had Matthew's a few days before. Her filthy hand cleared some of the mud from that man's hairline. Anna-Kate was stunned to see white hair. She dropped the man's hand when his eyes opened and the brilliant blue eyes of the man she felt she knew from somewhere gazed at her. She stepped back.

He struggled to stretch his hand out to her. AnnaKate saw the gloved hand reaching for her. *Where had she seen that before?*

She looked into the man's eyes. For a brief moment, he smiled the warmest, most loving smile she had ever seen. His lips parted.

"Katherine! I've search so long." He worked harder to stretch his gloved hand out to her. "Katherine. It's time." The eyes closed. The hand dropped and the smile faded. And Anna-Kate, for some odd reason, felt a deep aching loss in her heart.

"I vow to fiercely love you in all your forms, now and forever. I promise to never forget that this is a once in a lifetime love."
Leo, The Vow (2012)

Nine

Bridey's headlong flight back to the City was uneventful. The trip was less frustrating since she knew what to expect and had something to occupy her mind. So much had happened and yet she was going back empty-handed.

That man, Grant, was perfect for the campaign. Bridey knew exactly what Lana Markham would say. But if she wanted this man, Lana would have to go out there and convince him herself. However, Bridey was sure she'd had her fill of the Wild West. If she ever saw him again, that cowboy would have been the one coming to her.

As luck would have it, Lana was off on a cruise when Bridey got back. The cruise was a typically Lana last minute thing that just couldn't wait. Over the next few days, Bridey threw herself into catching up on missed work and trying to forget the cowboy.

Neither her head nor her heart would let her completely forget him though. Everywhere she went, she saw him. Sometimes he was in a pose struck by a model she was photographing. Sometimes she heard his voice from another man's mouth. Once she even thought she saw him walking across the street. The stranger turned around before she embarrassed herself. He was everywhere and nowhere and wouldn't leave her alone.

Late one evening after a heavy week of shooting, Bridey went to her darkroom. She stepped into the cool, calm cave. Chemical smells wafted up as she filled the white enamel trays. This was her quiet place where no one came unless invited. Nothing bothered her here. Roll after roll of pictures appeared in the chemical baths, many discarded. Only the best were good enough for Bridey Deane.

Suddenly, there he stood, fixed in the golden light. The horse and the man glided in sunset gold. Sleeves rolled to the elbow. His light hair reflected the sunset into her camera lens. Bridey stood and watched the hauntingly perfect picture take form and found herself lost in thoughts of the man. Everything else was laid aside. Nearly every one of the photos she'd taken was perfect ... art gallery, prize winningly perfect. Her hand shook slightly as she lifted the last one out, both horse and man looking straight at her.

"Get a hold of yourself, Bridey," she told herself huskily. "He's country and you aren't. He's not interested in the City and you won't leave the bustle. He's ... he's ... Good Lord, he's handsome." Her hand reached to touch the chiseled cheek. She ran the same finger down the bare forearm. She had never understood her fascination with a man's sleeves rolled to his elbows. Something about that simple action stirred her deep inside.

She shook her head at her own foolishness and hurried to clean up the room, intending to put the photos away in the morning after they had dried. She stopped her silly thoughts and considered the early call she had to make in the morning. She slid between the cool sheets and felt the heavy duvet settle down around her. The big feather bed seemed to form around her like the arms of a lover she never had time to find, like *his* arms would. She drifted off to sleep with visions of the man, his horse and the possibilities.

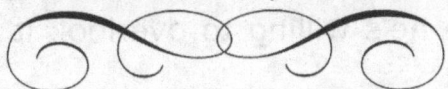

She overslept and nearly missed the shoot the next morning. As far as Bridey was concerned, that would've been fine. The only thing worse than a bunch of proud mothers fawning over their sniveling youngsters was a bunch of elderly matrons with the ugly little dogs they doted on. The morning dragged by as Bridey tried hard to work her magic on the fussy old ladies and their cantankerous little creatures. Bridey longed for the distant day she'd pick and choose her customers, when the choice would be more important than the client, the money, or the fame. But these ladies. Well, they were her mother's friends. Even when she got so wellknown everyone knew her by a single name, Bridey knew she'd still do this yearly duty.

This was her way of trying to heal the chasm her exhusband, Mark had made between her and her mother. On the few occasions, her mother would call to chat, she never failed to mention Mark and how successful he was in everything but finding a bride. But her mother didn't know the real Mark. The violent angry Mark who knew how to hide the bruises and make a woman feel like she was nothing. That Mark only came out when no one else was around. Bridey knew how lucky she was to have escaped and how hard she had fought to set up a new life.

"He loves you so much, Bridey," her mother fawned. "He's never gotten over you. He tells me that whenever I see him." A deep sigh came through the wires. "I wish you'd call him and talk over the problem, whatever it was. I'm sure he's willing to overlook it and take you back."

With each call, Bridey muttered noncommittal sounds and tried hard not to scream at her mother, knowing she'd never give up.

Bridey got back to her apartment late in the afternoon, longing for the peace and quiet. She loaded all her equipment in a precarious pile in her arms and walked inside. One flight up and she'd be home. Bridey climbed the stairs and stopped halfway up. Her door was open slightly. No one in the City left his or her door open and unlocked even when they were home. She'd lived here too long to be that careless. She put down her cameras on the narrow stairs and finished the climb on the tips of her toes.

At the scarred wooden door, Bridey stopped and listened for just a moment. A muffled voice came from inside. She pushed the door open quietly and stepped inside, her heart beating rapidly. The light in her dark room glowed under the curtain that separated the alcove from the rest of the room. Bridey shivered. The voice came from inside. Looking around for a weapon, she grabbed the umbrella leaning against the wall behind the door. It wouldn't do much damage, but it might frighten off a burglar.

Hands and legs shaking, she crept toward the dark room. Cautiously, she pushed the curtain aside. In the middle of the room stood Lana, cell phone in hand, talking away.

"You're never going to believe this!" Lana was looking at the pictures of Grant still hanging on the drying line. Admiration coated every word she said to whomever was on the other end of the phone line. "Yes, get over here! Right now! She's done it again. She is amazing! Totally brilliant. What? No, Bridey's not here but she will be soon!"

Lana turned and saw Bridey standing in the doorway, brandishing the umbrella. "Oh, Bridey darling!! You're here." Turning back to the phone, she said, "Bridey's here! Come now!" She slapped the cover of the phone shut and flew to the stunned photographer, bussing the air near her cheek when she reached her.

"Lana! What are you doing here? You scared the devil out of me! I thought someone had broken in!" Bridey scolded, but Lana just brushed her off with the flick of a wrist.

"Oh, darling, don't be so silly. I just got back from that wretched cruise. Remind me never to go on any boat smaller than 100 feet again! I just *had* to see the cowboy shots!" She guided Bridey closer to a long credenza over which the pictures of Grant hung. "Isn't he perfect? Didn't I tell you? Those arms! Those eyes!" She threw her hands in the air and slapped her against her cheeks. "Absolutely divine!" Both women stood still for a moment staring at the rich colors of the pictures. Lana swirled toward Bridey and continued, "So when do I meet him? When is he coming?"

Exhausted by the morning and Lana's exuberance, Bridey sank onto the stool nearby and let Lana rant on while she calmed her own frazzled nerves. The umbrella clattered to the floor at her feet. Lana stopped talking long enough to realize Bridey wasn't at the table with her.

"Bridey? Darling? What's wrong? Are you sick?"

Bridey took a deep breath and looked at the excited woman. "You can't have him. He won't do it."

"What? You can't be serious. He's perfect. Offer him more money. Get him here."

Bridey stood up and sighed long and deep. *This was going to be tough,* she thought as she walked out of the apartment to get her equipment. Lana never gave up on what she wanted. With an exasperated sigh, Lana sat down on the sofa and waited impatiently, fingers tapping and foot swinging, for Bridey to finish bringing the cameras inside. Making Lana understand took two hours and two bottles of Chablis. Lana wasn't happy. When her ad people showed up, they weren't happy either. This was the man they wanted. Bridey refused to go back. She offered to give them directions to the ranch, but they told her getting him to change his mind was her job. After an hour of bickering, pleading and cajoling, Bridey pleaded with then to leave her alone. She agreed to meet them the next morning to decide what to do next.

Practically pushing the last person out the door, Bridey leaned against the wood and rested for just a moment. Those damnable pictures, she cursed as she walked into the dark room and began gathering them up. If she had just had time to put them away this morning, she wouldn't be in this situation. Lana would never have seen them. But Lana didn't wait to be invited anywhere. She could have lied and told Lana the cowboy wasn't photogenic. But now that Lana had seen them, there'd be no stopping her.

She couldn't keep from admiring them herself as she stacked the photos to be put away. They were so perfect. Between his looks and her genius with the camera, the effect was astounding. She'd welcome a few hours alone with the man, in her studio, photographing him. Her skillful eye made him look so good anyone would buy anything from him.

Who are you kidding, she asked herself. *He'd look great with or without your camera.* She lingered over the golden hued one a few moments longer, fingers tracing the shape of his face. She was so lost in her dream that she jumped when the phone rang.

Damn!!!! Why couldn't she have just one minute's peace today! She jerked the handset out of the cradle and almost screamed, "Yes!?"

A throat cleared on the other end. "Uhmm, I'd like to speak with Ms. Deane please?"

Bridey's brows knit. She should know this voice. "Who is calling?"

"Cordry Grant."

Bridey's eyebrows lifted high. The cowboy?

"Is she there?"

Bridey cleared her throat. "Mr. Grant, this is Bridgette."

A moment's silence strung itself over the phone line. "I, uhm, wondered if we could talk."

"Talk? About what? You made yourself perfectly clear on the ranch." More silence. Bridey could almost see the man fidgeting with what to say next. She decided to let him off the hook a bit.

"How's your jaw?"

"Not bad. Hurt for a long time though. What'd you have in that bag?"

Bridey smiled. "Nothing much. Just extra film, batteries and a small computer. You know, the notebook kind."

"No wonder it felt like bricks." Bridey could hear a smile in his voice. "So? Can we get together? I really want to talk with you."

"Well, I'm not able to travel again for a few weeks. I have several ..."

The voice on the other end interrupted her. "I can come to you. In fact, if I have read these maps right, I can be there in about twenty minutes. Or tomorrow morning if it's too late."

"Wait a minute. You're here? In the City?"

"Yes. I got in this afternoon." Silence filled the phone lines as Bridey thought this over. Her pride still stung over the way he'd treated her. Maybe she'd just make him work for her attention a little bit.

"We'll, I'm tied up right now. I'm not sure when I'll be available."

"Look," Cord interrupted her excuses. "I can't stay here long, and I need to discuss something with you. You have to eat. Have dinner with me. We can talk and then, if you chose, you'll never have to see me again."

Bridey's heart jumped and thawed a little. If he only knew. She paused and let the uncomfortable silence linger a moment or two longer.

"Are you still there?"

"Yes. I think I can clear my calendar within the next two hours. Shall we meet for an early dinner? Where are you staying?"

They made arrangements and agreed to meet two hours later at a small Italian café Bridey liked near his hotel. Both agreed she should come to him since she knew the City. He nervously joked at being able to find his way across miles of open country, but he'd probably be lost within a block of the hotel.

Bridey smiled when she hung up and thought, *now we'll see how he likes being so far out of his element.*

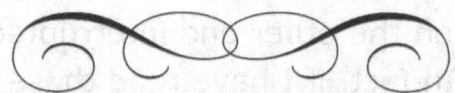

The café was a quiet little place away from the busiest section of the City. The Italian atmosphere welcomed her with the scent of warm bread and garlic as she entered the door. She smiled at the sign just inside the door that had a picture of a laughing chef saying, "If you don't like garlic, you best go home." Red and white checked clothes covered unsteady wooden tables scattered throughout the small quaint room. The traditional wax-coated Chianti bottles stood guard over each table as if watching to be sure the diners ate everything with proper gusto.

Cord was seated in a booth in the back of the room. He had already removed his jacket and was in the process of rolling his sleeves up. Bridey paused for a moment to watch. Almost immediately, he looked up. Flushing at being caught ogling him, she walked through the maze of tables and past the more intimate booths to where he waited. Moments before she reached him, he slipped out of his chair gallantly and stood. She couldn't remember the last time a man respectfully stood at her mere entry as he did. He dropped his head lightly and said, "Ms. Deane."

Bridey tried not to stare at his distinctive eyes as she extended her hand to greet him. This time she didn't shake or faint from the sight of his outstretched hand though her knees felt weak at the warmth and electricity that flowed from him to her. He held her hand a moment too long as they looked at each other.

Bridey heard a waiter come up behind her and clear his throat.

She shifted and pulled her hand back.

"Mr. Grant," she said pleasantly, as she slid onto the chair opposite him. "Nice to see you again. I trust *your* trip was uneventful." The stress on the word *your* was not lost on him. Since he hated flying only slightly less than the idea of major surgery, he chose not to comment.

The waiter shifted his feet and smiled at them. "Do you know what you want or shall we order a drink first?" Cord asked.

She looked up at the waiter and gave him her most dazzling smile. "Bring us a bottle of the Chianti from the owner's stock please." The waiter raised an eyebrow but, dipping his head slightly, he spun on his heel to get the wine.

"Owner's stock? Do you know the owner?" Cord asked.

"No, that's a New Yorker's way of saying I want the good stuff. He understood." Bridey smiled over her clasped fingers. She'd teach this hick a thing or two before he left.

"I guess I'll take your word for it." They looked over the menu as an excuse not to speak for a moment. The waiter returned with a bottle in the traditional straw weave basket. He placed two glasses on the table and poured the wine. Bridey watched Cord as he looked over the menu.

"Do you know what you want?" Cord looked up to see the green eyes smiling at him as if expecting him to flounder. Confidently, he ordered antipasto, linguine with shrimp sauce followed by spumoni in perfect Italian and gazed back at Bridey with a smug look in his own eyes.

"My mother was a cook on a ranch. The owner loved good Italian." He grinned at her. Bridey tipped her head sideways slightly in admiration of his knowledge. She looked at the waiter and asked him to double the order. There was nothing left to do but talk to each other. Both fidgeted with the silver and napkins for a few moments, reluctant to start the conversation they knew they had to have. They talked about weather and other simple things until Cord lost patience with the game.

"I guess you want to know why I'm here."

Bridey settled into the bench, thinking *ok here it comes*. "Well, you must admit after the totally hospitable way you treated me, I'm a bit curious. I figure you're either here to threaten to kill me unless I give you the film or ..." She paused a moment for the effect. "... you're going to give in and be our spokesperson." She snorted ungraciously. "I doubt the latter is true."

"Well, actually ..." The waiter appeared with their meal. Cord watched every move he made rather than look at Bridey. Unwilling to discuss business in front of the waiter, Bridey waited impatiently for him to leave.

Cord lifted his fork and started to lift a bite. Bridey stopped him with "Actually, what?"

Carefully, Cord laid his fork back down. "Actually, I have rethought the idea and decided to agree. If I can make a few stipulations."

Bridey eyed him suspiciously. "Like what?"

"First, I need to know exactly how much money we're talking about."

"That's something to talk to the client about. I can tell you she saw the pictures and she loves them. Thinks you are just right for what she wants. You can command quite a price ... almost anything you want"

Cord sat back in his chair. "You said you weren't going to show them to anyone."

Bridey held her hands out, palm up. "I didn't do it on purpose. I told you there were other things on that roll of film. I developed them all at once. I hung them to dry, intending to put them away the next morning, but I overslept and had to run out to a job. When I got home, Lana – that's the client – had sweet-talked my super into letting her into my apartment. She saw them still hanging."

Cord relaxed a bit. "So, does that mean I'm in?"

Bridey simply nodded and lifted a fork full of fragrant linguine to her mouth.

"Why the sudden change of heart?" she asked innocently. She watched as he tasted his food and washed it down with the Chianti.

"Hmmm, that is good." He said as he set the glass down. "To be honest, I still don't want to, but I don't own my own place. That horse you spooked is mine, but he's more of a pet right now than anything. On a cattle ranch, a horse can't just lie around and eat all day. They have to be able to work for their keep. The boss man said make him work or we get rid of him."

"Get rid of him? That beautiful animal?"

Cord's eyebrows shot up quizzically. "You like horses?"

"I may be just a city kid, but I took riding lessons long ago. And, yes, I like horses."

"Well, beauty isn't good enough when feed is so expensive." Cord lifted his fork again. They ate quietly for a few minutes.

Bridey broke the silence. "What would happen to him?"

"Well, there aren't many choices. No self-respecting breeder would want him since he has no papers, so that means a rodeo or the dog meat factory."

Bridey dropped her fork in shock. "Dog meat! Rodeo? A bucking horse?" Cord nodded and continued to eat. "You can't be serious! That's so cruel."

"Actually, it's not cruel at all. It's a pretty good life. The horse would be fed regularly. Once a week or so, he would spend eight seconds trying to get some cowboy to eat dirt. They don't allow spurs or whips any more. At least not in professional rodeos."

Bridey felt her mouth drop open. Quickly, she snapped her lips shut and reached for the wine glass. The idea of that beautiful horse killed or mistreated wrenched her soul. Her hand shook as she thought about the practice.

"So, you're doing this for the horse?" she asked. Cord nodded. "What's in it for you?"

"Well, I think the best thing would be to make enough money in a short period of time to buy part of the ranch or a nearby place. Then I could keep Kin on my land but still work for Stallings. I'm sure he'd throw some fine colts. I'd buy a few mares and start my own herd."

"That's his name? Kin?"

"Yea. The first horse I ever saw was named The Devil. He looked just like Kin. All fire and speed, but not a mean bone in his body. Like Kin, he was simply a one-man horse. No one could handle him but his owner. That was the man my mother worked for." Bridey watched his eyes take on a special glow as he talked about the horse and its owner. Obviously, he had some fond memories of that time.

Cord continued, "When I was young, I sort of apprenticed myself to the head horseman, who eventually became my stepfather. The man who owned the place was impressed with how quickly I learned. I was the only other person The Devil would let into his stall. On my sixteenth birthday, he gave me the last colt from that stallion. I called him Devil's Son. This colt, the one you saw, looks so much like them both that I named him Devil's Kin."

Bridey sat in amazement as she watched the changes wash over the face of the solemn man as he talked about things he obviously loved.

"Was this all in out West?"

"No," Cord responded. "Virginia. Not far from Washington, D.C."

D.C.? Bridey was surprised again. So this country hick wasn't from the sticks after all. "So where are your parents? How did you end up in out there?"

A shadow descended over Cord's face. He looked down at his nearly empty place. "They died and the horses are long gone, too. Listen, do you want anything else?"

The quick change in subject told Bridey there was a lot more to the story than he had told her. "No, I'm full. So now what?"

Cord looked at his watch. "It's only 8:00. Is there anything to do around this place besides smoky, loud clubs?"

Bridey smiled. "Do you like movies?"

Cord nodded and signaled the waiter to bring the bill. They walked to an old theater near the restaurant. They bought tickets and went into the cool dark theater. Cord let Bridey choose seats. He was pleased when she chose seats close to the door. He slid into the old leather seat at the end of the row beside her. The film was about a country sheriff, a real he-man macho type, in love with a delicate fragile British ballerina. A fated love story if he'd ever heard of one. He thought about how the story would unfold if he and the woman next to him fell in love. *A lot of the same*, he thought, *doomed to fail from the start*.

Bridey sat still, feeling the warmth coming from the arm that rested next to hers. She'd seen this movie years ago and loved the concept and the presentation. The film was not a man's movie with gunfights and speeding car chases. She wondered how long the movie would keep his attention until he began to shift around restlessly. To her surprise, he seemed engrossed in the plot. Only once did he fidget. He leaned over and whispered in her ear. His warm breath caressed her neck as he asked, "Would I be crowding you too much if I laid my arm across the back of your seat? I'm not used to these little seats."

Bridey didn't trust herself to look at him or answer out loud. She just nodded and waited as she felt his warmth on the back of her neck and shoulders. She shuddered lightly.

"Cold?" he asked.

"A bit." The arm drew down around her and she nestled deep into its circle.

Cord felt her settle back and thought, *what in the world are you doing, man?* But he didn't move the arm.

The movie ended and they walked back in companionable silence out into the dark night. They strolled back toward Cord's hotel.

"So? What do we do now?" He asked her as they stood in front of the building.

"I have a meeting with the cologne people in the morning. If you want to come along, you can meet them and see what they're offering. That's the time to make your demands and negotiate whatever you want with them."

"Negotiate, huh? I haven't done a lot of that before. I guess I'll just have to wing it."

Bridey smiled. "Well, since I know why you want the money, I might be persuaded to help you a little bit."

Cord smiled down at the green-eyed beauty. He was still surprised that he could ever have thought of this gentle, fragile creature as a shallow-minded groupie for some movie star. He resisted the urge to take her in his arms. His body reacted to the idea with a hardening in his loins. Thank God, he was wearing a long jacket.

"OK, then. Where and what time?"

Bridey pulled a pen and a card out of her purse. "Let's meet for breakfast and we'll talk over a game plan." She wrote an address on the back of the card. "Give this to the taxi driver in the morning. It's a diner near the office. I'll meet you there at 8."

She turned to walk away. On the street, a taxi stopped for her almost immediately. Before climbing into the back seat, she looked back at the man standing there watching her. She shook her finger at him and said, "Don't be late, hear?"

He lifted his hand in a mock two-finger salute and watched her climb into the cab and ride away. *Cute,* he thought, *definitely cute.*

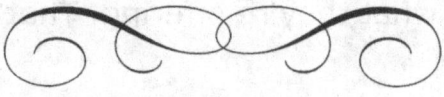

Cord walked into his room and slumped down on the bed. That meeting hadn't been as tough as he had anticipated. Bridey accepted his explanations without asking too many questions. He couldn't believe he'd told her about his parents. She was a good listener. In fact, she was too good at everything; too good to look at, too good to be with, and too good in his arms. He felt his body tighten again at the thought of her in his arms.

He had sat in the dark theater, paying half attention to a fair movie, fighting the urge to fold her close and kiss her breathless. He wanted her so badly, but they weren't through with business yet. Tomorrow, they'd meet again. He sighed. Tomorrow. He had decisions to make before then. Decisions he couldn't make with a woman on his mind. He headed for the shower. His body refusing to stop thinking of hers. This was going to be a long shower.

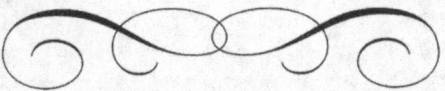

Bridey had no easier a time. The ride home was short, but not so short she couldn't daydream a bit. She could still feel the warmth of his strong arm around her shoulders. The faint aroma of his natural scent stayed in her nostrils. With great difficulty, she'd stayed focused on the movie. More than once, Bridey was tempted to turn her head just enough to see if he'd kiss her.

She climbed the stairs to her apartment and headed straight for the shower. She stood in the hot spray and let the water run sensuously over her. The shower was supposed to relax her and make her drowsy but, if anything, her senses turned against her. Her body melted into the feelings the silky water heightened and turned her thoughts to Cord's eyes, broad shoulders, and lean hips. She crawled into bed and spent the night tossing and turning with dreams of what could have been if he'd just kissed her.

"I think I'd miss you even if we'd never met."
Nick, The Wedding Date (2005)

Ten

Who beat whom to the restaurant the next morning wasn't clear. Cord walked around the corner from where the cabbie dropped him just as Bridey almost fell out of her cab. Cord rushed forward to catch her as the heel of those ridiculous boots she wore caught on the edge of the car door.

Bridey gasped as she fell against a broad chest. She struggled to free herself from the iron arms, ready to give the person touching her without permission a piece of her mind. The arms tightened and she looked up into the silver blue eyes that had kept her awake for most of the night. She relaxed against him for a moment and then remembered they were practically in the middle of the street. She could almost hear her mother's most proper voice in her ear, "You don't need to be throwing yourself at a man, Bridey. Men like the hunt."

"Well," she said, stepping back a small step. "Looks like you're always catching me falling on something." She brushed invisible dust off the front of her jacket.

Cord smiled at the flustered woman. "Looks like," was all he said. A car horn blared. Cord took Bridey's arm and escorted her to the sidewalk.

"Did you sleep well?" he asked.

She jumped a bit when he touched her arm and wondered if he felt that same little jolt of electricity. "Fine.

Why? Don't I look like I did?" she asked defensively.

Cord laughed nervously. What was the matter with him this morning? He felt like a teenager on his first date. "How about you?" Bridey asked. "Did you sleep OK?"

"Oh, sure," he said with a sigh, "As soon as I got used to all the tires squealing and the party people carrying on, I slept just fine." Bridey looked up at him. The light gray bags under her eyes that she'd hidden with make up were mirrored under his.

"Liar," she laughed and stepped into the restaurant. Cord stood for a moment, surprised at her honest reaction and then followed her inside.

"Do you know what I realized last night?" Bridey said as they seated themselves at a table.

"What?"

"You never smelled the cologne. What if you don't like it?"

Cord looked at her in surprise. "Is that important? I mean, in a magazine who knows whether I'm really wearing the stuff or not?"

Bridey laughed out loud at the perfect logic. "Either way. You really ought to try it. Here." She bent over and pulled the sample bottle out of her bag. "Splash a little on."

Cord took the bottle and looked at it for a moment.

"What's the matter?" Bridey asked. "You aren't wearing another kind of cologne, are you?"

Cord shook his head. "Nope, I've never been a cologne kind of guy." He smiled at her and opened the bottle. Shaking a few drops in his hand, he carefully lifted it to his nose, looking at Bridey over his fingers.

She smiled and said, "You can't tell that way. Perfumes and cologne all smell different on different people when the chemicals mix with their body chemistry. For instance, my mother adores White Shoulders perfume. On her, the scent is wonderful and delicate, but on me, an old tennis shoe smells better." She threw her hands in the air at his expression. "Don't ask me! I don't understand either."

Cord lifted his palms to his cheeks and spread the fragrance over his face and neck. "Whew, it's strong."

"Give it a few minutes."

Over bagels and cream cheese and fresh brewed coffee, they made plans. How much time spent on shoots and how much money should he settle for? What questions should he ask? What signals did they need?

Things were pretty much decided when Cord sniffed his arm where the cologne had dried. "I can't tell if this is good or not."

Bridey sniffed, but she was too far away to smell anything. "It's definitely not too strong. I can't tell from over here."

Cord slid his chair closer to hers. "Here. Try now. Is it good or not?"

Bridey struggled to shake off the torrent of sensual attacks her body reacted to. Good? It was Heaven. She had to make herself sit back when all she really wanted was to bury her nose deep in the bend of his neck and lay there breathing. She cleared her throat and answered. "It's good."

Cord caught the quick glint in her eye and smiled. "Are you sure? I could walk around and ask a few of these ladies if they like it?"

"They'd eat you alive." Bridey laughed.

Cord looked at Bridey and licked his lips. Her challenging smile and those lips were beginning to make him think of things other than business. He leaned close enough for his breath to pass her neck. "How about you? Would you be driven crazy?" He leaned back to see a look in her eyes that made his blood raise further. She looked shocked, unnerved and subtly interested ... for a brief second.

Bridey had to gasp to get air into her lungs. That whisper in her ear and the smell of him ... not the cologne ... *him*, unnerved her but only for a second. She shuddered slightly, sat upright and moved her chair away from him.

"Yes, uhm, well..." She ran a hand over her hair and pulled her coat around her. "You are welcome to work the room if you'd like." She cleared her throat. "... but as for me, I'm here for business, Mr. Grant. Nothing else."

Cord leaned back and smiled as he watched her fidget with her silver and water glass. She could deny the fact she was interested but she couldn't hide the truth. If he had to be in the City, he might as well have a little fun.

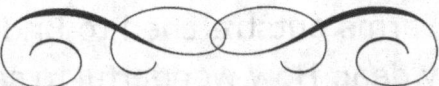

They were down to the last twenty minutes before the meeting. Having exhausted all the other topics, Bridey asked, "By the way, you haven't told me what reservations you have about using your picture? Want to fill me in now?"

Cord stood up and picked up the bill. He pulled his wallet out and laid the money on the counter. He slowly rolled his sleeves down before putting his jacket on again.

"Nope," he said and turned to leave her standing in his wake.

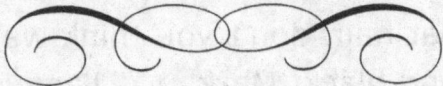

"So! That's my demand. Take it or leave it." Cord sat back in the tall leather chair and waited for the final decision. Three hours earlier, they'd walked into the huge oak paneled meeting room. The room was dominated by a highly polished table the size of a small swimming pool. He was seated at the foot of the table. Lana sat at the head with her designers, copywriters, printers and myriad other yes-men spread out down the table on either side of her. Bridey had placed herself near the middle of the table to his left. She was clearly visible to both parties and seemingly nonpartisan.

The sweet-talking he expected started the minute he came in the door. The heavy door swung open as he and Bridey were halfway across the room. He'd suspected a hidden camera had announced their arrival. Lana flounced down the side of the great table to greet them, arms outstretched to Bridgette.

"Bridgette, my dear. How wonderful to see you again."

Cord grimaced. She sounded as if she hadn't seen Bridey for weeks instead of days. He braced himself as she turned her attention to him. "And this. Well, this is Mr. Perfect." She stuck her hand out. When he took her heavily ringed hand, she drew him into a quick hug. "Mm, mm, nice!" she whispered as she pressed herself against his chest. Cord stepped back and tried to pull his hand back. Lana held tightly. Without taking her eyes off Cord's face, she began to discuss him as if he weren't in the room.

"James. Just look at those eyes. Those shoulders. Diane, with that hair, don't you think we should dress him in silver and black. Mark . . ." Lana issued orders. Her people took notes, scrambled closer to look over their new piece of merchandise. He was measured, discussed and questioned until he looked to Bridey. The plea for rescue in his eyes made Bridey smile. She waited just a few more seconds to step forward.

"OK, you guys! OK. Let the poor man breathe. He isn't a professional model. He's not used to this stuff."

Cord visibly relaxed as Bridey pushed her way into the small crowd and took his arm. She guided him to a chair. "Besides, Lana, we still have some issues to discuss before we actually have Cord's permission to use the pictures."

"Oh, details." Lana rolled her eyes. "There's all that messy money business." She clapped her hands. "Everyone out. Everyone except Franklin and Janey. You two need to stay and get us together on this."

The group left the room and closed the door behind them. To Cord, the room immediately felt more like a meeting place instead of a three-ring circus with him center stage as the dancing bear. The secretary and the accountant sat on either side of Lana who looked down the table at Cord.

"So, let's have it." She clasped her hands in front of her on the table, speaking in no-nonsense tones. "I want you for our campaign and I don't like to dicker. Just tell me the bottom line. How much do you want and what concessions do you want me to consider?"

Cord looked directly back at the woman who'd changed from smooth talking schmoozer to hard-nosed businessperson in a split second. "You make me an offer. You know better than I what the going rate is. I hope I can trust you to be fair. I see this as being a onetime thing. If the campaign is as successful as you seem to think, we might renegotiate later. But there are two things I must insist on. If you don't agree to this, I won't do any of the campaign." The people in the room collectively held their breath. No one demanded anything of this woman. Lana raised an eyebrow and slowly nodded. Cord cleared his throat, and with a quick silent prayer, laid his demands on the table.

"I agree to do whatever you want as long as Bridey stays on as the photographer."

Lana waved her hand and waited for the next part.

"And I agree to let you use my picture for magazines, billboard, subway stations, whatever you want BUT . . ."

Lana leaned forward. Cord continued, looking her straight in the eye. "I will NOT do any personal appearances, and no one is to have access to my name or address except Bridey. There it is. Take it or leave it."

Both parties leaned back. Bridey looked back and forth between the two. Personal appearances were important to a new product. But Cord's good looks were so perfect that might be enough. Lana stood.

"Excuse us for a moment, will you?" She strode out a door near her chair with Janey and Franklin in her wake. The door closed softly. Cord looked at Bridey.

"What do you think?"

Bridey shrugged. "I don't know. Personal appearances are vital to the promotion of a new product. There might be important people who want to talk with you about new jobs."

Cord held up a hand. "No. This is a one-time thing. You know why I'm my reasons for agreeing. I don't like the idea, but I'm doing this."

Bridey stood up and walked to a window. "Why is it you really don't you want to be out there?" She spun around to look at him. "Are you hiding from something? Or someone? Are you a criminal? Is that why you didn't want me to talk to you at the ranch? Is that why you were so angry that I found you?"

Cord stood and walked over to her. Her eyes blazed with anger. She hadn't thought to look into his background. A criminal couldn't represent the product. Cord put his hands on her shoulders. He could see the wheels turning in her mind. "Relax. I'm not some guy on the lam from the police. I have good reasons though.
I just . . ."

The door opened to let Lana back in. She settled herself back into her chair without a word and gestured to Cord to return to his seat. She waited patiently for him to sit down.

"I just talked to the people in charge of the layouts. Bridey is our favorite photographer. She was always meant to shoot this job. That's not a problem. Normally, I'd show you the door for refusing the promo appearances. But my people assure me you photograph excellently. That elusive quality we're searching for is all over you. Not letting you appear in public might enhance that elusiveness, even add mystery. We've been searching for months. No one else has come close. So . . ." she gestured at Janey who carried a small sheaf of papers to Cord. "On the last page of that contract, you'll find what I'm willing to pay you. Anyone will tell you this is a fair price for a nobody who is new to the business. With royalties, you'll be sitting pretty for the rest of your life."

Cord lifted the pages. He almost whistled when he saw the figure. All that was needed now was his signature and his face would belong to these people. He looked at Bridey. Her green eyes still held some questions. He shifted his gaze to Lana.

"Don't even pretend it's not enough." Lana slid a slender silver pen down the length of the table. Cord picked the pen up and felt the weight in his hand. Eight years had passed since he left the ranch with Edson's rage ringing in his ears. He'd traveled and covered his tracks for the first three years; living with the fear Edson would find him sleeping one night and kill him. Gradually, he'd relaxed and found his job on the ranch. Praying he wasn't making a mistake, Cord signed the last page.

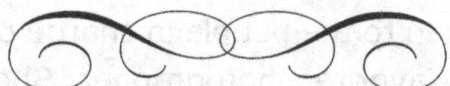

Halcyon days followed. Cord had never changed clothes so many times in one day in his life. Every time he turned around, someone new was measuring him or checking the makeup they made him wear. Lights flashed. Sets and people changed.

He sat on horses and motorcycles. He stood half naked in streams created in studios. Women draped themselves over his lap and across his shoulders. All he had to do was stare at the camera and look sexy. That he could do – as long as Bridey smiled at him from behind the lens.

And smile she did. Bridey told Lana that usually out of a day's shoot she'd get five, maybe six usable photos with the most professional of models. Cord gave her more quality than she'd ever seen. Lana smiled and asked sarcastically if she was complaining or what. At week's end, they were ready to wrap things up. They had at least a year's worth of good shots.

Nights found Cord exhausted, falling into bed, asleep before his head hit the pillow. Bridey worked late to get the photos developed and into the hands of the ad people by the following morning.

On the last day of shooting, the set had the delicious air of celebration. Cord stood in front of a poster of a white Lipizzaner stallion rearing up behind him. A woman he'd met moments before was collapsed in his arms. Bridey knew this would be a good shot.

"Wait," she called before taking that shoot. "Cord. Roll your sleeves up to the elbow."

Careful not to drop the woman in his arms, Cord unbuttoned the cuffs of his shirt. "You do like that look, don't you?"

One of Bridgette's helpers snickered, "Are you kidding? That's her signature pose. You can always tell a Deane photo." The young man stood up and pretended to strike a pose while rolling his sleeves.

Bridgette swatted at the young man while the rest of the crew laughed. She looked at Cord who waggled his eyebrows and slowly finished rolling. Flushing furiously, she called out, "Alright! That's enough! Let's get this done."

When she called a wrap at noon, a cheer went up throughout the group who'd worked so feverishly. Cord merely sat down. People walked by and patted him on the back or shoulder, murmuring words of congratulations to which he merely nodded his thanks. Nothing could be said that was as good as the feeling of relief now that he could go home.

He watched everyone leave. Bridey put away her equipment and watched as the workers took down lights and sets. Like a sexy diminutive field marshal, she rallied the men into one last burst of careful energy before turning them loose. Not until everything was secured and everyone else was on his or her way did she turn to see Cord sitting on a step watching her.

She stood arms crossed, weight resting on her heels, and looked back at him. "Just what do you think you're staring at?"

Cord shook his head. "I had no idea how hard just standing here and trying to look good was until I did this. It's astounding!"

Bridey sauntered over to sit down beside him. "You did great. I'm sorry we haven't had much time to talk or anything. I've been working late and I knew you were sleeping when I finished."

"So? Honestly," he looked at her with slightly hooded eyes. "How do the pictures look?"

Bridey's head tipped to one side. "You mean you can't tell?"

Cord shook his head and looked out across the room. "Nope. Never thought of myself as particularly good looking. Always took a lot of teasing for this gray hair. The kids in school always called me Grampa. So, I guess I figured I was just another guy. Now, I've had all these people telling me how good I look." *That is,* thought Cord, *everyone except the only person I care for an opinion from*.

Bridey laid her arm across his broad shoulders. She laughed and stretched up to give him a light peck on the cheek. Just as she was about to make contact, he turned to face her. Their lips met. Eyes wide open, they drew back slightly, each looking at the other to see the other one's reaction. Cord moved first. He leaned in and touched her slightly parted lips gently with his. When she closed her eyes, Cord felt the breath she'd been holding slip out over his chin. He moved closer and kissed her gently. When she parted her lips further to accept his exploring tongue, he wasn't sure who moaned first. What he knew for certain was he felt like he'd come back from a long journey. For the first time since he left his family in the ashes of the fire that destroyed his life, he felt like he was home.

"Love is something eternal;
the aspect may change,
but not the essence."
—Jeff Zinnert

Eleven

The sound of shattering crystal against a stone hearth rang out just after a high-pitched shriek of rage. Edson Stanton the Fifth, multimillionaire recluse and borderline madman, paced back and forth in a fury built up over the past years. A tattered magazine lay on the floor in front of his late father's favorite chair. Cord's hated face looked up at him from the glossy page; ice blue eyes half closed, a taunting half smile playing around his lips. The conquered woman draped over his shoulders seemed in the throes of some sexual game Cord was about to finish.

Edson stormed in circles around the magazine glaring, swearing at the picture. He screamed at the photograph, "How dare you end up happy and famous? The sniveling little coward who caused me so much trouble! You sorry little bastard. I want you to be miserable and alone. I have everything you wanted! I'm the rich one, the one with the house and land you coveted, the one with important influential friends all over the world. You have the nerve to flaunt your success in my face. I should've killed you when I had the chance!" Another glass shattered against the slick paper picture.

Edson kicked an empty liquor bottle out of his way and threw his head back, roaring out his rage. No one would answer his cry. Even the dog he'd brought home to be his companion had run away. Maids refused to stay in the house with him, afraid of his temper and strange behavior. Every agency he tried refused to send anyone else out. His demanding, heavy-handed ways left him alone in his own filth. Far above cleaning anything himself, Edson simply moved from room to room in the house. Twice a year, he went to Europe. At that time, a cleaning crew came in and made everything right. The only way the cleaning company would send anyone was if he, Edson, wasn't in residence.

Sniveling little weasels. How dare they? That's all paid minions were for – to do what he wanted when he wanted. Edson grabbed a half empty bottle of scotch and tipped it to his lips. He was an important man, the only heir of an important man. He was meant to have people begging to do his bidding.

Furious, he threw the bottle against the fireplace and watched the scotch ooze out over the filthy carpet. Edson liked throwing things into the fireplace. Fire was a warm pleasant thing that always did exactly what he wanted. He smiled thinking of times fire had done his bidding. He tilted his head back and laughed at the thought of the pain he'd caused that fool Cord. Too bad, dear old dad didn't live long enough to see what happened to the servants he left behind.

Edson strode over to the liquor cabinet and yanked another bottle out. Ripping the cap off, he guzzled the liquid straight and then flopped down onto the leather chair. The same kind of leather chair he'd sat in the night he sent dear old dad to the hospital with a heart attack. Poor dad. Edson laughed again as he remembered the looks on their faces – all of them – when he focused the shot and Deborah's face became clear. They were all too stupid to realize he'd superimposed Deborah's head on the body of one of the hookers he'd hired to party that week with his friends. He'd even offered them extra cash if they could seduce Cord. What interesting parties they'd all had in his rooms after the country folk retired for the night. Edson laughed again and leaned forward to slap his thigh.

From the slick pages of the magazine on the floor, Cord stared up at him. The laughter stopped. Edson ground his heel into the paper image.

Cord. That bastard. He had to pay. Edson's life would have been so different if Cord hadn't come along and stolen his father from him. Edson leaned down a bit closer. In the corner of the photograph in small letters was the name of the photographer – Bridey Deane Photography – New York.

Edson reached for the phone and pushed one of the buttons he'd bullied his last secretary into setting up for him. He'd use the photographer to find Cord and then destroy him once and for all. An answering machine responded.

Livid with anger, Edson held the phone away from his ear, put the mouthpiece squarely in front of him and screamed, "Elks! Dammit Elks. You'd better call me immediately. For what I pay you to be there, you have no right not to answer me."

He slammed the phone back down and began pacing around the tight circle again, kicking the debris out of his path. He hadn't completed a full circuit when the phone rang. Edson leapt across the circle, stepping on an empty container he'd thrown aside days ago. Landing heavily on his backside, Edson cursed and moaned as he reached for the phone. Through clenched teeth, he muttered, "This better be you, Elks."

The calm voice on the other end of the phone belonged to Marcus G. Elks, former ambulance chasing, cheating-husband-following private detective. He'd once made his living following the lowlifes of the world, doing whatever he could to make money – from tracking down felons to finding lost dogs. His 12 x 12 one room apartment served as his home and office. He never turned down a job, no matter how distasteful it might be. All he needed to do was make enough money to survive.

But that was before he answered the advertisement. Twelve years ago, a small advertisement appeared in the local paper seeking "discreet professional assistance of a personal investigative nature." Elks liked the way that sounded.

He called the number and spoke with a nervous secretary whose voice trembled as she took his name and number. Softly, she assured him that Mr. Stanton would return his call within the hour.

Stanton? Stanton? He knew that name. The laptop, he'd put himself in debt to get, lay on the table next to the phone/fax machine. Elks opened the lid, connected his only phone line to the modem and logged onto his favorite search engine. The next half an hour he spent finding out details about the Stanton family. The father had a reputation as a philanthropist and humanitarian. He seemed to be well thought of by the media. No wife was mentioned. There was a son, but little was written about him.

Almost the second he disconnected the line and reconnected the phone, the instrument rang. He picked the handset up casually and announced his name. A demanding voice boomed through the handset without introduction or simple courtesy.

"Tell me what you know about my family." Assuming the caller was Stanton, probably the younger by the voice, Elks told him what he'd gleaned from the archives. The voice let him talk for about five minutes and then rudely interrupted, for which Elks was grateful.

He'd come to the end of his notes.

"Well, at least you're smart enough to know where to look for information. What did you do? Go online? Or did you visit the library?"

"Online." Elks waited. Only the sound of breathing let him know Stanton was still there. No wonder the secretary sounded so timid having to face this brutal behavior all day long.

"I'm going to reconnect you with my secretary. She'll give you the details." The line went dead. So, was he hired or what? Elks barely had the time to think about the question before the trembling voice answered again.

"M-m-mr. Elks? M-m-mr. Stanton says to . . ." Elks interrupted, unable to stand the trembling voice any longer.

"Wait a minute. Are you OK?"

"Why yes, I'm fine," the surprised voice answered.

"Are you in some kind of trouble or does your voice always shake that way?" He tried to sound like as if making a joke.

"I, hum," a small nervous giggle slipped out. Then he could hear the fear creep back in. "I'm sorry, sir. This is a business phone and I'm not interested in a personal conversation. Now, if you'll give me your mailing address, I'll send the contract which I'm SURE you'll sign and return.

The emphasis on the word SURE made Elks smile. "So, I'm hired then?"

The trembling, but business-like, voice on the other end of the line answered in the affirmative. "At the risk of becoming personal, let me ask you this. Does your boss frighten you?"

A monotone response followed. "No sir, Mr. Stanton is a good person to work for. He is very good to his employees."

She must have rehearsed that line often, he thought as he gave her his address and then hung up. Interesting call.

The contract was indeed a lucrative one, more money for a retainer than he'd make any time soon as a private eye. There was also a generous allowance for expenditures plus extra money to be paid by the hour for any work he did for Stanton. As he read and reread the contract, all he could see that was being demanded of him was to be available at a moment's notice and, once he signed the contract, the job would begin in four days.

Elks sat down and thought the job over. He'd have to give up most of his other clients. He laughed at himself. What other clients? He looked at the contract once more to make sure he hadn't missed anything. He tipped it up and shook it. A small piece of paper fluttered out and landed at his feet. A simple message in black stood out against the stark white paper – *555.8312 after 7 PM*. Hmm, a mystery all ready. Elks looked at the clock. 10 AM. He had plenty of time for a few details including a lunch date with a lawyer friend of his. The lawyer looked over the contract and pronounced the paperwork sound, so sound that he wanted to know where to get one himself. Elks signed on the dotted line right there in the restaurant.

Promptly at 7, Elks dialed the number. The phone rang only once. A cheery young female voice answered,

"Morten residence."

"This is Marcus Elks. I was asked to call this number." He heard a slight sigh on the other end.

"I'm so glad you called. This is Maria. I'm the one you spoke to this morning at Mr. Stanton's office."

"Are you sure?" Elks laughed. "You don't sound like the trembling little mouse I talked to earlier.

Elks was rewarded with a tinkling laugh on the other end. "Here at home, I'm not." The words "where I'm safe" were clearly implied by her tone of voice. Elks was more and more intrigued about his new employer and the relationship he seemed to have with his secretary.

"Have you signed the contract yet?" she asked quietly.

"Shouldn't I? It sounds awfully good. Is there something I should know?"

"Well," Maria lowered her voice conspiratorially. "First, never let him know we talked. Please. He pays me very well too, but he has very strict rules. I need the money for my family. I can stand his temper and outbursts for the money to send my brothers to college. Second, never try to have a personal conversation with him or anyone you call on that line. He listens all the time. When he's out of the country, he tapes the calls."

Elks listened and tried to picture the man in his mind. "What does this guy look like? I found a lot of information on him, but no recent pictures."

"I don't know. I've never met him."

"Excuse me? Don't you work in his office?"

Maria replied, "Yes, but he's never here. I answered an ad just like you did. The only time I ever hear from him is when I've done something wrong. Rarely, I do something perfect for him and never get even a bit of praise. Sometimes I do a job well enough to get a grunt from him and, then the next time, I do the same thing done the same way and he screams at me. You just never know with him."

"So, why did you give me this number? To warn me?"

"Sort of. But mostly because I wish someone had told me before I started working for him. The money's great. It's always on time, but the feeling that you're being watched and that whatever you're doing – even when you aren't doing anything – is wrong – well, that's pretty tough to handle sometimes."

Elks thought her words over and decided he was a lot tougher than Maria. He'd deal with the intimidation of Stanton ... for that amount of money he'd put up with a lot of garbage.

"Thanks, Maria. But I think I'm going to try the job out. I'll drop the contract by tomorrow. Where's the office?"

"NO!" Maria screamed into the phone. "Don't go there. I'll make arrangements for our courier service to pick up the paperwork at 10 AM. Will you be at home? "Yes, but . . ."

"Trust me. Never come to the office. He doesn't like that." Maria bid him goodbye and hung up.

The first check arrived two days after Elks sent the contract back and checks had arrived religiously each month since then. Elks had grown used to his employer's oddities. The jobs were small, mostly dirt gathering on people who had, in some way, offended Stanton. When Elks was assigned to find dirt on the younger woman the older Stanton married and some cook and her family that worked at the Stanton home, he experienced what Maria had warned him of firsthand. There simply was no dirt to be found. They were good, law-abiding, hard-working folks who their lives quietly.

One evening, three weeks after being hired, Edson roared for over an hour into Elks' ear deriding him for not doing a thorough job, screaming at him to find skeletons, make up dirt if he had to. Elks listened quietly to the sound of madness raging throughout the diatribe. If this man wasn't crazy now, he was well on his way. Still the money was worth listening to occasional ravings as Elks looked around his new office and thought of his nice apartment not too far away and all the other things he could now afford thanks to this madman. As the months moved on, he took note of how Stanton moved closer and closer to the madness that threatened to overtake him.

Of course, Elks had read about the tragedies at the Stanton ranch. The newspapers and all the local television stations carried the story in-depth. No fingers were ever pointed at anyone. Life had moved on past the tragedy. Elks continued to dig up information for Stanton.

Tonight's call was normal. Nearly midnight and Edson expected Elks to be in his office. Elks made a habit of forwarding all his calls to his home number to maintain that illusion. The phone rang and he heard Edson's screaming message from a sound sleep. Rather than jumping up to answer the call, he took a few moments to splash water on his face and get a soda from the refrigerator.

Elks dialed the number and leaned the chair onto its back legs. He knew from experience there would be no need to say anything.

"Dammit, Elks, what the hell took you so long? When I need you, I want you now, not when . . ." Edson was off and gone on his ravings. Elks pulled the phone slightly away from his ear and took a long drink. He assumed Edson would carry on for his requisite twenty minutes. He let his mind wander to other things, like the sleep he was missing.

"I want you to find him and find him now. Do you understand me?"

Elks let the front legs of his chair hit the floor again. For the first time, Edson actually got to the point quickly and he'd missed the orders given. This wasn't good.

"I'm sure I can find him, Mr. Stanton. Spell his name out for me."

"Grant. Cordry Grant! What's so hard to spell, you moron. He's staring up at me from some magazine. You find him! Do it fast! And don't you dare let him know!"

"Mr. Stanton, have I ever . . ."

"Don't! Just find him now." The receiver slammed down. The silence rang in Elks' ear. Moments later, the fax machine churned out a picture. Stanton must have called Maria to send the photo to him. The picture was too dark to see clearly but seemed to be an advertisement for a man's cologne. Gleaming teeth smiled through a blurry face at him. An equally blurry womanly shape draped itself around the man's shoulders. Elks snickered to himself. *Saracen,* the logo proclaimed, *bring out the warrior in you and win her heart forever.* What a claim.

The fax machine quieted. Elks picked up the picture. The face wasn't clear enough to recognize let alone find someone from it. In the bottom left corner written sideways was the photographer's name – Bridey Deane, Photography – New York. A clue at last. Elks snickered again as he turned back to his bed. This could definitely wait until morning.

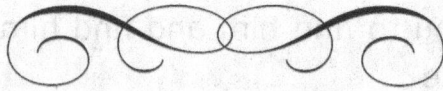

"Photography." Elks listened for a second to see if he had a real person or a machine. If the voice was from a real person, she was very distracted.

"Ms. Deane?" Elks asked, deliberately sounding uncertain.

"Yes? Yes, what can I do for you?" Bridey was less than thrilled at being interrupted as she developed the newest shots for *Saracen*. Cord looked great. She'd answered her phone only because she was expecting a call from him.

"My name is Andersen. Thomas Andersen. I wanted to talk to you about the ad layout you are doing for Saracen."

Bridey straightened up and leaned against the counter. She'd been working since 4 AM. Both exhausted and excited over the pictures, she was in no mood to talk to anyone but Cord.

"Look, I can't ... She started to answer, but the man on the other end cut her off.

"I won't bother you for long. I just need to know if you and your new cologne model are available to do some other work. Don't worry! It's not a competitor of the cologne. I deal in outdoor equipment. That guy has just the right look."

Bridey visualized Cord dressed in backpacking gear, tramping up some mountain and smiled.

"Yes," she said, "he does. But Mr. Grant is under a very tight contract for at least the rest of the year. You'll have to deal with *Saracen* and him at the end of the contract. I can't do anything to help.

Doodling the name Grant, Elks continued to stroke the woman for information. "Well, maybe I could just talk to the guy for a few minutes on the set."

"No, I'm afraid not. The shooting is done for now. Mr. Grant is leaving this morning to go back to his ranch."

"So, he really is an outdoorsman. I thought so. He just has that ... that aura about him."

"Look, Mr. Andersen." Bridey rubbed her exhausted eyes and tried to wake her brain a little, too tired to remember her promise to Cord. "I really can't discuss this. When Mr. Grant comes back from New Mexico, you might be able to talk with him then. I'm not even sure when or if he'll be back, but I'm really not the one to talk to."

"I understand." Elks put just the right note of disappointment in his voice as he scratched N.M. next to the man's last name. "I guess I can just wait. In the meantime, who can I talk to at *Saracen*?"

Bridey gave him Lana's office information and hung up. Lana would be upset with her giving the man her contact information, but right now Bridey just didn't care. Lana was the reason she'd worked so late last night and gotten back to the job so early today. Lana insisted on that one last shot even though Cord and Bridey were exhausted. Bridey looked at the last picture. Cord was looking right at the lens – right at her – the exhaustion showed in his eyes. But there was a hunger there as well, like a man obsessed by a woman, a man blinded by love and lust. Bridey shook her head. Lana was right. This was the best shot of them all. Bridey smiled as she realized he was looking at her. Her body gave an involuntary shudder. Lana thought Cord was getting on the plane tonight, but she and Cord would make other plans. This one evening she'd have him all to herself. One night to show him why she lived in the City. Their ongoing argument about why anyone would want to live in or out of the City had come down to this final night. She was determined to make this night the time of his life.

Bridey hung the last photos on the line to dry and looked at the clock. She could get a three-hour nap if she went to bed right now. *No problem,* was her last thought as she fell onto the bed and instantly to sleep.

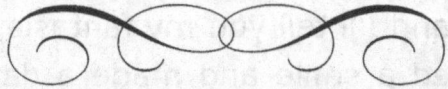

Before long, Elks found more information about Grant. He took a trip to the *Saracen* headquarters to see what he could find. At the main desk sat an overly made-up secretary obviously bored with her job. She saw Elks walk in the door and checked her lipstick, smacking those too bright red lips like a hungry predator. Elks forced a smile. He'd dealt with this type before. According to the talkative secretary he sweet-talked for half an hour, no one knew much about Grant. His first name was Cord. He was a rancher in New Mexico, but that was all anyone knew except that he was perfect for the image. Everyone who'd seen the proofs could tell, the almost gasping woman proclaimed, clutching her chest. There was just no information floating around. He was hired, did a great job, had a contract and was leaving tonight.

The secretary batted her heavily made-up eyes and sighed, "I tried hard to get to know him. Even invited him to my place once. But he said he couldn't make it. Said there was someone waiting for him at home. Always the same ... the great ones are already taken."

Elks smiled and thanked her for her help. As he stood to leave, the woman reached out and touched his arm in an attempt to keep him in the seat. She looked at him from under heavy false lashes attempting to be seductive. Elks shuddered again.

"How about you, you handsome brute? You know young studs are nice, but I like my men a bit more mature, and, shall we say, talented. Meet me for a drink tonight and I'll tell you my fantasies."

Elks flashed a smile and made a date he had no intention in keeping. As he walked out the door, he used all his self-control to keep from brushing the feel of her hand from his arm. *Scary woman,* he thought to himself as he walked back to his office and settled down for the call to Stanton. Predictably, Maria answered the phone. Though they'd met and even dated a couple times over the past decade, Elks was very careful with her.

"Good morning. This is Elks. Please tell Mr. Stanton that I have some information for him." His tone very business-like and distant.

Maria's voice was equally business-like, but less steady. "Yes, Mr. Elks. Mr. Stanton is on another line but

I'm sure . . ."

Maria was cut off by Stanton's brusque, "Tell me."

Elks heard the soft click as Maria put her receiver down. Elks gave the information as succinctly as possible.

"That's it? That's all?" Stanton was less than pleased. Elks could almost see the smoke coming out of his ears like the old cartoons when a character got so angry his brain began to boil.

"That's all that's available. They have a very tight hold on this man's bio and no one is talking." Elks waited for the explosion. When a quiet but stern whisper came through the lines, he felt his first tinge of fear.

"Understand me! I want this person! Are we clear?" Stanton paused briefly for effect, then continued at slightly louder but no less unnerving tone, "I want to know where he lives and what he does and who he sees. You are to do nothing else until I have this information. Understood?" Stanton didn't wait for Elks to answer before he hung up.

Elks took a taxi to the building that housed the Deane office. In the little café across the street, he nursed cup after cup of tepid coffee waiting for her to appear. Figuring his best way to find the man was through her, he planned to follow her for a few days. He didn't have to wait long. At 5 PM, he saw Bridey and Cord get out of a taxi and enter the building, arm in arm. Half an hour later, a silver limousine pulled up to the apartment building. The driver double-parked, got out, and walked to the door to ring the bell.

A few minutes later, a dazzling Bridey, dressed in a lovely scarlet dress with a matching satin wrap, alighted followed by Cord now attired in a tux. *Damn,* thought Elks, *this is going to be a long boring night.* He watched the driver handed the couple into the back seat of the long silver machine, knowing he had no time to go home and dress accordingly. He'd just have to follow the limo around and sit outside the clubs until the couple decided to go home again. He shook his head. Too bad he couldn't go inside with them. That little photographer was worth having to hang around just for the opportunity to look at her. He left the waitress a hefty tip, stepped outside the café, and hailed a taxi.

Man, how he envied that cowboy.

"Love is energy: it can neither be created nor destroyed. It just is and always will be, giving meaning to life and direction to goodness... Love will never die."
–Bryce Courtney

Twelve

They laughed. They danced. The night was full of sounds and yet, for them, empty of anything but each other. There were other people around, of that Bridey was certain. You couldn't go anywhere in the City and be totally alone. But as far as Bridey was concerned, there was only Cord and her feelings for him.

That last photograph stayed etched in her mind. Every time she looked at him, she thought she saw the hunger that had been in his hooded, half-open, very sexy eyes. She remembered the shudder that had run through her body when she realized that look wasn't for the woman wrapped around him, her hands running over his chest and her lips playing with his ear. Nor was that look for the camera alone. He'd looked at the camera too many times without that elusive look. Bridey knew that look was for her. His disturbing eyes followed her as she stepped away from the lens, taken aback at the emotional power of what she saw. Her body responded like the strings of a finely tuned instrument waiting for fingers to caress them and coax the music from them. That picture alone was going to sell a lot of cologne. For a brief moment, she felt jealous of every other woman who'd see the picture and felt like he was looking at them.

Bridey shook that thought out of her mind and looked over her glass of wine at Cord who appeared engrossed in the menu. When they entered *Gallow Green* at the top of the world famous McKittrick Hotel, the host escorted them to a perfect table immediately, close enough to get to the dance floor, but far enough away for relative privacy. A half wall of hothouse flowers created a fragrant barrier between the other tables. With a little imagination, they could feel like they were alone.

Remembering the hooded seductive looks that came through the lens at her, Bridey could hardly pull her eyes away from Cord. *Gawd, he's handsome,* she thought. She shuddered lightly, her body responding to the emotion he aroused in her. Cord looked up to see her staring. There were questions in his eyes. Bridey hid her own thoughts quickly. "What?" she asked.

"Have you looked at these prices?" he said in amazement. "Back home, I can get a whole calf for the price of some of these meals."

Bridey laughed and reached out to touch the back of his hand. "You don't get it, do you? You're going to be a very wealthy man soon. You can afford this kind of stuff." Cord shook his head and looked back down at the menu.

Cord raised an eyebrow. "Just because a man can afford something ..."

"Besides," Bridey continued, "if it makes you feel better, we're riding on Lana's nickel tonight. This is considered work. I'll write the cost of the meal into her bill when she pays me. Believe me, she won't blink an eye."

Cord shook his head again and, without looking up, turned his hand over under Bridey's. Bridey felt the fingers close gently around her own. Her heart skipped a beat or two. For a brief moment, she forgot to breathe. Cord looked up and smiled. There was that look again, want coupled with desire, clear as anything. Bridey stared back and let her own feelings show in her eyes. *Here we go,* she thought, *I sure hope I know what I'm doing.*

A white-coated waiter cleared his throat discreetly. Bridey reluctantly withdrew her hand and picked up her own menu. In her element, Bridey questioned the freshness of the vegetables and the preparation of the meat. She told the waiter what to bring and in what order. Cord simply sat and watched in amazement. She made ordering a meal sound like an executive decision of the utmost importance. His admiration for her grew by the moment.

As soon as the man left with their order, Cord stood up. "At the risk of causing you to faint, would you care to dance with me?" Towering over her, he held his hand out, palm up, the same way he'd done that first time. Bridey smiled at the memory. Without a second's hesitation, she laid her hand in his and let him pull her from the chair. He laughed as he offered his arm to her and escorted her to the polished wooden floor. "I do a mean Texas Two Step, but it's been a long time since I waltzed. I hope you have a couple extra toes around."

Bridey put her hand on his shoulder and stepped into the circle of his arms with a smile. "Fortunately, I seem to be in a risk-taking mood tonight."

They started out holding each other loosely. By the time, the first song ended, neither was interested in letting the other go, each of them experiencing new feelings that were too good to leave alone. The second song, a sweet, dreamy love song, began. Cord pulled Bridey closer to whisper in her ear. "Back home we call this kind of song a belly rubber."

Bridey felt his strong, lean body press against hers and mumbled something into his chest. Cord pushed her back slightly. "Pardon?"

Bridey looked up with a mock fierce look. "I wish you'd stop talking about back home. I have you until 9 AM tomorrow morning. Back home can have you after that." She pressed herself back into the space she'd been seconds before.

Cord sighed as he felt her soft warmth mold itself against him. She was just tall enough for him to fold around and not have to stoop over. She fit him perfectly. The smile on his face softened at the thought. Common sense told him this evening was a big mistake. He was going home tomorrow; quite sure he wouldn't see her again for a while. What in the hell was he doing here dancing with her, holding her, wanting her like he'd never wanted another woman since ...? Immediately a vision of the dark head lying on the carpet filled his head. He pushed the thought of Deborah out of his mind. Nothing from the past was going to ruin this evening for them.

The exquisitely presented meal was on the table when they returned. The perfectly seasoned steaks and crisp vegetables were cold, but neither noticed. Cord wanted to slide his chair around to be closer to Bridey, but she looked so beautiful through the candlelight between them, he stayed where he was and stared.

They talked, stared, and danced some more.

Neither of them paid any attention to the waiter as he removed their plates and poured the last of the wine an hour later. They were completely engrossed in holding hands across the table and staring as if to memorize the other's face. The waiter asked if there'd be anything else. Bridey shook her head without taking her eyes from Cord.

"Just the bill," she said, dismissing the man.

"One more dance?" Cord asked softly.

Bridey's voice shook slightly. "Not here. Let's go."

"Where?" Cord pulled her hand to his lips and kissed the knuckles.

"It doesn't matter," she gasped. She quickly signed the bill and gathered her things. "My place. Your place.

Anywhere we can be alone."

Cord wrapped his arm around Bridey's shoulders when she stood. She leaned back into his warm solid body. Determined to keep as much contact as possible between them, Cord guided Bridey out to the waiting limo. The driver jumped to open the door. Cord directed him to take them back to Bridey's place.

They cuddled down in the soft leather of the back seat, Cord's arms around Bridey, her head on his shoulder. Neither said anything for a few blocks.

"You know this is foolish," Bridey whispered against his chest.

"Yup."

"We should stop this now and just say good night, shouldn't we?"

"Yup." Cord's hand cupped Bridey's chin and lifted her lips to his.

"We aren't going to be sensible, are we?" she said, staring into his glistening eyes.

"Nope."

Cord kissed Bridey deeply. He gloried in the sound of her quiet moan and the way she shifted her body to make access easier for him. His hands caressed her where the backless dress left her skin exposed for a few seconds before allowing his hand to gently slip forward under the loose material to cup her unclad breast. Bridey gasped as she felt his cool, slightly rough hand on her warm, sensitive body. She eased her own hand down his chest to his lap and felt the evidence of his desire.

"Touch me," he whispered. "Touch me please." He slid the loose material of the dress away from her breast, dropped his mouth and suckled gently. Bridey's hand struggled with the zipper of his pants. Cord shifted to offer her more access. Just as she accomplished her mission, the limo pulled over and stopped. Bridey opened her eyes long enough to realize they were home. The driver's door slammed. Cord lifted his head. While Cord zipped his pants, Bridey started to pull the dress back to cover her exposed breasts. Cord's gentle hand stopped her. "Leave it," he whispered and pulled her wrap around to protect her from the cool night air and the driver's eyes. Cord stepped out and turned to help Bridey.

"Hello." The simple word made Bridey falter. There, standing just beyond Cord stood Mark, obviously coming out of her building. Surprise and dismay raced through Bridey. Despite her mother's continued attempts to get them back together, she hadn't seen him since that last party, the night he'd showed her the real Mark. All the anger, hurt and shame of that evening flooded into her mind as if trauma had only happened the night before. Of all nights for Mark to try to crawl back into her life. After all this time, what did he have to ruin this beautiful night?

She pulled the wrap tighter over her exposed breast and answered coldly. "What are you doing here?"

Mark didn't answer right away. The look in his eyes made clear he was still mourning the loss of the gorgeous defiant creature that stood in front of him, her hair tumbling down her back in riotous waves, makeup smeared, and a sensual kind of hunger radiating from every pore. The memory of her silken skin, her loving embrace, the time when that look he seen on her face as she climbed out of the cab was for him, twisted in his gut. Why she'd left him, he still didn't understand. He tamped down the rising anger at the audacity of her leaving him and shifted his shoulders inside his jacket before answering.

"I've been hearing about how well you're doing. I thought we could go out to dinner and then you'd show me your studio. A sort of a private ..." he glanced pointedly at Cord who remained quietly at Bridey's side, tensed to defend her if she needed his help, "... showing, if you will."

Bridey took a deep breath of the cool night air that surrounded her. She felt Cord's warmth coming from close behind her and drew strength from his presence. She looked Mark square in the eyes and said, "You ended your chance at anything private between us long ago, Mark."

She felt Cord's warm hand wrap itself around her waist. "There's nothing left between us."

She looked up at Cord, smiled and tried to step around the man. Mark's hand shot out to stop her from going into the building. He had more to say to her and dammit, she was going to listen. Intent on grabbing her arm to make her face him, he missed her arm and grabbed the material covering her shoulders. The stole slipped down revealing the open dress. Mark's shocked face turned red with fury. All this time, while he had been trying to talk some sense into her, that cowboy had been touching her as only he had a right to touch! He dropped his hand as if burned. He looked at her, at Cord, and then back again.

"So, you got some cowboy to treat you like the cheap whore you are, did you?" Cord tensed beside her. Reaching out to grab her breast, Mark spit words like a viper on the attack, "Hell, I could've done that if that was all you wanted."

Cord reacted immediately. He shifted Bridey to his other arm, away from Mark's groping hand, and planted his fist firmly under Mark's beautifully shaven chin. As Mark crumpled to the ground, Cord folded Bridey into his arms and led her into the building.

At the door, Bridey looked back at the crumpled heap on the filthy sidewalk. She looked at Cord and said, "We can't leave him there." Cord placed his lips over hers to silence her and turned her back toward the stairs. He stopped to pick her up in his arms and said, "Where I'm from we leave pigs in the dirt."

Cord struggled up the stairs, trying to kiss Bridey while carrying her. Halfway up, he swore and paused. Cord dropped her legs and leaned her against the wall. He kissed her as if he'd never stop. She felt his hands kneading the exposed breast under the satin wrap. Bridey felt control leaving her body. If she didn't have him soon, she was sure she'd die.

"Cord," she gasped, "We ... have to ... get inside."
Cord groaned and, without breaking the kiss, lifted her
again, struggling to the door.

"Where are your keys?" he breathed against her
mouth. He felt her searching for the small bag she
carried. Keys jangled. She pulled away from him and
turned her back to slip the key into the lock. Her hands
shook as Cord nibbled her neck and hairline. As the
door opened, she turned back to him. He bent to kiss
her again and pushed the door further open. They fell
through, landing in a tangled heap on the soft rug that
covered the hallway floor. Cord wrapped his arms
around Bridey and rolled over on top of her, kicking the
door closed on his way.

"My keys," Bridey put her hands on his chest and
pushed away from him. "Cord, this is New York. You
can't leave the door unlocked or the keys hanging in
the lock. Besides, the bed is so much more comfortable
than this rug."

Cord swore and fell back to lie beside her on the
floor. He took a deep steadying breath and turned to
look at her. Lipstick smeared and hair tousled, half out
of her dress already, Cord was certain he'd never seen
anyone more beautiful. "The last thing I care about
right now is comfort!" He reached for her again.

Bridey rolled out of his reach, struggled to stand
up in the tangled dress and pulled him after her,
laughing. "There's a thing or two I need to take care
of. There's scotch in the cabinet in the living room. Get

the keys. Lock the door. Make yourself a drink and I'll be right back."

She looked into his tormented eyes and reached up to touch his cheek. He covered her hand with his and turned her fingers to kiss the palm. Bridey promised, "I swear I'll hurry."

Holding her hand as long as he could, Cord took a deep breath as he resigned himself to the fact that she was really going to leave him in this condition. He watched her stagger away from him, aroused even more by the fact that she seemed as affected by him as he was by her. Cord smiled and opened the door to retrieve the keys. He turned the locks and shot the bolt through, shaking his head. At home, he just shut the door and went to bed. Home. Damn.

He took off his wrinkled jacket and walked into the living room to pour a stiff drink. "Do you want one?" he called toward the room Bridey had disappeared through.

"No." The soft whisper close by made him turn around. He nearly dropped the decanter when he saw her standing in the doorway wearing nothing more than a smile. "I have something more interesting in mind." She turned her back and glanced over her shoulder at him, mimicking the hooded look she'd seen in the camera. Crooking her finger in a seductive *follow me* gesture, she sauntered slowly away out of his view. Mesmerized, Cord carried the glass in one hand and the decanter in the other, too astounded to do anything but follow her.

She stood by the bed, waiting for him. He walked up to her and fastened his lips to hers. Her arms wrapped themselves around his neck and pulled him close. His arms, weighted by the glass, wanted to respond. She let one arm drift down and took the decanter from him. Without breaking the kiss, she set the crystal on the night table. The glass slipped to the wooden floor as her hand found the front of his pants and this time unzipped him with no trouble at all.

He stepped back from her and watched her face as he unbuttoned his shirt. The smile of a conqueror played on her lips, a winner who knew she was about to enjoy the spoils of the battle freely given.

Cord shrugged to get out of his shirt, anxious to feel her bare skin against his. He loosened the cummerbund and let both drop to the floor. He stood in front of her, muscular chest and banded arms glistening with sweat from the trip upstairs. He lowered his eyelids slightly and watched her as he undid his belt. The dark material drifted down his sleek haunches and exposed his erection.

Smiling, Bridey placed her hands on the broad chest and ran her hands through the soft curly hairs. He moaned and tried to take her in his arms. Bridey gave him a small shove that sent him toppling gently onto the soft mattress. Staring at him through glazed eyes, Bridey dropped to her knees. He watched as she untied his shoes and removed his socks and pulled them off with his pants. Just seeing her there made him want her more. He moaned as he felt his erection tightened. She stood pulling his pants with her and threw them over her shoulder. Then she leaned in seductively to kiss him again. Cord pulled her down to kiss her. He had full access to her body. His hands struggled to touch every part of her all at once. He ran his hands over her arms from wrists to shoulders and down, pausing briefly to touch her breast when he heard the catch in her breath. One hand stayed there, gently kneading and rubbing, while the other wandered down to the V of her legs. He touched the soft curly hair and pressed further. Gently pushing her lower lips apart, he ran a finger into the channel, already slick and wet with desire.

Bridey gasped and broke the kiss, unable to breathe in her arousal.

"I take it you like that?" he asked, a smile playing on his lips.

Her answer was to push him back and lay on top of him, kissing his face and neck while rubbing her body against him. Groaning with desire, Cord understood her unspoken need and rolled her over into the middle of the bed. He pulled back to look at her once more, eyes heavy with lust, lips swollen and parted, chest heaving, and sweat glistening. She let him look for only a moment before whispering, "I want you so badly,
Cord. I want you now. Don't make me plead with you."

He didn't.

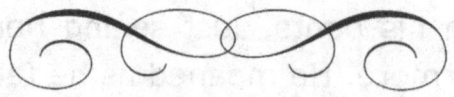

Bridey woke halfway when she felt the bed behind her shift. She ached in every part of her body. She couldn't remember a time when she'd felt so loved and desired. She flopped an arm back to find Cord gone. She heard water running in the bathroom down the hall. She heard footsteps coming back to her and felt the bed sag slightly again. A cool body pressed up against hers.

"You awake?" he asked. She made an affirmative sound deep in her throat. "Sorry. Didn't mean to wake you." She heard a smile in his voice as his hand reached forward to touch her swollen breast. She felt her nipple rise up to meet his gentle fingers. No longer interested in sleep, she rolled over to look at him.

"Liar!" She smiled at his impish grin. "What time is it?"

"Around 5," he said as he kissed and teased her nipple with gentle nips.

"That means, if we had any sense, we'd get some sleep. You have to be at the airport in a couple of hours." She pulled his head up and looked into his eyes. She knew he wasn't any more interested in sleep than she was at the moment. He smiled and leaned down to take her lower lip between his teeth.

"Have you always been this worried about being sensible?"

"Always. Well ... before tonight." She said and lifted her head to kiss him one more time.

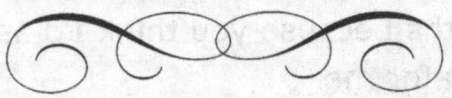

He barely made the plane. The cab they'd ordered for 6:30 A.M. sat at the curb blowing its horn as they gathered scattered clothing. Cord put his tux back on. Bridey dressed herself in Calvin Klein jeans and a Hilfiger sweatshirt. They raced back to Cord's hotel to get his things together and then to the airport. They arrived just in time for the first call of passengers.

Cord walked Bridey over to a fairly secluded corner and leaned her against the wall. "I'll miss you. A lot."

Tears glistened in her eyes as Bridey nodded. "You know," he continued, "we can't do this. I'm not geared for long distance love and neither of us wants to give up the lives we have."

Bridey nodded again. Cord took her in his arms and held her. The last row was called for boarding. "Come with me," he whispered into her hair.

Bridey shook her head and pushed him back. "Why? For a lot of great sex? It's wonderful, but I doubt that's enough for either of us." She slipped out of his embrace and turned her back. He watched her slender shoulders sag in despair. Torn between his desire for her and his need to go home, he stepped forward and put his arm across her shoulders. "Ok! Then I'll go home, sell everything and be back."

Bridey flashed around. "No! I saw how you were out there. That's where you belong. You love that damned horse and those stinking barns and that desolate country. I won't watch you grow to resent me in a few months because you think I'd ask you to give up everything for me."

She looked at him in defiance and listened as the final boarding call was announced. "Get on the damned plane."

Time froze as he watched a tear roll down her cheeks and remembered those eyes filled with passion just a few hours ago. She watched his eyes as they darkened with pain and wanted more than anything to skip into his arms and beg him not to go.

Somehow, she found the strength to break the spell, whispering, "Just get on the damned plane."

He started to walk past her. Just as he stepped by her, he stopped for a moment. "I'll call you when I get there."

"Please do." No longer able to control her pain, Bridey threw herself into his arms and kissed him once more. He carried his bag and her toward the boarding ramp. Their kiss deepened with each step. They reached the stewardess and he handed over the ticket, his eyes never leaving Bridey's.

"Sir, you really must get on the plane. We're ready to take off."

With one more stroke of her cheek, Cord turned and walked away. Bridey let the tears flow freely as she watched the man she loved walk away and chided herself for letting him go alone.

"True love doesn't mean being inseparable; it means being separated and nothing changes." –Anon

Thirteen

Elks reported to Stanton. Cord Grant lived on a ranch in New Mexico. He owned no property, was well liked in the community and seemed to be deeply involved with the photographer. He expanded on how he followed them to the airport and watched their tender good-bye. While Bridey and Cord were engrossed in each other, Elks bought the last remaining seat on the plane.

Following Grant back to the ranch was frighteningly simple. The cowboy was totally engrossed in his thoughts and memories, not paying a bit of attention to anything around him. Elks remembered how beautiful the photographer had looked like the couple had come down to the limo. He'd have trouble, too, if he had just spent the night with such a woman and had to leave her. When Grant got to the ranch, Elks drove around to find nearest small town where ranch hands might go to unwind. That would be his best opportunity for gathering information. The classic idea of the tightlipped cowboy was a myth. Given a bit of alcohol and some good-natured ribbing, they'd all spill their guts.

Upon his return to the City, Elks called to report to Stanton. "Seems to be well liked, no problems. The guys who work with him say he doesn't talk about himself much."

Stanton snorted. "I'll just bet."

Sitting back in the soft leather chair Stanton's money had purchased, Elks waited for his next assignment. Stanton was quiet for so long, Elks was beginning to think he'd hung up. "Mr. Stanton? Sir? Do you want me to proceed?"

Ignoring the question completely, Stanton asked, "What do you think would be the easiest way to get to the man?"

Elk's brow furrowed. What did he mean *get to*? "Well, you can always go out there. Depending on what you have in mind, he seems approachable enough."

"No, no, I don't want to leave the area right now."

"Simple then. Get to the photographer. She seems to know him, uhm, extremely well." "What do you mean?"

Elks described the scene at the airport for Stanton. As he finished, he heard the unnerving sound of Stanton's laugh. Elks shuddered and wondered briefly if he should warn the woman. As if reading his mind, Stanton came back on the line.

"No, Elks. You aren't to proceed. In fact, you're to forget this conversation. It never happened. Do I make myself clear?"

"Yes, I understand you perfectly." The connection ended abruptly. Elks held the phone away from his ear and replaced the handset. Sometimes he really didn't like that man.

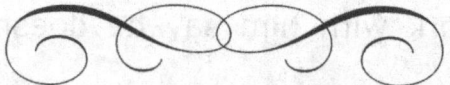

Edson turned his mind to the job ahead with joyous abandonment. For days, he had thought out carefully staged, deliciously evil scenarios, only to shoot each plan full of holes and start again. He planned kidnappings and murders, torture and blackmailing. Until he finally hit on the perfect idea. He was finally going to get that conniving little bastard out of his life. When the plan was perfect, the arrangements only took a few days to complete.

The last night before he put his plan into action, Edson went to the den where he'd ended his father's rule and sat in the chair across from the one in which his father had preferred to hold court. Once or twice, he got up, walked over and sat down on the butter-soft leather of his father's favorite chair – the throne. But he was up again in a few seconds. No matter how often he tried, the chair just never seemed to fit him right.

Edson thought about his life and its horrors, imagined or otherwise. He knew all his troubles had started when his mother had abandoned him by dying when he was so young. He couldn't forgive her. He rubbed his eyes as the vague memories of a sultry perfume and soft arms that held and rocked him as an infant closed in on him. All his life he'd searched for that feeling of those arms around him, holding him with love and compassion. No one ever came close. He pushed them all away sooner or later.

He threw his empty glass at his father's chair. "And you were the worst, you old bastard! How dare you send me away and then put every stray that came along in my place. How dare you!"

Some days he wished his father was still alive so he could make him suffer even more for sending his only child away. Other days, he wished he could make amends and try harder to fix things.

Edson woke up the next morning, stiff and sore from spending the night in the high-backed chair where he had drank himself to sleep. He immediately began putting his plan into action, calling the cleaning service to let them know he would be out of town the following week. The private jet he bought shortly after his father's death was waiting for him at the airport. Once in New York, he registered at one of the city's finest hotels and immediately tried to contact the photographer. Her answering machine came on every time he tried calling during the day. Edson left no message. He wanted to hear her voice when he put his plan into action. Torn between his excitement to get to Cord and his anger at continually getting the machine, Edson waited restlessly until the next morning. At 7:30, he tried once more.

"Ms. Deane?" He carefully modulated his baritone voice to its most pleasant timber and smiled the entire time in hopes that he sounded much friendlier and warmer than he felt.

"Yes, this is she. What can I do for you?"

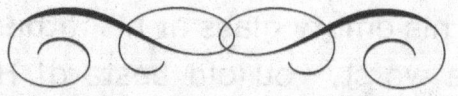

Lying in her bed, Bridey stared at the ceiling, wrapped up snugly, and wished Cord would call. Each morning since that glorious night, talking herself out of the bed they'd made such glorious love in took longer and longer. Everything in her life was going so well. Her business was booming. She had so much to do. The *Saracen* campaign was a huge success. Her answering machine was so full some days that she was actually considering hiring a secretary. She should be bounding out of bed every morning, yet without Cord, nothing seemed to be as exciting as before him.

They'd talked often. More than once, Cord called her just as she was waking up. Sunrise in New Mexico was a reasonable time in the City if you were a working person. This particular night she'd dreamt of their last night together, tossing and turning restlessly. When she finally fell asleep, the dream with its whispering insistent voice came to haunt her.

She reached for the ringing phone and was sorely disappointed not to hear Cord's voice on the other end.

Edson turned on the charm. "I was given your name by Senator Armand, whose portrait you did a few weeks ago."

Bridey tried to remember that portrait. She'd done three senators since *Saracen* hit the market.

"Yes," she said noncommittally.

"I'm in need of a similar portrait and wondered if we could get together to discuss it. Say, at dinner? Tonight?"

Bridey ran a hand through her tousled hair. Her calendar was in the dark room, giving her the excuse she needed to get up. "Uh ... I'm going to have to check my book. Can you give me a minute to find it? I don't usually get business calls this early."

Edson's jaw tightened but he smiled into the receiver. "Of course, I'll be glad to wait for you."

Bridey carried the cordless with her in search of the book. She was pretty sure her evening was free. Just as she put the phone back to her ear, the incoming call tone sounded. "Excuse me, Mr. ... uhm . . .."

"Staley. Edward M. Staley."

"Yes, Mr. Staley. I have a call on the other line. Give me a second to get rid of them." Edson murmured consent and heard the line go quietly.

"Hello? Deane Photography."

"Bridey?"

Her heart nearly skipped out of her breast at hearing Cord's voice. She plopped down on the nearest chair and smiled. "Cord! How are you? I was just thinking about you a few moments ago?"

"Where you now? Are you still in bed?" He chuckled at the thought. She heard the laughter in his voice. He loved to argue about how city people lay in bed all day while country folks were up and working.

"No, Smarty, I'm not. In fact, I'm ... Oh no! I have an important client on the other line. I have to get back to him. Do you want to hold or shall I call you back?"

"Just called to say good morning. That I was thinking about you. I'll be out moving stock all day today. We leave in about 30 minutes. You go do your business and I'll call you another time, OK?"

Bridey sighed. She heard him whisper into the phone. "I do you know."

"Do what?" she asked.

"Think about you. All the time. I try to sleep ... and I dream that you are there just far enough away so I can't touch you. I ride in the car and sometimes hear your voice on the radio." Bridey sighed as she listened to his seductive confession. The sensual voice conjured up images of their time together.

"Worst of all is when I have to move the cattle. Sometimes there's one little heifer with a particularly nice sway in her hips." He smacked his lips loudly. "Always makes me think of you!"

Bridey screamed into the phone. "You shit!" His laughter roared back in her ears. Bridey cradled the phone tightly to her ear trying to get closer to him. She wanted more than anything to spend time in any way she could with this man.

"I have to go, OK? Oh, wait a minute? How's the horse?" Cord snickered and told her about the colt's latest trick. They talked and laughed for about ten minutes until Bridey remembered her other call.

"Oh, God help me!" Bridey cried when she remembered the call. "I have to go. There is some big mucky muck businessman waiting to take me to dinner."

Cord's voice lowered a notch. "Should I be jealous?"

"I hardly think so, Cord." Bridey smiled. "You seemed to have left a very lasting impression in my life. Ruined me for other men in some odd way. I'm practically a nun these days. Besides, you have those gorgeous little cows to keep you company."

Cord groaned as she turned his words back on him. His chest swelled with emotion. He'd give anything to be there right now. "OK, go to your big businessman then. I'll wait till next time to tell you that Lana has summoned me."

"When? Are you coming back soon?"

Cord loved the sound of her breathless excitement. "In a few days."

"How long can you stay?" She sounded like a child at Christmas. Cord laughed at her joy.

"We'll have to play that by ear. Lana has something for me she said and I, well, I have some news myself." "What? What news?" Bridey asked, giddy with joy.

"Bridey?" Cord asked slyly. "Did you forget your big man on the other line?" He laughed again at her gasp and said good-bye. Bridey hung up reluctantly and then turned her attention back to the other call.

"I apologize, Mr. Staley. Turned out to be a ... uhm ... Trans-Atlantic call I'd been waiting for."

Sensing a lie, Edson swallowed his anger. He seethed with fury. No one ever kept him waiting like that. *No one*. The brighter tone in her voice told him she'd probably been talking to that stinking cowboy. He felt the rage rising up in his chest. His anger doubled as each minute passed. If he'd been in the same room with her, he doubted she'd live out the day. Breathing deeply, he worked hard to control the rage by adding her body to the list of things he'd steal from Grant.

"Why, of course," he said, saccharine sweetness dripping from his lips. "I understand that business must come first; however, I'm also a busy man. Do we have a date for this evening?"

Hardly a date, Bridey thought. But, now, she felt like she couldn't decline. "Of course. Where shall I meet you?"

"Oh, no. I'll send a driver for you. I don't know much about how things are done in New York but, in Virginia, where I was raised, a gentleman never allows a lady to walk into a restaurant without an escort. 7:30 a good time for you?"

Bridey's eyebrows raised and then lowered again. Hmm, a gentleman, was he? This could be interesting. She gave him the address and then hung up. By the looks of her schedule, the day was a full one, starting in less than an hour. She'd have to rush things in order to make dinner. She had no intention of making the man wait again – unless, of course, Cord called. Bridey smiled on her way to the shower and lightly chided herself. Everything took a back seat to Cord's calls.

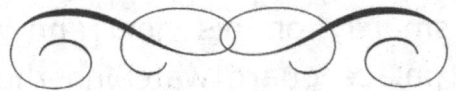

Promptly at 7:30, Bridey heard a sharp rap on her door. Outside stood a chauffeur dressed in white, complete with gold braid and decorative buttons rather than the traditional black. He held his hat under his arm and waited patiently as Bridey opened the door.

"Good evening, Madame," he bowed at the waist with a flourish and produced a small envelope in his gloved hand. "I understand you are dining with Mr. Staley this evening."

"Yes. Yes, I am." She smiled at the man who looked more like an Eighteenth-century coachman than a limousine driver. The uniformed man held the note out to her.

"This message is from Mr. Staley, if you please." He bowed slightly again.

"Thank you." Bridey accepted the envelope and stepped back inside her apartment to read it. The note was simple, written in a copperplate style.

"Slightly detained by work. Taken liberty of arranging dinner in my suite. Dress formal."

She smiled at the Old World charm of the situation and opened the door again. "I'm going to need to change. I won't be long."

The man bowed again and said, "Mr. Staley expected a slight delay, Madame." Did she imagine the emphasis on the word slight?

"Do you want to wait inside?" she asked.

"No, Madame, I'm fine right here. Thank you." The man turned smartly on his heel and assumed the position of a palace guard watching the door of the Queen's residence.

Wow, thought Bridey, *I could get used to this. Quickly.* She closed the door and stepped into her bedroom to change.

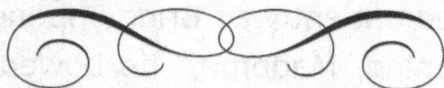

Edson had been detained but hardly by business. He ordered the concierge to find a discreet hairdresser to come to his suite. She arrived at 10 AM. By noon, Edson had darker hair and eyebrows with distinguished silver at his temples. Freshly shaven, he looked into a full-length mirror and was shocked to see his father staring back at him. Bile rose up in his throat. His fists clenched. The hairdresser came up behind him and looked at him in the mirror over his shoulder.

"Nice. Is that all you wanted? We do offer other services." The young woman smiled seductively. Edson returned the smile and lifted one eyebrow. He stared at the woman in the mirror. Both of them knew what other services she was offering. He needed a way to work off his fury. She could help. He turned and locked his hands, viselike, around her upper arms and smiled at her grimace of pain. "It's almost everything I need."

He began kissing her, hard and furious. Backing her to the bed, he lifted her up, only to throw her down on the bed and fell on top of her. He tore her blouse open and pushed her bra up to expose her breasts. He just needed to see them. Then he ripped the thin cotton uniform pants and lacy underwear off her and drove himself deep inside her without preparation. Her cries, whether from pain or pleasure, delighted him. Fighting off the impulse to beat the wench senseless and careful not to leave bruises, Edson spent his rage on her body in less than two minutes, finishing with a roar. He rolled off the woman and casually stood up. He took a linen handkerchief from his breast pocket and cleaned up, tucked himself back in and straightened out his suit that was barely mussed. Without looking at her, he casually threw money on the rumpled bed and addressed the woman, "I'm assuming you know this is a one-time thing and how to keep your mouth shut." The woman lay on the bed, breathless. She carefully took account of her bones. None were broken despite the violence of his attack, but her clothes were beyond repair. She nodded at his words.

"How do you expect me to get out of here?" she asked.

Edson turned from the mirror and smiled viciously. "That, my dear, is your problem. Never offer services without being prepared for every possibility. Number one rule of business." Edson straightened his tie and broadened the feral, almost evil grin. Suddenly realizing that this session could have been disastrous for her, the woman shuddered, gathered up her things and fled to the bathroom to clean up. Her coat would cover most of the problem and she had an extra uniform downstairs.

When she came out of the room, Stanton was gone. On the bed were scattered ten one-hundred dollar bills. She hadn't expected so much violence from such a genteel looking man, but she sure as hell got paid well enough to keep her mouth shut.

With the edge off his anger, Edson coldly focused his mind on the rest of the evening, arranging the car and driver to pick Bridey up, a fine meal to be delivered to his suite at 8:30, and a new tuxedo. Tonight, everything would begin to fall into place. He rubbed his hands in glee as he thought of the possibilities.

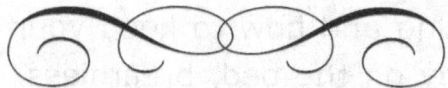

Bridey took less than fifteen minutes to change to a lavender sheath with a matching jacket that complemented her hair and skin. When she stepped out into the hall, the driver snapped to attention. As she turned to lock her doors, the man reached for the keys. With a gentle "Allow me," he locked the door and then stuck out an arm to escort her down the hall.

At the curb sat a gold Rolls Royce limousine, the kind of car she'd seen in movies about the 30's and 40's. No stranger to chauffeured cars, this one seemed just a bit more elegant. The chauffeur handed her into the back seat with yet another bow.

The trip took half an hour. Traffic was light and the ride was as smooth as coasting down a lazy river. Bridey felt the tension of the day roll away. She'd spent a tough day at a furious pace to get everything done in time. The promised gentile civility of the entire evening seemed to be designed to make her relax. When they arrived, the driver escorted her inside to the elevator and used a key to access the penthouse for her.

"Good evening, Madame. I've been instructed to return here to pick you up at midnight." Bridey smiled. The witching hour when all the Cinderellas needed to be back in their ashes. The driver caught the smile and returned the grin. "However, I'm at your disposal all evening. Simply dial the concierge and he'll summon me immediately ... should you need me."

"Thank you." The elevator doors closed on the man's smile. Bridey regarded the plush appointments and thought, *Whoever this Staley guy was, he sure knew how to dazzle a woman.*

The elevator opened directly into an elegant foyer. Staley was waiting as she stepped off.

"Miss Deane, I assume?" He offered her an arm as she stepped onto the deep pile carpet.

"You must be Mr. Staley." Bridey shuddered slightly as she heard her mother's prim voice coming from her lips.

"Oh my dear. Call me Edward."

They walked down a short hall, discussing the weather and other inconsequential topics. The suite was huge, complete with crystal chandeliers and a stunning view of the City from spotless ceiling to floor windows. Candles glowed on every surface. Tropical flowers spread their pungent fragrance in the air. Soothing classical music drifted through the room. Even though she was used to a fairly elegant life, this vision astonished her.

"I hope you won't get the wrong impression, my dear." Edson gave the hand on his arm an almost fatherly pat. "In Virginia, when we dress for dinner, we truly dine. I'm a big fan of candlelight and soft music whenever possible in this harsh world we live in." "Actually, this is perfect. I like to know what my potential subjects like. Seeing this gives me insight into how you should be portrayed if we come to an agreement."

"Oh, my dear," he spoke softly. "I really don't think we'll have a problem with that, do you?"

Bridey allowed herself to be led to a sofa on a small dais in front of the center window. She seated herself and basked in the view while Edson decanted sparkling white wine for them both.

He sat down beside her and began talking more. Dinner arrived but did nothing to slow their conversation. Both were conversant on a wide range of topics, from their favorite museums and musicals to foreign ports they had visited. Their tastes were very similar. The clock gently tolled 11 PM and they hadn't even discussed the portrait yet.

As interesting as the evening had been, Bridey stifled a yawn. Edson saw the move and stood, "I'll call for the driver, my dear. I fear I've kept you too long."

"But we still have the portrait to discuss." Bridey hid another yawn.

Bitch, Edson thought, *how dare you be bored with my company? I should throw you on to the floor right here and show you ...* Edson stopped his runaway thoughts and smiled down at her. "You poor dear. I insist we call it a night. I'll call you tomorrow and we'll discuss the photo session. What time do you usually rise?"

Edson handed her back into the elevator with a fatherly kiss on the forehead and watched as the door of the elevator closed around her. He nearly ran back to his room, closing the door behind him before he cursed in his rage and began to pace the floor. His control was nearly spent from the stress of pretending to be his father all night. He called the concierge.

"Get a woman up here. Now! And don't send me some sweet little wallflower either. I want someone who knows what she's doing."

He slammed the phone down and waited, pacing like a caged animal.

"I will spend an eternity loving you, caring for you, respecting you, showing you every day that I hold you as high as the stars."
−Dr. Steve Maraboli

Fourteen

The next days flew by. The morning after her meeting with Staley/Stanton, Cord called and told Bridey he'd be in New York the following Saturday for three or four days. She had only a few days to clear her schedule completely. Bridey planned, schemed, and rescheduled for hours to rearrange things. The only person she wasn't able to reach was Staley. Messages left at his hotel went unanswered. At 2 PM, right in the middle of a photo session with a rising young movie star who needed a portfolio, her beeper went off. Bridey ignored it.

Within the next few minutes, the shrill beep sounded two more times. Finally, Bridey threw her hands up with a resigned *Fine!* and called a ten minute break. Exasperated, she reached for the beeper. She was just getting the wannabe actress to relax and begin showing herself beautifully. Now, they'd have to start over again. *This better be good,* she thought as she read the number on the display. Staley.

She called him immediately.

"I must apologize, my dear. I've been in meetings all morning and just got a free moment." Stanton breathed into the phone, trying to sound like he been rushing to the phone when in reality he was still lying in bed. He'd just sent another whore the concierge had arranged away after using her viciously to stave off his anger. He thought about the woman's cries of pain, how she'd tried to fight him off when she realized the violence he planned to mete out on her and how her feeble attempts to get away had aroused him. Smiling, he turned his thoughts to the woman on the other end of the phone, *soon it'll be your turn, my dear. And, if you're good, we'll let your little boyfriend watch while he dies.* Edson choked off the gleeful laughter that threatened to escape him. Edson sat up and tried to focus on what Bridey was saying.

"So, you see, Mr. Staley. This thing has just come up. I either need to squeeze you into a session today or tomorrow – which I'd prefer not to do – or wait till I come back."

Come back? Come back from where? He'd missed what she said. "Well, dear. I really want this to be a good portrait. I don't want it rushed." He paused for a moment. "Tell you what. I'll be in town for a couple more days and then I need to go back home. You agree to have dinner with me again tomorrow night and we'll set a date for the sitting. How does that sound?"

Bridey breathed a sigh of relief. This was good, very good. She agreed and hurried back to the job at hand. She'd cleared everything now, leaving Saturday through Tuesday open for Cord.

Cord. Cord was coming back! She almost danced with the joy that filled her, feeling like a teenager with her first crush.

Dinner with Stanton, the man she knew as Edward Staley, again would be enough to delight and enthuse most women. And more than once, Bridey thought about how easy falling for such a man might be. In fact, if Cord, who now owned her heart and interrupted her thoughts constantly, hadn't been in the picture, she might have let herself go with this man but he had found her too late. The love of her life was already in place.

This time Stanton took her dancing. The evening was warm, the wine rich and the music perfect. They danced on the terrace after a perfect meal. Stanton stared into Bridey's eyes, trying to make her think he was falling for her.

That wouldn't be too hard, he decided, *to fall for such a beautiful woman.* But, again, that bastard Cord was in the way. Stanton pulled Bridey up against him as they danced. She didn't resist. He smirked over her shoulder as he let his hands roam over her back, drifting ever lower.

When the music stopped before he reached her full rounded bottom, he held her a few moments longer. When she gently pushed away from him, he dipped his head for just a small taste of those succulent lips.

Bridey turned her head at the last second. Stanton stiffened in anger but controlled the rage. He dropped his hands and apologized.

"I'm sorry, my dear. That was wrong of me. I'm afraid I was caught up in the moment." Offering his arm, he escorted her back to the table. He pulled out her seat and waited for her to settle before going back around to his chair. Bridey reached for her glass of wine with trembling hand.

"You must think me a complete idiot to have tried to kiss you like that. I hope you'll accept my apologies." Stanton looked earnestly at her through the candlelight. *She looks lovely in the flame of the candles,* he thought stifling a delicious shudder as the memory of fires he'd set and the damage they'd done danced in his memory.

Bridey waved him off and held her hand out across the table to him. "You are hardly an idiot, Mr. Staley . . ."

"Edward!" He chided, stopping her with a look and a cluck of his tongue. "I have just tried to kiss you and professed a growing desire for you. Do you think you could use my first name?" He smiled as Bridey looked shocked. She didn't know his first name.

"Edward, please don't think I'm put off by your attentions. I'm flattered. You've been a perfect gentleman and you do, indeed, know how to turn a girl's head. I'd have no hesitation if . . ." She paused and looked at her plate.

"If . . ." Stanton stared at the top of her head.

She seemed to make a decision as she lifted her face to him again. "There's someone else. In fact, I'm not really going away next week like I told you this morning. The truth is he's coming here and I want my schedule clear to be with him."

Red furled before Stanton's eyes as he struggled to keep the smile in its place. *Look at her! Look at that face. She's in love with him. The stupid bitch. Couldn't she see what a sniveling snake that man was?* He cleared his throat and smiled graciously.

"I'm glad you told me, Bridey. I had a feeling there was more to that story you told me this morning anyway. There was just something in your voice." He let her hand go and lifted his glass in a small salute. "So, tell me about this very fortunate man." Stanton's eyes glistened as he drank from the champagne flute and listened to her talk. The rage lessened as he realized that she was playing right into his hands. She'd bring that cowardly little bastard right to him. He'd make sure she did.

Bridey chattered nervously for a few moments about her plan for his portrait. She didn't want to ruin this contact. Suddenly, she felt an odd creeping urge to leave his presence.

"Look, I don't want to bore you with details. It's been a lovely evening, but I think I need to get back." She pushed her chair back. Stanton stood and quickly stepped around to help her with the chair.

"Yes, yes, of course. Just promise me that I haven't offended you."

Bridey lifted her eyes to meet his serious ones. *He was truly worried,* she thought. *What a nice, gentle man he was.* She placed her hand on his cheek and reached up to kiss his other one. "Of course not, Edward. I'm just tired that's all. Will you excuse me for just a moment?"

Stanton took care of the bill. While he waited for Bridey to return, he called his hotel. The concierge answered. Edson growled, "Get someone up there. Now! And make it a red head!"

"But Mr. Stanton that may take longer..." stammered the concierge.

"I don't care," bellowed Stanton. "Do it!"

He hung up just as Bridey stepped around the corner. The surprised look on her face made him calm her by saying, "Business, dear. Just a reluctant supplier." Bridey smiled weakly.

Grinning broadly, he held his arm out to Bridey and walked stiffly beside her to the waiting car. As he watched Bridey's long legs disappear into the limousine, he thought about the woman who'd be waiting for him. *Whoever the whore was, she'd better be a lot stronger than the last one.*

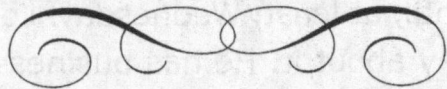

Bridey ran like a crazy woman for the next two days from photo session to meetings to hours in the darkroom trying to finish everything. *Cord's coming! Cord's coming!* Ran though her mind like a mantra, driving her on to finish all those little projects that were near deadline.

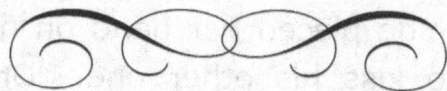

Saturday morning, she awoke to the jangling of the phone. She rolled over and grabbed the handset, breathlessly excited. "Cord! Are you here? Shall I come get you? Where are you?"

A laugh that wasn't Cord's answered her. "I'd love to believe you were talking to me, Bridey, but I think you might have been expecting someone else's call. Am I wrong?"

Bridey fell back into her pillow. "Good morning, Edward. You're right, I expect Cord today and I thought this call would be from him."

"Oh, so he *does* have a name. You neglected to mention that at dinner." Stanton let the pause stand for a moment or two. "No matter. I just called to let you know I'm leaving this morning. When will this Cord fellow – of whom I'm terribly jealous, by the way – be leaving?"

Bridey smiled at his teasing tone of voice. "Cord will be here until, at least, Wednesday. Longer if I have anything to say about it. He has business to take care of and news he wants to share with me."

I'll just bet, Stanton thought viciously. Careful to keep his voice light and easy, he continued, "Wednesday you say. That's good. I have to come back next Thursday. If you're free, I have the morning open.

Do you think you'll be back from cloud nine by then?" Bridey giggled self-consciously and answered, "For you, I'll be ready. Thank you for being so understanding, Edward. I really appreciate your kindness."

They spoke for a few minutes longer and hung up. While Stanton called the concierge, ordered packing service and a limo, Bridey lay still and thought about the kind man she'd just hung up on and drifted back to sleep dreaming of Cord.

Cord arrived three hours later without a phone call. Bridey was wakened by a loud pounding on her door. "Just a minute!" she cried, looking for something to wrap around her. She ran to the door and stretched up to the peephole. Nothing but blackness. Someone had their finger over the glass.

"I'm not opening this door until I know who's out there." Bridey heard Cord's booming laugh followed by, "Smart lady!"

She threw the bolt and undid the locks. Wrenching the door open, she flew into his arms. He lifted her up to kiss her as he stepped into the apartment. She reached her hand over his shoulder to close the door. He let her slide down until her feet met the floor, breathless from the depth of the kiss and the emotion that went that overwhelmed them both. He'd missed her terribly. He smiled at her rumpled, sleepy face and said, "I know. This is New York. Lock the doors."

He did and turned around to kiss her again. His hands roamed freely over her back and sides. He was pleased to note that the flimsy satin robe hid nothing from him. Without taking his hands from her, he stepped back and looked at the robe that threatened to fall open with her every breath.

"Here I spent the whole trip dreaming about ways to get you out of your clothes."

Bridey laughed out loud and stepped out of his grasp. Slowly and seductively, she slipped the robe off her shoulders and let it fall to the ground in a shimmering pool. "Give you any idea of how hard that would be?"

Cord ran a hand through his hair and leered at her. "It might not be hard for you, but you're sure making this very hard on me."

Bridey glanced down at the bulge in his pants. She laughed and turned toward the bedroom. "Well, we better hurry. We don't want to waste any time. Oh, and just to let you know, I do have an appointment next Thursday." With that, she took off on a dead run for the bedroom. Cord tackled her as she leapt for the bed.

They spent the day loving each other. Out of bed, they laughed and played, like a pair of ten-year-olds in a newfound friendship. In bed, they exhausted each other, trying to make up for lost time.

When Bridey realized they hadn't eaten all day, she ordered in Chinese. Cord took her to the shower while they waited for the deliveryman. He was in the middle of showing her once again how much he'd missed her when the bell rang.

Breathless, they stepped apart. Bridey stepped out and wrapped her hair in a towel and her body in a terry cloth robe. Cord let the water run over him for a minute or two longer, astonished at the effect this woman had on his body. She never seemed to tire of him. Her passion for him matched his own longing to levels he'd never experienced before. The water turned tepid and he stepped out.

He smelled incense burning as he left the steamy bathroom. The living room had been converted to a candle-lit sanctuary. Small white boxes sat on the low table. Bridey sat on a pile of pillows on the other side, struggling to open a bottle of sake. Cord dropped himself onto a similar pile of pillows next to her and took the bottle. He opened the vial with ease.

"Have you ever had sake?"

Cord tipped the little bottle and looked at it. He returned his eyes to her and shook his head.

"Sake is meant to be drank when it's slightly warm. About body temperature." With a silly smile, she watched his puzzled face as he tried to decide how to heat the rice wine. He looked at the bottle and then at her. A Groucho Marx leer crossed his face as he made his eyebrows dance. Quick as a rattlesnake, he grabbed the front of her robe and threatened to put the bottle against her chest. "Can it be warmed here?"

Bridey grabbed her robe and closed the fabric, laughingly, fighting off his attack.

"No! No! Wait!" She grabbed the bottle away from him and reached for a simmering teapot. "This is how it's done." She swirled a little of the hot water in a small cup and dumped the water into a waiting bowl. Bridey carefully filled the warmed cup with the rice wine and handed the drink to Cord.

"Ohhhhh! That's how it's done. I like my idea better." Still smiling, he asked, "Is this yours or mine?" "I thought we'd share it while we eat."

"Good. But we'll need more soon." A wicked glint leapt to his eyes as he lifted up his own robe and gently placed the dark ceramic bottle between his thighs. "Ahhhh!" he said, settling down around the cool glass. "That should be warm soon. I hope! If you want any more, you'll know where to find it."

Bridey fell back against the pillows laughing riotously. Cord looked at the beautiful woman across from him and cleared his throat. "If you want something to eat, we better get at it. Seeing you against those pillows like that gives me other ideas."

Bridey sat up. "As much as I like the thought of you getting ideas, I'm hungry." She reached for one of the paper cartons. "Besides you have news for me, remember?"

"Oh, yeah." Cord watched her spill a fragrant mixture onto his plate. "What is all this stuff?"

"Don't they have Chinese food in New Mexico?"

"Yes, they do but mine usually comes in a can labeled Chung King."

"You poor child. You haven't eaten until you have experienced real sweet and sour shrimp and moo shoo pork. Try this." Bridey lifted the chop sticks to his waiting lips. They ate with as much lust as they had loved, savoring the food and their time together.

After demanding more sake but refusing to dive for the vial, Bridey said, "Soooo? What does Lana want you for? I haven't been able to talk with her this week." "She's decided we need a new contract."

"Already?" Bridey was astonished. Lana usually took forever over contract negotiations.

"Yeah," he sipped the strong wine. "Seems as though sales are going so well; they want to lock me into a longer contract. I told her I'd have to discuss that idea with my business manager." He tipped his cup toward her slightly. Bridey frowned.

"What? You don't think it's a good idea?" he demanded.

Bridey shrugged. "I guess I just didn't know you had a business manager now." She looked at him. "Am I going to have to make appointments now?"

Cord reached a long arm out and pulled her head toward him. After a deep kiss, he said, "Only with yourself. I was assuming you'd take the job."

"'ll think about it. But then I'm for anything that gets you back here as often as possible." Another shadow crossed her face as she thought about how little time they had together. Brushing away the thought, she continued. "I guess I'm just worried about what that contract means for you."

Cord waited for her to finish thinking.

"I mean, is this what you want to do?" she finished.

"You gotta remember I never really wanted any of this in the first place. Some little New York city woman bewitched me in to taking the job. All I wanted was enough money to buy my own spread and my horses. I have plenty for that now."

Bridey giggled and said, "Guilty as charged. But what if you decide you want to keep working while you can? In a year or so, when *Saracen* is no longer the hot item, you'll have a hard time getting another job. You'll be the *Saracen* man to everyone. Highly recognizable. Is that what you want?"

Cord held up a hand. "Let me stop you right there. This was a onetime thing. I have almost everything I need now."

She took his hand. "But that camera loves you, Cord. After your contract runs out with *Saracen*, you could do a lot more with it ... if you wanted to, I mean."

Cord settled back against his cushions and beckoned her to come to him. Without a moment's hesitation, Bridey slid over and curled up next to him.

"I never told you about how I got that horse you spooked, did I."

Bridey shook her head lightly, content to listen to the sound of his voice reverberating in his chest. Cord told her the story of the beaten, almost dead horse and how he'd rescued him. She listened without comment.

"That's why I was so upset with you for spooking him. I had worked so hard to get him to trust me. Your carelessness ruined months of work in less than a second." Bridey started to sit up to defend herself. Cord held her down. "Don't get riled up. I know you didn't mean it. I've seen you work, the intensity you have is astounding. I'm sure something there took your eye and you focused completely on that without any other thoughts. Besides you're just a City kid. You'd never make it out there." She jabbed him hard in the ribs.

Cord grunted and lifted her chin. "The news I wanted to tell you is that the old man who mistreated that colt died with no heirs. Someone went over and found him dead in a corral with another half-starved horse he was saving. I lucked out and was able to buy his place for back taxes."

This time Bridey did sit up. Cord held up his hands. "It's a mess. The old geezer didn't care for anything but turning a buck on horses he bullied. There's a ton of work to be done but the house and the barn are sound. I've already hired a crew to go in and clean out everything while I'm here. Next week we start rebuilding and painting the place. I figure, if you'll help me renegotiate with Lana, I can have the place pretty much rebuilt and turning a nice profit in a year or so."

"Then what?"

Cord rubbed a hand over his eyes. "Well, that remains to be seen. I want to breed horses. That's all I have ever wanted to do. Devil's Kin is a good stud and I'm sure he'll throw strong colts, but he has no papers. He'll have to prove himself. In order to do that, I have to find some blooded mares to breed with him to prove his worth. All that's going to take money."

Bridey sat up, leaned her elbows against the table and rested her chin on her curled fingers. "So, your dreams are coming true?"

"Yes, they are. Thanks to you, Bridey. I know how much I owe you. I can never repay you for all this." She dropped her hands into her lap, her eyes downcast. Somewhere in the deep recesses of her mind, she'd held a slim hope that he'd change his mind and move to the City with her. Tears glistened in her eyes as she realized what a fool she'd been but there was a Mona Lisa smile on her face when she looked up again. "I did nothing, Cord. It was all you and the magic you do in front of the camera."

Cord reached out and pulled her gently into his arms. Just before he kissed her, he whispered against her lips. "Sure. Whatever you think."

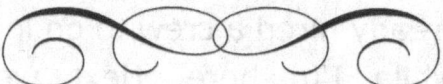

They spent the rest of the weekend enjoying the city and its offerings. Bridey acted as his personal tour guide. They visited museums, saw shows and did all the tourist things. They talked about everything except when Cord had to leave.

Sunday afternoon, Bridey took Cord to meet her grandfather. She wasn't quite ready to share Cord with the rest of her boisterous Irish family yet but she knew he'd be alone on a weekday. She wasn't sure Cord was ready for the family either. He and her grandfather hit it off right away. They talked of sports and horses. Until that very moment, Bridey didn't know her grandfather had once ridden the Queen's horses to the Steeplechase.

"Aye, wee Bridey." He winked at Cord. "There's a few secrets I still have of my own, you know." All too soon the time to leave arrived. Cord shook hands with the old man and invited him out to see the ranch any time he wanted to. The old man laughed and asked him just to send a jar full of that deep horse smell. The two horsemen looked at each other, well aware of what that meant.

Bridey leaned over to kiss her grandfather goodbye. He whispered in her ear. "You should hold on to this one, Bridey Darlin.' He's more for you than that other one. He reminds me of our Michael." Tears rose in Bridey's eyes at the mention of her father and she turned to walk away from her grandfather.

On Tuesday, they met with Lana who made a lot of noise about being taken advantage of but eventually signed Cord to a new very lucrative, two-year contract with all his stipulations intact. They celebrated late into the night with dinner, dancing, and a magnum of expensive champagne.

Bridey woke up before Cord on Wednesday, which wasn't easy since her idea of early was about four hours later than his. His body was still on New Mexico time. A weak sun tickled the blinds on her bedroom windows as she woke and snuggled closer to Cord's warm body. Instinctively, his arm wrapped around her in his sleep.

She lay still, watching him sleep and thinking about the look in his eyes as he told her about the place he'd bought until sorrow over what might have overwhelmed her. Tears slowly leaked from her eyes. She caressed his face and watched his mouth curl up in a sweet smile.

Slowly, she slipped out of bed, not ready to wake him. Bridey padded into the bathroom and splashed water on her face to erase the tears. She didn't want Cord to know how unhappy she was that he was leaving today. She was now sure how deeply in love she was with him. He'd given her little indication of how he felt about here ... besides the sex, of course. Seeing him for a few days two or three times a year wasn't going to be enough. No other man would ever live up to what Cord had given her.

She leaned over the shiny countertop at her reflection. "Well, what are ye goin' ta do now, Bridey me girl?" she asked herself in a perfect imitation of her Grandfather's brogue. She let her head drop and closed her eyes.

"What *are* you going to do?" Bridey started. There stood Cord in the doorway behind her, looking impossibly sexy in a sleepy, tousled sort of way. "Bridey suits you better than Bridgette, you know. He walked over and placed his hands on her slender shoulders. When she turned to him, he saw the tears threatening. Casually, he continued, "I liked your grandfather, you know. And I think he liked me." Bridey nodded in agreement. Cord turned her to face him. She looked up and the tears she'd tried so hard to hold back fell. She wrapped her arms around his neck.

"What's this all about, Bridey? Are you upset because I'm leaving today? Or is it because I haven't told you yet how much I love you?"

Bridey jumped out of his arms, astounded at his casual delivery of such important news. "How much?"

"I love you. River strong, mountain high, as the old song goes. Simple and clear. I was sure the last day of that session. Well, actually, I knew before but the realization hit me that last day. You keep telling me that I do magic with the camera. Well, I know I don't about that but ...," he held his arms out to her. "I know I do magic with the woman behind the camera."

She stepped into his arms and felt him rock her gently.

"You haven't told me how you feel. Could you learn to love me, Bridey?"

She looked up into his ice blue eyes and said, "I loved you when I saw you in that corral. I thought so then and I'm sure now." He carried her back to the warm bed. Tucking her in beside him safe and tight, he whispered sadly into her hair, calling her the loving nickname he'd heard her grandfather use. "What are we going to do, wee Bridey?"

They made slow gentle love full of wonder at their newly discovered feelings, savoring each kiss, caress and moment of love. The alarm went off three hours before his flight left. They showered and he packed quietly, each lost in their own thoughts. Bridey insisted on riding to the airport with him. Once more he checked in and found that secluded corner to spend the last minutes with his love.

Bridey wept openly. "I don't know how often I can do this, Cord. I love you so much. My heart's breaking to let you go."

He stroked her hair. "Then don't. Come with me."

Bridey made a sound somewhere between a snort and a growl. "Right! I almost killed myself out there once. As you so like to point out, I'm a city kid. I love the City. It's too quiet out there in the wilds. I worked too hard to build this business to just walk away from it."

"Bridey, my love," Cord took her face in his hands. "I'm not asking you to walk away from this. Just relocate your offices. You could shoot wildlife and waterfalls instead of people and pets. Lots of folks buy that kind of thing. Hell, we might even find a person or two for you to photograph." He smiled, trying to ease her pain. His heart ached to see the negative answer in her eyes as she dropped them away from his gaze.

"Fine. I guess that pretty much says everything. There's no sense hurting each other any longer. Just stay in your precious City and your business. Go! I don't need to sit here and watch you cry until my plane leaves."

Bridey nodded, keeping her eyes on the ground. She turned and walked away. She hadn't traveled more than a few yards down the corridor when she heard footsteps running behind her. She looked up to see Cord running toward her. She raced back to him and jumped into his arms.

"I can't let you go this way, Bridey. We'll make it work, you'll see."

Bridey silenced him with a finger to his lips and a shake of her head. "No. You wouldn't be any happier here than I'd be there. We just have to think it out and see what happens." She kissed him. "I love you. They're calling your plane. Go back. Call me when you get home." Cord kissed her deeply and whispered a dozen *I love you's* as he backed away from her.

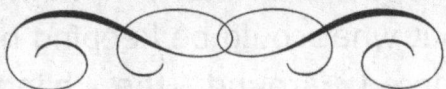

From the other side of the corridor, a shadowed figure watched. Wrapped in a red haze of anger, the man's fist pounded the unforgiving marble again and again until the side of his hand bled. His hatred roared and spread toward the lovers, not quite reaching them, frustrating him even more.

They separated. The woman watched through freeflowing tears as her man walked back to the boarding area. The shadowy man silently vowed vengeance and destruction on both of them – soon.

One day, someone is going to look at you with a light in their eyes you have never seen before. Wait for that look. –Anon

1879 – Deep South

The room was uncommonly quiet as Katherine Angeline Bondurant sat poised on the small wicker stool and gazed wistfully out the floor-to-ceiling, paned window. Dozens of people strolled around the lawns, waiting for her to come down. They'd been sitting so long waiting for her that many were walking around gossiping about what could be keeping her inside. The guests wandered around the blindingly white, bloomladen bridal bower and stood beneath the heavy limbed magnolia trees. Cream-colored satin ribbons that matched the blossoms pirouetted in the light breeze. The heavy scent of the full-blown flowers drifted across the manicured expanse of the lawn and into the cool, dark, still room. Katherine took a deep, ragged breath in an effort to steady her jangled nerves.

Heavy damask drapes had been pulled back to reveal the awe-inspiring views of distant hills, wooded to the edge of the sky. She let her eyes travel along the horizon so far away, hoping beyond hope that she would catch a glimpse of the dream. Her gloved hands tightened across her midsection as she tried to steady their shaking. The brilliant white of her gown stood in stark contrast to the dark wood in the room.

The dress was too tight. She could still feel fingers of the maids running all over her as they tugged straps, adjusted seams and buttoned dozens of tiny seed pearl fasteners. Their hands felt like spiders and ants, hungry and skittering, everywhere. When she was finally able to send them away, every part of her wanted to pull off the dress, leap off the balcony and run as far and fast as she could.

How did she get here? Not that long ago, she'd been happily ensconced in Lady Tuttle's Seminary for Young Women in Boston, perfecting the finesse she needed as the daughter of an ambassador to foreign countries. Helping her parents would prepare her for the life she fully expected to live when she became a socialite wife or the wife of a member of the diplomatic corps like her mother had. That was the life she loved, the life she knew so well.

But then tragedy had struck in the form of influenza which swept through the family taking the lives of her beloved mother and younger brother. Since her mother had passed away, the demanding duties for which she had only just started preparing for had fallen at her feet. No one had asked her to leave school and take over her mother's duties. Everyone just assumed that as the only daughter she would step into the void at her father's side. To be the wife of a country plantation owner in the South – she had not prepared for this!

She loved the travel, the different countries, cultures and customs. The gala parties and beautiful clothes that came with them would all go to someone else now. She'd have parties here, of course, but certainly no kings, rajahs, or emperors would be gracing these halls. That grand life was gone, only to be played out on a much smaller scale in a place where she would always be the outsider even though married to the most powerful man in the area.

Tears welled up as she thought of her mother. She'd have loved to have her here just to talk to so she could reassure her that she was doing the right thing now. Blinking away the tears, Katherine stood and walked carefully to the paneled French door. The only sound in the room was the swish of the heavy skirts of her wide dress against the carpet. Stopping on the brink of the marble balcony, she looked over what was to be her home for the rest of her life. Her marriage, brokered by her father, would leave her and her future children wanting for nothing for the rest of their lives. She would be trapped here but her sons would be leaders. Her daughters would be debutantes of the highest echelon. She herself would be one of those magical people whom others sought out and the curried favor of in this small part of the world. Her brow knit as she wondered about the extremely high price she was about to pay.

She closed her eyes to erase the miserable feeling and conjured up the long-held dream that had made her happy for years. She envisioned a young man on a huge black horse racing across the lawns, intent on getting to her. His clothes were working clothes, jeans clean but well worn, sleeves rolled to the elbow. His silver blonde head was bare. Everything about him was a complete contrast to the well-dressed, refined gentry that awaited her arrival. The love she felt for the man filled her so completely that she was afraid the whalebone corset that encased her body would burst.

She heard her name being called, softly, insistently. "Katherine! Katherine!" She gasped, hoping beyond hope, praying the voice she heard was his. She let her eyes open and gazed longingly at the distant horizon. No silhouette of a dark horseman. Her heart fell. He wasn't coming to her rescue. She heard the door behind her open softly. Loud footsteps crossed to her side as she continued to search the horizon. She felt the heat of a body standing at her shoulder.

"You're holding everything up." The man beside her put a hand on her shoulder and squeezed hard enough to get her attention but careful not to leave a bruise. "You're embarrassing me."

She took a deep breath and turned to look at the man who'd told her last night in no uncertain terms that she belonged to him. She'd never be allowed to leave him. If she ever tried, he'd use all his influence to ruin her father and destroy any chance for her remaining brother to succeed in life. She tenderly rubbed her side where he had emphatically left a reminder that he could hurt her any time he wanted.

He knew exactly where and how to leave such reminders.

Suddenly, he dropped his hand from her shoulder and reached his kid gloved hand out toward her, palm up ... not the hand she wanted but the hand she had to take. She reluctantly laid her hand palm down on the proffered hand and tried to ignore the pain as the fingers closed too tightly around her delicate hand. She knew the cruelty underlying the man's elegant façade. Life with this man will be like walking a very narrow beam, but she had no choice. Without looking at him, she stood.

The strong fingers tightened a bit more and she winced. The voice hissed, "Stop thinking about him. You are mine. You will always be mine. There is nothing you can do to change that. Now behave yourself ... or you know what will happen." He released the pressure slightly and hissed, "Katherine. It's time."

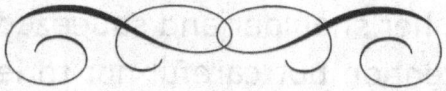

She stood on the third story balcony of the great house above the porch where the other women and watched the men ride out under the massive magnolia trees that lined the main drive. The sounds of sobbing rent the air as those who would miss their men lamented loudly. She wished she could conjure up one or two tears to make her act look better, but she couldn't wring another tear out of her eyes. When she saw her husband turn to look at her, she started to raise her arm to wave to him as she knew she should.

The painful memory of his warning from the night before almost made her cry out. She could only lift her arm halfway in a weak gesture. Hopefully, the others would see it as a gesture of her sorrow.

As the last man disappeared through the iron gates to join the war and defend their lifestyle, she pulled a delicate handkerchief from her sleeve, lifted the scented linen to her eyes and looked down at the faces of the women who now expected her to run this plantation.

She went down to join them.

"We must be strong, ladies. Hopefully, those dreaded Yankees will not come this deeply into our beloved state before the war is over and our men have returned." She paused to draw a breath. "We have much to do to keep the home fires ready for their return. I know, like my dear Charles, your husbands have left you instructions. Go about your days. Stay busy and be cheerful. We'll meet in the drawing room each afternoon and take our rest together." She reached over to take the hand of the woman nearest to her and said, "We're not alone, ladies. We have each other, and our children and never forget that the hand of God is on our side."

She stood stiff-spined until the last lady left the room and only then sunk slowly on to the nearest chair. A gentle hand rubbed her shoulder. She looked up into the face of the only person who knew what her husband was really like, her sister-in-law, Arabella.

She'd been his punching board before Katherine had married into the family.

"You shouldn't feel bad," Arabella whispered.

"About what? That we have all this work to do? That there are no men to do the heavy work? That we have no defense should anything happen?" Katherine sighed.

"No," Arabella laughed gently. "That you're happy he's gone." She slid into the chair beside Katherine's. "Did you tell him?"

Katherine didn't look up but merely shook her head. "I was afraid to."

"Afraid to? Why? You know how much he wants a son."

Katherine blew out a half-laugh, half-sigh. "Honestly, I was afraid he wouldn't leave if I told him." Then she began to laugh, uncontrollably. She laughed and shuddered until she fell into her sister's arms weeping. "What am I going to do?"

Arabella wrapped her arms around Katherine's shoulders and whispered, "Exactly what is expected of you. You'll do your best to keep the home fires burning and grow your child. You must be happy as you can be, so your child doesn't feel your grief. Together we'll pray for your safety and that of the child. When we get together with the other women, they'll pray for the safe return of their loved ones while we pray in our hearts for a deadly sniper bullet to end our terror."

Katherine nodded. What else could she do?

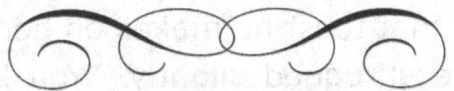

"It's a girl!" Arabella cried out into the hall where the other women waited. "They're both fine."

A sigh of relief flowed from the other women as they turned back to their duties. Katherine had been in labor for many hours. With no doctor to be found and no medicine, they'd had to depend on the local midwife, an elderly black woman. The woman did what she could, but all were glad to have the ordeal over and that mother and child were safe.

Arabella returned to Katherine's side and knelt by the bed. The baby was snuggled in Katherine's arm, sleeping soundly. "She's so beautiful. Have you decided what to name her?"

"I think the best name for her is your mother's, don't you? I mean, Charles is going to be angry enough that she is not a boy and I know he loved your mother."

Arabella nodded and reached out to stroke the babe's cheek. "He was so young when she died. I think he'd like that. Though to saddle such a tiny thing with a name like Eugenia Evangeline seems unkind."

Katherine laughed. "You're right." Katherine tipped her head slightly to one side and looked at her sisterinlaw. "Why have we never talked about your mother?"

Arabella continued to stroke the delicate face and shrugged. "I guess no one really wants to talk about her. She was a very sad, unhappy person. Charles remembers her better than I, but he never brings her up except for that toast he makes on her birthday and holidays." She shrugged slightly. "You know how he gets then."

Katherine, returning to a happier topic, said. "I think we'll call her Daisy for now. She does look so bright and I want a happy name for her."

She gazed down at her sleeping child and wondered what would happen when, if, her father returned.

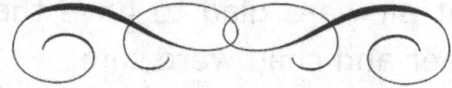

Three years later

"They're coming! I saw them from the barn!" Young James ran screaming toward the house. "They're coming up the road!"

Everyone inside rushed down to the massive portico at the front of the house to see their men returning for a short visit home. Everyone except Katherine. She stood on the same balcony where she'd bid them farewell and watched the much smaller parade return. She heard cries of delight when a child or a wife saw their loved one. She heard screams of pain when someone realized their loved one wasn't in the line. She felt a tremor of fear when she saw Charles at the front of the line.

Her eyes travel over the rest of the disheveled group. She gasped out loud when she saw the man who rode directly behind her husband. He might not be familiar to anyone else, but she knew him. Her hands flew to her face when she recognized the massive black horse he rode, the curve of his cheek and the silver hair that stood out against the tanned face. Oh yes. She knew him. The man in her dreams, the one she had known from childhood. He was here. He was finally going to take her from this place. All she had to do was wait until she saw the gloved hand reach out for her and heard the whisper of her name.

At that joyous moment, she saw Charles' face and her joy crashed into pieces along with her heart. The scowl told her he wasn't happy. A tremor of fear raced down her spine. She turned to the bed where Daisy lay sleeping and wondered what would happen next. She pulled the curtains around the small bed and moved to the large, gilded mirror that hung on the other side of the room. She checked her hair and her clothes to be sure she was presentable. As she gathered her courage to go downstairs, the door burst open.

Charles filled the space. "So," he spoke in a low dangerous tone she knew so well. "Are you hiding up here?" He took a step forward. Katherine held her place. "Ooo, I know! You are too overcome with emotion and joy to make your way downstairs..." He reached out, grabbed her arm and yanked her to him. "I'd have thought you would know better than to embarrassed me after all this time."

"Charles." She gasped his name weakly. "Charles, I..."

She didn't have time to say more as his lips crushed hers in a bruising kiss. His hands began ripping at her clothes. "I don't want your excuses. You know what I want." He pushed her back toward the bed and advanced one more step. Then he stopped short. A stunned look fell over his face as he looked beyond her. Katherine turned and saw Daisy standing just behind the curtain.

"Mommy?" Charles's eyes flew open wide.

Katherine ran to snatch Daisy to her side.

"Mommy?" Charles asked. "Mommy!" He demanded.

"Charles, I want you to meet your daughter, Eugenia Evangeline. We call her Daisy. Daisy, this is your daddy."

Charles's face ran the gamut of emotions. She saw shock, elation and then a bit of fear. She put her hands on Daisy's slender shoulders and urged her toward him. "Daisy. Go say hello to your daddy and give him a big kiss."

She took a step toward him, but Daisy had other ideas. She began to struggle and cried out, "No! He's a mean man. He's scary! No! NO!" She wiggled out of Katherine's arms and ran out onto the balcony.

Charles' scowl darkened further. "Whose child is she? Who've you been screwing while I was gone?" He advanced on Katherine like a lion intent on a bit of prey. Katherine ran over and grabbed Daisy once again.

"Charles! No, Charles. She's your child. I found out I was pregnant a few days after you left." "I."

He took a long step toward her.

"Don't." He grabbed her and shoved her further out to the balcony.

"Believe you. If she was mine, she'd know me. Children always know their parents."

Katherine shuddered as his fingers tightened around her arms. She had to get Daisy out of his reach. She looked toward the door and froze. There, in the doorway, he stood, his hat in his hand. His collar was damp from where he had washed in the horse trough. Katherine gasped when she saw the sleeves rolled up exposing tanned, strong forearms. She stared at his brilliant blue eyes and silver hair and felt her legs go weak. *He's here! I'm safe!*

The stranger in the doorway stood still, staring at Katherine. She was the woman he'd seen in his dreams for so many years. He knew that auburn hair and those green eyes – he knew them well. And now the woman he'd been searching for all his life was his Captain's wife. He'd seen the cruel ways of his captain as they'd fought battles. He knew he had little, if any, compassion and God help anyone who crossed him on purpose or only in the man's demented mind. The thought of the callous man's hands on her made his blood boil, but he willed himself to remain calm and think of something quick.

"Captain?" The man in the doorway stepped forward and called out. "Captain!"

Charles' face never left Katherine's. "What?" he growled.

"The men are wondering what to do. Shall I tell them to bed down?"

Charles tore his face from Katherine's and looked at his second-in-command. "Yes. Now get out! This is a personal matter."

"Begging the Captain's pardon sir, but you can be heard outside and downstairs. They might even be able to hear you in Nashville, sir!"

Charles looked at Katherine and saw the beseeching look she was giving to the other man. He whipped his head back around and saw the concern in the younger man's eyes.

"I said get out!"

Knowing he couldn't leave her, the young man stepped forward again. "Captain! We need you downstairs."

"Oh, I just bet they do. I get it! I see what you're doing," Charles' menacing voice filled the space between them. "Trying to get between me and mine, man? Always wanting to be the hero. You want to help this lying cheating whore? Fine. Save her!"

With that, the Captain ran forward, grabbed Katherine by the shoulders and pushed her backwards. Roaring his anger and shaking her slender body, he backed her up until she leaned against the railing. He looked into her eyes and was thrilled to see endless fear. With a smile and a mighty heave, he picked her and her child up and threw them off the balcony.

"NOOOO!" The younger man screamed and raced to the ledge. He looked down at the cobblestone below him and saw two broken bodies. As he stared, Katherine summoned up her last bit of strength and reached for him. He stretched out his gloved hand even though he knew he couldn't reach her and watched as her hand fell and his love slipped out of his grasp. He sobbed her name, "Katherine."

> *"I feel like a part of my soul has loved you since the beginning of everything."*
> *—Emery Allen*

Sixteen

"I must say, my dear, you look like a small child who just lost her puppy." Stanton fussed with his cuffs in an effort to hide the bandage wrapped around his hand that covered the bruised knuckles from his last session with a hooker. He smirked and thought, *a hooker who'll never be right again. How dare she snicker at him!* Bridey pretended not to notice the wrappings as she adjusted the studio lights shining on him.

Bridey peered around the camera at her subject. That was precisely how she felt, like she'd lost something too valuable to replace. She tried hard to hide it but apparently wasn't doing so well. Going back to her apartment without Cord had been harder than she expected. She tried to focus on her work but, for the first time since she discovered her gift, the work wasn't enough. She wandered around the too-quiet apartment, mindlessly tidying up the place, touching the pillows Cord had lounged on, and reluctantly changing the sheets they'd loved on.

Bridey smiled weakly at Stanton. "I'm sorry. I guess I'm just distracted."

"Your time with your young man wasn't as good as you thought it would be?" Stanton sneered, without looking directly at her, still fidgeting with his tie and cuffs.

Bridey stepped behind the camera and looked at a tight-lipped Stanton. Something wasn't right about him this morning and she couldn't put her finger on it.

"No," she answered. "That's not the problem. In fact," she stood up again and walked over to move a light. "If anything, it was better than ever before."

"So, what's wrong?" Stanton's narrowed eyes followed Bridey as she shifted props subtly and then moved back to the camera to check the view again.

"I don't know exactly." She felt unwilling to open up to this man.

"Problems in Paradise, I guess."

"No," Bridey stood up and leaned against the top of the huge camera. She looked at her subject and shook her head. "Let's just say I'm not so good at long distance relationships, but I'd really rather not talk about it if you don't mind. This session is supposed to be about you, not me."

"Hmm," Stanton murmured noncommittally. He watched as she scanned the set. "Is something else wrong?"

"No ... uhm, yes. Yes, there is and I can't quite put my finger on it." She looked at him quizzically. "It's like

238

there's something here that isn't right and I just can't place it. I'm usually pretty good at this." She rubbed her forehead and looked around him again.

Stanton cleared his throat and stood up from the small stool she'd perched him on. "I know what it is," he stepped toward Bridey with his hand extended. "I know exactly what's wrong."

Bridey hesitantly took his hand. His cool fingers closed around hers and he pulled her from behind the camera. "Your mind simply isn't on this job."

Bridey started to protest but Stanton stopped her with a wave of her hand. "No, don't protest. It happens. Your mind is in ... well, wherever this young man of yours is. That's definitely not here." He reached over and shut off the hot lights. Keeping a firm hold on Bridey's wrist, he forced her gently to follow him across the opulent room.

"But fortunately, I know exactly how to fix it." He opened the door and led her through. "I'll distract you from thoughts of the *other* man." He laughed at her shocked look. "First, we'll have lunch on the terrace and then we'll go for a drive and chat about anything but that cowboy. After that, we'll have an early dinner and then see a show. Tomorrow morning, we'll begin again.
If I've done my job well, you'll be right back on target."

Bridey stared at the man in front of her. He seemed such a gem. She couldn't remember a client who'd been as understanding as this man. Without thinking, she put her arms around him and hugged him tightly.

Stanton closed his arms around her and smiled wickedly, pleased with the way things were going.

"There, there, dear," He patted her back in a fatherly fashion. "I was just joking about being the other man." Bridey laughed and slid away from him. "I know. I just can't believe how nice you're being about this. Not all of my clients would be so kind. I mean, you're a busy man and still you're willing to help me deal with my silly distractions."

"Ms. Deane," Stanton lifted her hand to his lips and whispered over it, "*love* is never silly." He kissed her knuckles and looked back into her eyes. "Though it can certainly be a delightful distraction."

Stanton's plan worked perfectly. By the end of the evening, Bridey was laughing and smiling like herself again. Never once did she mention *that* cowboy. When he dropped her off, she kissed him lightly on the cheek and thanked him. She climbed out of the limo, turning on the steps of her apartment to wave and remind him to she'd be back to do the portrait at 9 A.M.

Stanton watched her go through the door and sat back in the deep back seat. He pulled a linen handkerchief from his breast pocket and wiped away her lipstick. "You'll do more than just kiss my cheek soon, bitch. Very soon."

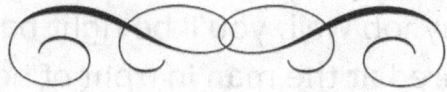

Although the photographic part of the session went perfectly the next morning, Bridey's sixth sense said there was something about the subject himself, but she just couldn't see what was off. He was perfectly dressed, looking as sharp and debonair as any model. His tone was light and airy when they spoke. There seemed to be something in the light – a shadow she couldn't subdue – that lingered around his face.

Other than that, Stanton was a perfect subject. They shot different poses for over an hour when Bridey finally said she was happy with the outcome. She began packing up her equipment, chatting idly with Stanton. She was putting away the final bank of lights when he said, "You know, I had an idea last night."

Bridey kept working. "About what?"

"Your young man."

Bridey paused before she closed the last clasp. "I thought we agreed that subject was closed?" Stanton smiled, shrugged his shoulders and held his hands out, palms up, looking for all the world like an apologetic child. Bridey smiled back.

"There's nothing that can be done." she said wistfully. "We're from two different worlds."

"Here's what I have in mind." Stanton directed the bellhops he'd called to load the equipment and walked Bridey out to the terrace for another look. "I have to go to California next week. On business. Why don't you accompany me part way?"

He turned to face Bridey. She looked up at him in confusion. "Accompany you?"

"Sure. I'll use the private jet, of course. We'll drop you off in New Mexico and you can visit your young man. When I come back, I'll pick you up."

Bridey stepped back; eyebrows knit in concern. "How do you know he lives in New Mexico?"

Stanton brushed her question off. "You mentioned it somewhere along the line."

"No," Bridey said. "I didn't. I'm sure. Cord asked me never to mention where he lived to anyone."

Stanton stepped over to her and put an arm around her shoulders, turning her back to the view. "Now, Dear, I'm sure you never meant to break his confidence, but what harm's been done. I mean, is he on the run or something?"

Bridey thought for a minute. Cord never really answered her questions about why he didn't want to be found. He'd reacted so strongly when he thought she was a groupie, she'd just assumed he didn't want a bunch of people traipsing all over his property disturbing his horses. He was too kind and decent to be a criminal.

All her senses told her to trust him. She shook her head.

"I don't know."

Stanton gave her shoulders a quick squeeze and dropped his arm. "You think about it. Today's Friday and I need to leave by 7 A.M. Monday morning. Call me if you want to take me up on my offer. If you don't call, I'll see you when I get back. We'll get together to view the ... what do you call them ... rushes?"

Bridey laughed brightly. "No, that's movies. You'll get proofs to decide which you like best."

"OK, then." He escorted her to the door and opened the heavy wooden exit. "You'll let me know?"

Bridey nodded and stepped out of the room. Stanton closed the door softly and leaned against the jamb. He had her. He was certain now. His wild laughter filled the room. Soon. Very soon. That damned cowboy would be in his hands and this time he wouldn't get away. Stanton danced across the floor in celebration and reached for the phone.

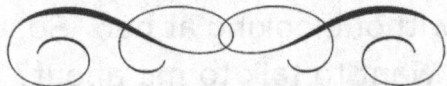

Sunday afternoon found Bridey at her usual place – in the company of her grandfather. One of the things she loved about him was the sameness of his house. Everything was always exactly the way she left the house when she visited again. Sometimes there were more people than other times, but mostly the draw was the constancy of the love in the house that called to Bridey, the calm quiet loving ambiance. She carefully placed heavy ceramic mugs on a wooden tray beside the plates of cookies, or biscuits as her grandfather called them. The kettle whistled as Bridey measured the loose tea leaves into the old-fashioned metal balls her grandfather preferred to tea bags. Twice a year, Bridey ordered his favorite tea and biscuits from a little shop in Kilkenny, Ireland. Little things like that pleased the old man and Bridey was grateful she could afford to give back to him in such a way.

Her grandfather watched quietly as she settled herself on the other side of the low table and played *mother*. She poured half the mug full of warmed milk and the other half of tea for him and filled hers with tea, adding a good amount of lemon juice.

He snorted in disgust. "Bloody waste of good tea, if you ask me, ruining a nice drink with the habits of the *fine* folks." He accepted his own mug. Warming his hands and blowing the steam away over the lip of the cup, he said, without looking at her. "So, darlin' Bridey, what is it you want to talk to me about?"

Bridey looked up in surprise. She thought she'd carefully avoided giving any sign that something was wrong. All morning, she'd laughed and talked with her cousins and other family members as usual. Lunch was a typical joyous affair that everyone had gathered around the dining room table telling stories on each other. Soon after lunch, the others had left, drifting off to their own lives and homes, leaving Bridey to sit with her grandfather for a while longer.

Only once during the whole time had she thought of Cord and how much he'd have loved being here. She thought she'd covered her sorrow quickly enough, but she caught her grandfather looking at her across the table. The sly old man knew her too well.

"Now, Grandda, what makes you think . . .?"

"Just get on with it, Girl. I saw you mooning around this afternoon. And you lost at backgammon – to Jamie. You never lose and certainly not to Jamie." He leaned over and whispered conspiratorially. "He's not the freshest apple in our cart, you know."

"Grandda!" Bridey gently chided the old man whose eyes twinkled at her over the cup of tea.

She sighed "You're right, Grandda. I'm in too deep to know what to do."

"Do you need money, Bridey? I don't have much but . . ."

Bridey reached up and patted his arm. "No, Grandda. I'm doing just fine in that department." She took another sip of the soothing liquid. Silence wrapped around them.

"You're not ... uhm, you're not ... well, in the family way, are ye?"

"Grandda!! No! I'm not and I certainly wouldn't be here talking to you if I was."

The old man harrumphed and waited for her to begin.

"You remember Cord, the man I brought with me last week?"

"Aye, Girl. I'm old, but I've not gone 'round the bend yet! If I remember right – and I do – I told you he was a keeper. Don't tell me you've run him off." Tears began to fill her eyes as Bridey described how much she loved Cord and he loved her, how much letting him go hurt, and how she didn't know what to do to fix things. "I can't ask him to give up that ranch and that horse. If you'd seen him there, you'd know what I mean."

"You're right, me darlin.' If horses are in his blood, that call is hard to shake them out. I know. Your sainted grandmother, God rest her soul, put up with me for years as I got used to being without them."

"I know. And me? Well now, can you see me on a ranch, a rancher's wife? Shearing sheep and feeding chickens and whatever else a rancher's wife does?" "Darlin'," he said with a laugh, "I can see you wherever you want to be."

"I just don't know what to do, Grandda. I'm so unhappy without him and yet I . . ." Bridey's voice trailed off. The two sat and stared off into space for a long while, companionable silence wrapping around them.

Bridey thought her grandfather had drifted off to sleep when he began to speak. "You know, I grew up poor. The family had to struggle for everything. One by one, my brothers either died or went off to find their own lives until they left me and Ma alone. There wasn't a lot of joy in our town. I learned young that you have to make your own happiness. Find bits and pieces as you travel through life.

"I knew an old woman once. A dried up shriveled old prune of a woman she was. Had more wrinkles than anyone I'd ever seen. Her voice cackled and whined when she chose to talk which wasn't often. Everyone called her Meggie, Meghan the Lovely. I never could understand why – she was such an ugly old thing.

"One day, I was out on the roof of one of the shops where I knew I shouldn't be, hiding from some bullies intent on giving me a beating for something or other. I looked down at Meggie's house and there she stood in the middle of her small garden. The trees cast shadows all around her except the one spot where she stood. The sun shined through the leaves like a spotlight. I saw old Meggie dance. She swayed and twirled as if a handsome gentleman were holding her in his arms. Her smile was so beautiful. I lay on my belly and watched her for a long time. For the first time, I understood why they called her Meghan the Lovely.

"That night, after dinner when no one else was around, I asked me ma about Meggie. She told me a wonderful story about how Meggie was the daughter of a wealthy English lord, a very important man with land and properties all over Great Britain.

"One day, Meggie met James the stableman. Poor he was. Poorer than the dirt he shoveled from the stables every morning. But there was something about him that spoke to Meggie's heart. One day, Meggie's regular groom got kicked in the head by a draft horse. James was sent in his place to accompany the young mistress on her morning ride. Rumor said that they took one look at each other and, from that second on, there was no other for either of them. Their love seemed to be fated.

"The only thing Meggie loved more than James was to dance. She was light as a feather and moved as if carried by a breeze. She tried to teach the heavy-footed James to dance in the fields near her home. Whenever they went riding, they danced in the meadows and fell more deeply in love with each other.

"Meggie's father found them dancing one day. He was furious and thinking more than just dancing was going on. He sent Meggie to live in London. He had James beaten and put on a prison ship for Australia, but James escaped in Portugal where the ship had stopped for repairs. For two months he worked his way back to London. There he found his Meggie engaged to another fancy Englishman. James took a job in the rich man's stable until he had a chance to talk to Meggie. She clung to his neck and wept with joy. Her father had told her that he'd had James killed.

"Meggie told James she'd agreed to marry the Englishman. He was tired of waiting and he demanded that she say yes or no to his proposal. Thinking her only true love was dead, she'd agreed. James begged Meggie to marry him instead and to sail away to America with him.

"Meggie refused. She wanted to be with him, tend his hearth, and bear his children, but she was terrified of being poor. She told him she wasn't as strong as he was. She didn't want to be without her money and her cotillions and fine things. Heartbroken, James stowed away on a ship the next morning. Meggie married a man she didn't love. Before long she realized the man didn't love her either, though he did love the huge dowry she brought with her. He locked her away in his country estate and left her there, alone with no one but a few servants to attend her."

Grandda paused and sipped the cool tea.

"Did James ever come back?" Bridey asked.

"Oh yes, he did. He came back when he was old and so was Meggie. The Englishman had died of a heart attack in the bed of his mistress a few years before. Sad Meggie, who'd given up love and a family for safety, was free – and so was James. He found her one afternoon and fell on his knees at her feet, grateful just to see her again. She dropped to her own knees beside him, pleading with him to forgive her. Her foolish fears had caused them so much misery. James lifted her into his arms and begged her forgiveness for not dragging her with him.

"James only lived a year or so more. Consumption got him. Meggie nursed him herself. He died in her arms and Meggie never got over his death. All that wasted time. They say she lost her mind when James died. They say she still talked to him as if he were alive beside her and some even say they have seen her dancing in the back garden as if in James' arms.

"I never looked at old Meggie the same way after that story. She died before I came to America but, whenever I thought I was afraid to reach for something I wanted, I always thought of Meggie and all she lost for want of a little courage."

Bridey put her head on her grandfather's shoulder and said, "That's a lovely story, Grandda."

"'Tis, Bridey Kate, 'tis." He rested his hand on her bright hair, remembering his own dear wife and how he had nearly lost their love from fear. "Sweet Bridey, please learn from Meggie's story. Don't let your fears stand between you and real love. There's nothing more wonderful and nothing that can replace waking up each morning beside the person you love."

Silence filled the room again. Bridey sat up to sip her tea and think over the story. "There's another man, Grandda."

"I thought there might be."

"He's older than I, not much though. He's rich, handsome and treats me like royalty. We like all the same things and he lives near The City."

"Sounds like that other one, that Mark."

Bridey's hand flew to her throat. That was what was wrong! Her photographer's eye pulled up the picture of Edward sitting for the portrait. That was it! He looked like her ex-husband Mark – stiff, dignified, overconfident, a bit self-involved, hiding his true self as he tried to hide the bandage on his hand.

"Grandfather! I never ... I didn't think. I didn't see the similarity."

"Bridey, me darling, if you don't let your heart rule in this matter, you'll regret it for the rest of your life. I don't want to tell you what to do, *Hinny*, but you can be a photographer anywhere. People will come to you when they see your work, just like they come to you now. Your photographs haunt people. I know. I keep the photograph you took of your grandmother before she passed on the bed stand. That makes me feel like she is still here with me. You captured a part of her, not just her image."

Bridey leapt to her feet and threw her arms around his neck. "I love you, you very dear old man. I hope when I'm your age, I'm half as wise."

Her grandfather harrumphed and cleared his throat as he accepted the hug from Bridey. "You don't worry about being old, Bridey girl. You go get that young man and make a houseful of babies. Then you invite me to come visit. I've always wanted to see the wild wild
West!"

When she got home, the message she'd been waiting for was on her machine. She listened to Cord's voice explain over and over again why he hadn't called. The love she wanted sounded clearly through the lines. If she'd had any doubt about his feelings before, they were gone completely. Bridey picked up the phone and called Stanton's New York number. Another machine answered her call and took the message that she'd be at the airport in the morning ready to go. She'd gladly accept the offer of his plane to get her to her destination.

Stanton heard the message in the den of his home and laughed gleefully, like a child given the thing he wanted most for his birthday. He looked around, remembering the last time he and the bastard cowboy had been in this room together. He lifted his glass to the air and shouted, "Too bad, dear old Dad that you

won't be here to see the last act when I finally win."
He phoned his pilot and demanded the jet be ready to
take him to JFK airport by 6 AM tomorrow.

"My love, we were always meant to meet and fall in love. We were always connected with an invisible thread. Our hearts beat together and our souls are eternally entwined. We belong together and there is nothing in this world that can tear us apart whether it's time.
distance or death."
—Aarti Khurana

Seventeen

Stanton watched as Bridey pulled her suitcase behind her across the tarmac toward the waiting plane. As soon as they landed, he'd paged her to the gate where the plane waited. He'd watched her half run toward the plane as he instructed the pilot to prepare for immediate take off. His steward met Bridey at the stairs and took her suitcase. Stanton stood to greet her as Bridey walked into the cabin, flushed with excitement and breathless from joy.

"Bridey! I was so pleased to get your message." He kissed her cheek and led her to a deep leather chair near his. Almost choking on his words to hide the sarcasm, he said, "If I can't have you for my own, I'm very pleased to be helping you connect with the love you deserve."

Bridey squeezed the hand that held hers. "I don't know how I can ever repay you."

Stanton waved his hand as if to cast off her words. "Don't worry, my dear. One day something will come up. Who knows? Maybe you'll name your first-born child after me. Did you let your man know you were coming?"

Bridey blushed as she took her hand back to settle into the plush seat and fasten the seat belts. "I tried to, but phone service out there is patchy. Besides, he doesn't spend much time in the house and doesn't use his cell around the horses. When I got home yesterday, there was a message on my machine from him."

"Not to worry," Stanton smiled broadly and said. "I won't let you go until I know you're safe. I'm sure he'll be glad to see you." A mischievous grin spread across his face.

Bridey smiled and turned toward the window as she felt the plane begin to taxi. The engines roared carrying them high into the clouds. Bridey daydreamed about joining Cord again. Her heart flipped at the idea of seeing him.

Stanton cleared his throat. "By the way, I have another small surprise for you. Assuming you'd be coming, I had my staff do a bit of research. He found a small grass strip nearer the ranch where your young man works. We'll be flying to Phoenix and then changing to a smaller plane. That way we can fly directly there."

Bridey turned to look at the man she knew as Edward Staley. That odd, slightly evil, glint was in his eye again. The one she'd seen in the camera lens, like he had a secret he wasn't yet willing to share. For a brief instant, she was a bit unnerved. How much did she really know about this man? She shoved the thoughts back and wrote the feelings off to the nervous excitement of surprising Cord.

"How do you know what town the ranch is near? I'm the only person who knows and I'm positive I didn't tell you or anyone else. Besides, he quit one job and moved on recently. He didn't even tell me where his new place is."

Stanton leaned back and closed his eyes. "Like I said, not to worry. I've made a habit of knowing exactly where he is for years. Granted I hadn't had any luck with this last place until you came along. But the new place wasn't that hard to find since it's so close to the other."

Bridey felt an odd tightness in her chest as she stared at the man across from her. Without opening his eyes, Stanton continued, "I guess it's time to tell you, Bridey. Your *cowboy* and I know each other ... and quite well at that. Practically grew up together, we did. I've been looking for him for a very long time." Stanton lifted his head and glared malevolently at Bridey. "He took something that was mine and I mean to get it back."

"What ... what did he take?"

Stanton leaned forward as far as he could against the restraining belt. The vicious glint in his eyes took Bridey's breath away. The malevolent look told her she was dealing with a man on the edge of madness. "Everything. First, he stole my father's affection and then he stole my place in his life. Finally, he killed my father." Stanton's leer broadened. "Well, sort of."

Bridey struggled to unfasten her seat belt. She had to get away from him and warn Cord. Stanton laughed. "What's the hurry, Bridey? Where can you go at 7500 feet in the air?" He reached down and pressed a buzzer beside his chair. The door to the pilot's cabin opened and a huge, tough looking man with a deep scar running from his eye to his chin stepped out.

"Bridey, I'd like you to meet Kelleher, a good friend who sometimes does favors for me. He knows Cord very well too, don't you, Kelleher?"

The large man smiled a twisted, evil grin and nodded. The scar on his face deepened and reddened. He stared at Bridey in a way that made her cringe.

"Now, Kelleher," laughed Stanton. "Don't do that. Can't you see you're frightening our guest? Go back up front. When we land, you'll have someone of your own to play with. If you're very good, when I tire of Miss Photographer here, I'll let you have her." Kelleher smiled wider. His lips split open, showing a gaping dark space where there should've been teeth. A small trickle of spit dripped out of the corner of his mouth. Stanton laughed louder as Bridey tried to push deeper into the chair in an effort to get away from the man. He waved Kelleher off.

"Go back up front where you belong and be a good boy. I'll call you if I need you." The grotesque giant squeezed back into the cockpit and closed the door behind him.

Tears welled up in Bridey's eyes. *What had she done? What did Edward plan to do to Cord? How could she have been so blind to Edward's hidden agenda?*

"Edward…" Bridey started to question him. Stanton banged his fists on the arm of the chair and leapt to his feet. He moved to where he stood over Bridey, his furious face inches from her's.

"My name is Edson! Edson Lawrence Stanton the fifth. Stop calling me Edward."

Bridey pushed as far as she could into the seat to get away from the fury emanating from him. Then just as suddenly as he had jumped up, his face relaxed and a smile crept across his lips. He stood up, tugged imagined wrinkles out of his suit and returned to his chair.

Stanton settled back comfortably and said, "No sense crying now, my dear. You'll have plenty of time for that later when you find out my plans for your little boyfriend. Oh. And don't worry. I'll make sure you'll have a ringside seat." He chuckled and settled back. "You'd better get some rest. Things may get pretty hectic once we get to the ranch.

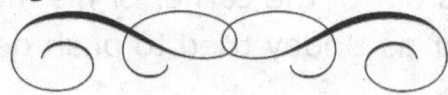

Cord couldn't shake the feeling that something was wrong. He'd left Bridey on Wednesday morning. By the time he got back to the ranch, he was instantly caught up in all the work that slipped while he was gone. But today he felt edgy, compelled to work at top speed and didn't understand why. He felt like something big was brewing.

Someone had messed up his paint order. Rather than cover his barn in the most noxious shade of green Cord had ever seen, the foreman of the repair job let the paint sit in cans. Cord was grateful to the man, but his sensible actions put them behind on all the other jobs. Assuming the painting would take all the time that he was gone, Cord had left no other instructions. The barn roof needed repairs and work on the house hadn't even started yet. Cord wanted everything done by the time the cold weather set in. But the contractor was, understandably, reluctant to start anything until he had Cord's final approval.

For three days, Cord had been running full speed, painting, sawing, hammering, running for supplies, and whatever else was needed. He barely had time to spend with Devil's Kin. Cord knew a few stolen moments were not enough. The horse was much calmer now, but not being able to work with the animal would set them back.

His frenetic energy wasn't good for gentling a horse. The more nervous or worried he was the harder to control the horse was. The barn had been whitewashed inside as well as cleaned and disinfected.

At night, Cord fell into bed, wishing like hell Bridey was there beside him. His arms ached to hold her as much as his body ached from the hard work he was doing each day. He meant to call her Thursday morning. Just as he picked up the phone, the sound of a large truck coming up the road brought him to the door. Fencing and more building supplies were being delivered along with the right color paint. Cord threw himself headlong into the job of getting everything organized.

The full-blown sense of foreboding overtook him in the middle of the day. A prickling feeling along the back of his neck, like something wasn't right, nagged at him. He walked through the house, outbuildings and the yards looking for signs of problems. He found nothing. Something was wrong somewhere. He felt dread deep in his gut. Half the night he was awake, walking the floor, thinking of Bridey. He finally fell into his lonely bed and slept fitfully.

Friday morning, several large trucks lumbered up the road to collect the scrap metal carcasses left by the previous owner from the yard. Cord worked beside the men all day, anxious to get the eyesores off his property. As soon as they left, he brought out the only piece of machinery that seemed to work, an old riding lawn mower. The blades needed to be sharpened badly, but the machine cut the grass that had grown wild for so many years.

The job took the rest of the day. Cord had to walk each part of the lawn before running the mower over each section. Hundreds of bits and pieces of decayed metal were hidden in the deep grass. Several times he stopped and searched the horizon. Adding to the sense of foreboding was a feeling of being watched. No one could sneak up on him here but he still felt as though he was being observed. After each scan of the horizon, he shook his head and turned back to his job. As he walked, his mind was on his Bridey. *What was she doing? Was she missing him as much as he missed her? Why hadn't she called him?*

Long after sunset, he crawled into bed, exhausted, but determined to call Bridey despite the time difference. He lifted the handset and punched the numbers. With a tired smile, he put the phone to his ear. No sound. He pressed the disconnect button and let go again. Still no sound. He pressed the button a few times in rapid succession to no avail. The phone was dead. He fell back to the bed thinking, *great! Phone's dead on a Friday night. I'll be lucky to get anyone out here before the end of next week.*

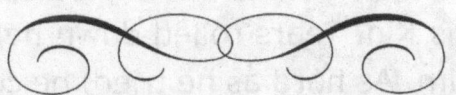

A few hours before Cord went inside for the night, a furtive man, at least half a mile down the road from the house, found the telephone juncture box. He knew no one was likely to see him, but he was careful anyway. This road might as well be abandoned for all the traffic that passed by him.

Carefully, he opened the box and surveyed the multitude of colorful wires inside the gray-green pylon. From that innocent looking little box, anyone who knew what he was doing could disconnect any phone he wanted. As he'd been instructed, he'd sat on the side of a hill all week, hidden behind a low rise, watching Cord work his property. The job was boring, but the money was great. He reported every little detail each morning and got new instructions for the day. This morning's orders were what he'd been waiting for. As soon as he cut the phone line, he was free to leave. *Too easy,* the man thought, as he walked back to his car.

Saturday and Sunday, Cord worked alone in the house. He was pleased with how well the job was going. The niggling sense of being watched was gone, but he couldn't shake the feeling something was wrong.

Saturday night he fell into bed, dreaming of Bridey. But this time, instead of being soft sensual dreams of loving her, he saw her dressed in an elegant gown, stained with dirt and mud. She was sitting on the back of his Kin. Tears rolled down her face as she reached for him. As hard as he tried, he couldn't reach her hand. Something heavy sat on his chest, preventing him from helping himself. He was trapped and needed her help but, if she got down, her life would be in danger. His hands ached as though they'd been badly cut or as if he'd been fighting with someone. He saw himself reach out to her and whispered, "I need you to take my hand." He woke from the dream, drenched in sweat, more convinced of the dread he felt had to do as much with Bridey as with himself. As soon as he got dressed, he climbed into his truck and headed for town to find a phone. He just needed to hear her voice. Since this was Sunday, he knew she'd be with her grandfather. Cord cursed himself for not having that number. He'd leave a message for her, trying not to frighten her. At least, she'd get his message and know why he hadn't contacted her. And how much he missed her, loved her.

Cord was just about to start the truck when he heard the sound of a small plane flying overhead. He looked out the windshield and saw a low-winged, fourseater plane circle a few times as if looking for a place to land. Cord thought he heard the engine sputter a few times. Maybe the plane was in trouble. He watched until he was sure the plane was landing just over the hill.

Half listening for the sound of an explosion, Cord started the engine and gunned the motor. He topped the hill just in time to see the plane roll to a stop at the bottom. The pilot climbed out and looked around as if lost.

Another tourist, Cord thought in disgust, probably flying off course on some sightseeing tour. He drove more carefully down toward the plane. The pilot waved at him and leaned back against the machine. As Cord pulled up nearby, he saw a side door open.

An enormous man wedged himself out of the tiny cockpit and dropped clumsily to the ground. Hat pulled down over his forehead, the giant hurried toward the bushes and disappeared behind them. Cord smiled at the thought of the big man answering nature's call in the brush. Some people just couldn't handle a little excitement. With a shake of his head, Cord turned his attention back to the plane.

The pilot reached a hand into the back of the machine as if to help someone out. Cord's eyes flew open as he saw Bridey's red head pop out of the door. Behind her another man appeared. Stanton! Cord slid out of the truck and started to run as Bridey screamed his name.

"Run, Cord! Get out of here!" Stanton reached forward and struck the back of Bridey's head. She slumped to the ground. Cord's rage burst wide open. He raced toward the plane without any thought but to save Bridey. Well-hidden by the scrub brush, the large man who'd appeared so big and clumsy stuck an iron arm out in front of Cord just as he passed him. The arm caught Cord in the throat, knocking him backward. Cord felt as if he'd been hit by a large stone. The ground knocked his breath from his body. He tore his eyes away from Bridey's limp form and looked up at the man who towered over him, an ugly sneer on his scarred face.

Oh God, no! Kelleher! Slowly, everything began to make horrible sense. Kelleher was with Stanton and Stanton had Bridey. They'd used her to find him. Smiling broadly, Kelleher lifted a huge meaty fist and slammed it into Cord's face. Cord's last thought as he fought the darkness was of Bridey.

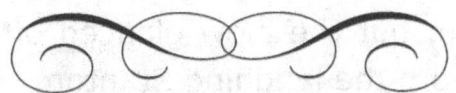

"Nice little place you got here, Grant." Stanton's voice was politely conversational as he watched Cord struggle back to consciousness. "Too bad you had to be so careless about letting people know." Cord tested his bonds. The stiff material around his wrists felt sticky and wide.

Probably some of the duct tape lying around here, Cord thought. *Nice job, Cord, why didn't you just give them a loaded gun?* Seeing Stanton in his little house made the bile rise in his throat.

From the carpet, Cord looked up to see a ghoulish grin on Stanton's face as he stood over him. Behind Stanton, Bridey lay motionless on the same sofa where he himself had lain her so many weeks ago. Near the door, Kelleher smiled and cleaned his nails with a sharp knife. The shining steel flashed dangerously each time Kelleher moved to a new nail.

Stanton leaned down and sneered at Cord, "Did you really think I'd give up tryng to find you? If you did, you're a fool. No one takes from me what is mine. The police may not be interested in you any longer, but I never forget debts that I'm owed ... and you owe me everything. By the way, how do you like these classy boots? Nice, aren't they."

Cord watched the silver toes of the sharply pointed cowboy boots as Stanton drew back his foot and aimed the metal toe squarely at Cord's chest. He stiffened and waited for the shoe to connect with his body. The pain was inevitable, but the blow glanced off him as Cord rolled away from the laughing Stanton.

"Now, we have a choice here. Just like before." Stanton strolled over and sat down on a wooden chair. "I can either return both of you to the scene of the crime and make you live it all over again or I can just kill you here." He looked up. "What do you think, Kelleher? Which would be more fun? Let them agonize for a while or get it over quickly."

Kelleher cackled like a little kid. "I don't care as long as I get to do 'em."

Stanton smiled like an indulgent father. "Now, isn't that great." He looked pointedly at Cord. "A man who knows how to defer to his betters. Kelleher, you restore my faith in Mankind."

Laughing, Stanton stood again and sauntered over to where Bridey lay. He gently stroked her cheek. "Too bad. She really is quite lovely." He turned on his heel and headed for the exit Kelleher opened for him.

"You wait outside the door. We'll give our lovebirds a last few minutes alone. I have to talk to the pilot about getting us out of here. We'll take them back to the scene of the crime. I think that's so much more fitting. Besides, I've always thought the anticipation of something was so much better than the actual performance."

Stanton walked away without further comment. Kelleher looked down at Cord, over at Bridey, and then back to Cord. He licked his thick lips, wiggled an eyebrow at him with a mean smile and followed

Stanton through the opening. As the door closed solidly behind them, Cord shuddered to think what was going on in the thug's mind. He had to get Bridey out of here.

"You are the song I love to play.
You are the movie I never get tired of.
You are the book I can never put down.
You are the one I will love forever." –
Anon

Eighteen

Cord rolled to his feet and staggered over to where Bridey lay. Pale and drawn, Cord was afraid she wouldn't respond to his voice.

"Bridey? Bridey, wake up! Are you OK, Baby?" Cord nudged her with his shoulder, trying to shake her awake as best he could. Her eyes fluttered open. Bridey threw her arms around his neck, sobbing out loud. He murmured sweet sounds in her ears.

"Oh, God, Cord, what have I done? I didn't know. Honestly, I didn't know. He seemed so nice. He offered to fly me here to be with you." Between words, Bridey covered Cord's face with short kisses.

Cord leaned away from her, trying to get her to understand their time was limited. "It's too late to worry now, Bridey. You've got to help me get us out of here. Can you do that? Are you OK?"

"Just a little dizzy is all. He hit me hard." Bridey rubbed the back of her head. She shook her head gently as if trying to clear a fog. "He said he knew you, very well. Does he? What is he to you?"

Bridey sobbed anew when she noticed his face, black and blue with bruises, one eye swollen shut. His lip was cut and bleeding. "Oh my God, your face. What did he do to you?"

Cord smiled a lopsided, painful grin. "We don't have time for me to tell you everything right now. We've got to get out of here. There's a knife over there in the drawer. See if you can cut this tape apart." Cord turned around so she could see his bound hands. "Hurry. They'll be back any minute. They're planning to kill us just like they did my parents."

Bridey stood and swayed a little.

"Careful," Cord cautioned her. "Don't stand up too quickly." She crawled over to get the knife. Sawing at the tough tape, she paused and asked, "This is about your parents, isn't it?"

Cord nodded and Bridey resumed her work. The tape gave way reluctantly after a few minutes of vigorous sawing on Bridey's part. As soon as he felt the bind give, Cord turned and grabbed her by the shoulders.

"I told you we don't have time to fill you in on everything now, but yes. Stanton killed his father, my parents, his stepmother and tried to kill me all because he was jealous of his father's interest in my career. He even convinced the police I killed his stepmother. He's a vicious evil man, Bridey. We have to get out of here." Cord tried to pull the sticky tape off his hands. The adhesive held tightly. Rather than waste more time, he let the gray shreds hang and ran to a corner of the room. Near the wall lay a little oval braided rug that he nudged aside with his foot. Underneath was a small trap door. Cord lifted the hatch.

"I found this a few days after I moved in. There's a kind of root cellar down there. Whoever built this place was either a misplaced miner or just paranoid about being trapped in the house. On the back wall, hidden behind a tall storage cabinet, is a tunnel out to a little hill behind the house. Some small bushes hide the door on the outside. It's the only other way out of here."

Bridey looked into the opening. She shuddered at the gaping hole, darkly festooned with spider webs and dust. The dirt floor was only a short drop but the room below looked so small. She wondered if Cord would be able to stand upright in the hole. Cord gave Bridey a quick peck of a kiss, wrapped his arm over his chest to protect his aching ribs and leapt in. Quickly, he turned and held his arms up to catch Bridey as she jumped in behind him.

"Now, hold the cover up until I find the flashlight I left down here." Bridey could hear him searching around. "Here it is. I'll need the light from up there to move the shelf. I'm not sure how fresh these batteries are so I don't want to turn on the flashlight until we need it. You wait here. Drop the hatch right away if you hear the door open. Do you see the lock bolt on the side there?" Bridey nodded.

"Lock it behind us. Hopefully, that will slow them down a bit." Cord gasped out the words as he struggled to move the heavy wooden storage cabinet. Slowly, he pushed and shoved until the large closet slid far enough for him to squeeze through. He called back to Bridey. "OK, grab that edge of the rug and close the hatch. Hopefully, the rug will hide the hatch long enough to buy us some time."

Bridey closed the cover. Darkness wrapped itself around her. The air smelled stale, like wet dirt and moldy food. She knew Cord's hand would be the only source of warmth in the place. He spoke to her in the darkness. She let his voice guide her and found his outstretched hand waiting for her. She took the long fingers in hers and felt his warm lips come down on them.

"And Bridey? In case I forget to tell you. I love you. Somehow some way, we're going to stay together." Bridey smiled at his voice. "Seeing you fall out of that plane did the trick for me. I just can't leave you alone. You get into too much trouble. I'll go to New York. Maybe we can buy somewhere nearby, like Virginia or Maryland, for Kin and my dreams."

Bridey raised the clasped hand to her own lips and kissed his fingers. He gently pushed her toward the tunnel.

"Not now. Let's get out of here. I'm right behind you." Bridey slipped in, took a few steps and leaned against the dirt wall. She heard Cord step in behind her and heard him trying to move the heavy cabinet back into place.

He cursed softly. "I can't move it back from here. Let's go." He slipped by Bridey grabbing her hand again as he passed her. A few feet down the narrow tunnel, Cord flicked the flashlight on. He knew the dry creek bed that hid the other end of the path from the tunnel was about 40 yards behind the house. By his reckoning, the run was about a fifty-yard dash to the barn. With the creek bed for cover, they should be able to get to the structure unseen.
Once in the barn, they had a better chance to get away.

Cord whispered his plan out loud. "If we can get to the barn and if I can get a leg over Kin, we can ride to the next place and get help."

"How far is it?"

"Only about a mile to the west of us."

"Have you ridden Kin yet?" Silence met Bridey's ears.

"We have to keep moving." Bridey felt Cord's taped hand take hers and pull her further down the tunnel stretching ahead of them, deep and dark. Rotten wooden boards held back the dirt at irregular intervals. Bridey bumped into the first one. A scattering of dirt and pebbles fell down on them.

"Careful," Cord whispered. Bridey smiled ruefully at the idea of someone digging for treasure in this rich farmland. What was he looking for? Gold? Diamonds?

Her musing was interrupted by the sound of crashing furniture behind them that broke the dark silence. Bridey cringed at the sounds of Stanton screaming and raving at Kelleher to find them. How could she have misread him so badly? Without a word, both of them moved more quickly away from the sound.

They heard Kelleher's triumphant cry out when he found the trap door. The sounds of heavy thuds as he jumped and kicked at the old wood echoed the tunnel. Bridey's grip on Cord's hand tightened as they heard the old boards give under his weight.

They'd just reached the outside door when they heard the cabinet crash to the ground behind them. Footsteps scrambled up the dark tunnel behind them, Stanton screaming filthy vile things at Cord and Bridey.

Cord unlatched and pushed the heavy doors open to daylight, thanking God no one had locked the exit from outside. Pulling Bridey up the few dirt steps behind him, he quickly dropped the old, weathered doors again. Just as he slid the bolt home, he heard Kelleher throw his weight against the door. They ducked away as bullets flew, splintering the old wood.

"You bastard. You stinking sniveling coward!" Stanton screamed. "Get back here. I'll kill you both. I swear I'll strangle you myself." Stanton's oaths and threats continued as they heard him race back down the tunnel toward the house.

Cord grabbed Bridey's hand and sprinted down the creek bed toward the barn, half dragging her behind him. In the pasture near the barn, Devil's Kin stood watching them run, ears flicking back and forth nervously. With no time to spare, Cord vaulted over the high wooden fence, groaning at the pain in his ribs. Calling to his horse, he waited to catch Bridey if she fell as she jumped off the top rail. They heard the two men burst from the house. Stanton still screaming their names. Cord pressed Bridey to the ground. Staying as low as possible, they crawled toward the barn, hoping shadows would hide them a few moments longer.

For those few precious seconds, the two men searched for the tunnel's end. Screaming at the top of his lungs, Stanton found the end of the tunnel and began firing his gun into the wood in anger. Cord saw Kelleher stop him and pointed at the black horse running toward Cord and Bridey.

"Shit!" Cord cried and grabbed Bridey's hand again. They fell against the small side door, pushed the wood and crawled into one of the stalls, collapsing breathless on the straw in the darkest corner. Cord wrapped his arm tighter across his chest, trying to keep the radiating pain at bay a little longer. The sound of Kin's cantering hoofs stopped just short of the door. A playful whinny sounded through the opening as if asking what this new game was.

"Now what?" Bridey whispered, hoping Cord had a plan.

Kin's whinny turned to a snort at the same time Cord heard Stanton's voice. Hoof beats raced away to the other end of the corral.

From outside the barn, they heard Stanton laugh. "This is too good. Too good!" He laughed the manic high-pitched cry of a madman. "You just stay in there. Both of you. I'll send your horsie in and we'll play bonfire. You remember what happened the last time we played bonfire, don't you Grant? Don't you!"

The big door to the paddock slid open. A few moments later, a gun fired three quick shots. Devil's Kin raced through the barn door, passed their hiding place, down the end of the center aisle. He stopped against the back wall, snorting and throwing himself against the wood trying to find a way out. The front door slid halfway closed again. Kelleher's joined Stanton's laughter.

Bridey pointed to the excited horse and whispered, "Cord! He's going to hurt himself." Cord held a handout to silence her and stood up. He looked toward the door to see if either man stood there. Neither was close enough to see him.

"Kin! Kin!" Slowly, Cord stood and called softly to the horse. For a few long minutes, the horse didn't react to him. His ears flickered back and forth in fear and fury until he caught the sound of Cord's magic whisper. "Kin! I'm here. Right here. Easy, Son. Be easy!"

Cord stepped out into the aisle, his back to the door. Bridey nervously tried to watch both the door and the horse. As Cord spoke, Kin whirled to face him. Cord and Bridey both held their breath, waiting to see if the horse would recognize the man who saved him or him attack as an intruder. Kin's nostrils flared, testing the air for familiar scents. Finally, he arched his neck and came toward Cord with the mincing little steps of a nervous horse. When he reached the man, the big horse put his head on Cord's chest and breathed deeply. Both Cord and Bridey let the breaths they had held so long go.

"Cord! Can you smell that?" Bridey whispered as loudly as she dared.

Cord whirled around. "Gasoline! He must have found the extra gas cans. That's how he killed my family and my other horse. He locked them in the house and the barn and set the buildings afire. We have to get out of here. Now."

Bridey ran to the aisle and looked carefully out the window near the door. She saw Kelleher tearing apart bales of straw and scattering them near the walls of the barn while Stanton danced around behind him sprinkling gasoline from a red can on the loose straw. As he danced, Stanton made up grotesque little songs. "Oh, Cord boy, oh Cord boy, won't you please come out and play" and "Little Bridey, little Bridey, oh my darling little Bridey, you'll soon be dead and gone forever alone with your lover."

"He's completely mad," Bridey called to Cord. The fumes were getting stronger. Kin was beginning to fidget again.

"He's been that way for a long time. Stay where you are. I know I can get a halter on Kin, but he may not like when I try to mount. Stay over there where it's safer."

Cord slipped the rope over the nose and ears of Kin who stared at the door as if transfixed. Every few seconds, his muscles twitched, but he held his ground as Cord crooned and stroked him.

From the back of the barn, they heard the massive door slide open. Stanton's voice echoed in, "I want to hear them burn, Kelleher. Pull that door open!" Both of the mad men cackled with glee.

"This is it, Big Guy." Cord whispered to the anxious horse. "I need you now more than you can know. You're the only hope we have of getting out of here. If you're ever going to trust me, please, please make it now.
Steady, steady."

His ribs still hurt too much to vault on to the broad back. Cord gently pushed the horse sideways to the stack of hay bales beside the stall. The bales reached from floor to roof. He stacked one on top of another and pushed the horse closer to them. Cord stood on top of the two wobbly bales for a moment to control his pain before he jumped.

Outside, Stanton threw the first match onto the gasoline-soaked straw. With a loud whoosh, the straw burst into flames. Thick black smoke poured in the door. Kin reared high into the air, knocking Cord backwards against the bales. The unsteady haystack collapsed and Cord disappeared underneath.

Bridey screamed. Cord's arm stuck out from under the bales, his fist clenching the rope reins. Bridey ran to dig him out. Moving aside the heavy bales, Bridey found Cord gasping for air as the horse danced around perilously close to him.

"Get back!" he cried to Bridey, afraid she'd be trampled. "Get back!" Bridey ignored his order and tried to lift him up. The cry of pain proved he'd done more damage to his ribs.

"What's wrong?" Bridey asked.

"Ribs. Stanton cracked a couple when he kicked me and I think I may have completely broken them now." Cord grimaced with pain at every word.

"He kicked you? With those boots? Damn his black soul."

Bridey looked up at the dancing horse and then back at Cord. Without a second thought, she grabbed the reins from Cord's hand. When he saw what she was about to do, he struggled to sit up and stop her. Afraid to cry out for fear of spooking the nervous horse again, Cord watched as Bridey walked to the sweating horse. Kin stood flinching, ears twitching, watching her every move. She whispered to him, trying to mimic the soft sounds Cord had made. Cord pulled himself over to a nearby railing and used the roughened wood to get to a sitting position.

Billows of smoke began roiling in the door. The quivering Kin stood his ground as Bridey reached up to pat his neck and sooth him. Patiently, she worked her way over to his shoulder and wrapped the rope reins around his neck. Quietly, trying not to let her own panic show, she led Kin over to a fence around a stall. He stood still for her. Cord held his breath, willing the nervous horse to stay still. With one look over her shoulder at Cord, Bridey clambered up on the rails. Without pause, she threw her leg across Kin's wide back. The horse ignored her slight weight.

Kin tensed every muscle. Seconds crawled by as Cord watched the woman he loved on the back of a horse no one had ever ridden. She clucked her tongue and Kin stepped forward toward Cord. With a mighty struggle, Cord got himself upright.

Bridey positioned the quivering horse next to Cord and looked down at him.

"Ride on," he said to her, indicating the open door. "Just put your head down and kick him hard. He'll run through the flames and clear the fence easily. The next ranch is just over the hill to the west. Go!"

Bridey shook her head. "We have to go together. We belong together." She slid forward as far as she could on the horse's shoulder, giving Cord enough room to slide on. He struggled to step up on the bales, still holding the fence rails. Smoke billowed around them. Another whoosh let them know Stanton had added more fuel to the fire.

"Come on," she yelled over the sound of the rapidly closing flames and Stanton's maniacal laughter. "Come on!"

He looked at her with pain-filled eyes. "I need your help! Please take my hand."

Bridey gasped. The dirty hand, the gray strips of tape that looked like a tattered glove, the bare forearms and the pleading voice. This was it. This was what the dream was preparing her for. This was her destiny.

She grabbed his hand and pulled as she held the big horse steady. As soon as she felt Cord slide in behind her and wrap his arms tightly around her waist, she dug her heals into Kin's side. The horse responded immediately, jumping forward with a scream toward the gaping door.

Stanton, never having understood horses, stepped out of the smoke directly in front of the racing horse. Kin never hesitated. Stanton threw his arms up and the horse reared. Kin came down with both front feet planted firmly in the middle of Stanton's chest. The sound of bones cracking and flesh tearing met Bridey's ears as the horse reared twice more. She felt Cord begin to slip behind her. Her heels pressed hard into the horse's sides as she urged him to move on.

Kelleher was so surprised that he stood stock still as the horse came toward him. He dropped the gun and ran for the fence as fast as his thick legs would carry him. Unable to climb the fence in his fear, Kelleher slid down the fence post, blubbering into the dirt. Kin reared up once more. The crack of hooves meeting bone reverberated through the air as Kin whirled and ran to the open gate.

Stanton lay in the doorway. Blood covered his chest where the horse had trampled him. He turned his head to watch the two, still astride the horse riding away from him. His eyes drifted down to the every-widening bloodstains on his chest. With a weak voice loaded with confusion, he shook his head.

"No," he whined, "the cannot happen. Not to me." Slowly, the flames reached his gasoline-soaked clothing and began to climb his legs.

Katherine urged Kin on toward the neighboring farm. Behind her, she felt Cord's grip loosen slightly. He moaned in pain but held on tight.

"My love for you is a journey starting at
forever and ending at never.
Anon

Nineteen

Bridey sat in the shade of the veranda that wrapped itself around the house. The late summer sun dipped low in the sky reminding Bridey of the first time she'd seen Cord. A breeze trifled with her hair as she watched the man she adored riding toward her astride the huge horse he called Devil's Kin. The stallion stepped delicately across the yard as if aware of the precious cargo he carried. Cord, controlling the animal with his knees, wrapped his arms around their nineteen month old daughter. Michela Deane Grant laughed as her father kicked the horse into a canter as smooth as a rocking chair. As they got closer, the little girl waved and cried, "Mama! Mama!"

Bridey waved back at her, marveling at the sheer beauty of the sight. She shook her head to think of how close she'd come to giving this up just to pursue a career and how close she'd come to losing the father of her child. She rubbed her hand over her belly. Soon, she'd tell him his son was on the way.

Her smile broadened. Nothing, not the fame, the fortune or the money she'd given up could ever take the place of the look of the man in love when he found out his child was growing inside you.

Devil's Kin slowed his rolling canter near the veranda. Cord guided the big animal to the edge. Demanding his share of attention first, Kin dropped his nose into Bridey's lap and nudged her gently. Laughing, she reached up and scratched the sensitive spot behind his ears. The horse groaned his pleasure and closed his eyes.

"I swear he thinks this is all I am good for," Bridey smiled up at Cord who leaned over and stretched a handout to his wife.

"I can assure you he's wrong. Come up with us." He tugged on Bridey's hand until she stood beside him.

"Come, Mama. Come up." Michela laughed, clapping her hand.

Devil's Kin stood still as Cord stretched his booted foot out straight. Bridey stepped up and used the boot for a stirrup. Swinging her leg over the broad back, she settled in behind Cord and wrapped her arms around him.

"Hmmm," Cord murmured as she hugged him tight. Devil's Kin stepped out on their nightly trek to the top of the hill. Watching the sun go down on a pleasant summer evening from the top of the rise had become a habit for the little family.

The horse stood still and they watched in awe as the brilliant gold and rosy light colored the hills. Cord rubbed his wife's hands as they lay locked around his waist.

"Kinda makes you miss New York, doesn't it." He ducked his head as Bridey ripped her hand out and gently smacked the back of his head.

"I'll take that as a no."

"No. I don't miss New York," she whispered in reverence to the beauty of the sunset. "I love you. I must have been a fool to believe I couldn't be happy here. Thank you, my love."

Cord twisted halfway around and kissed his wife as best he could. "You are welcome." He looked into the moist green eyes. "I think Michela is pretty sleepy. Maybe she needs a nap."

Bridey reached up and kissed the tanned cheek. She nuzzled his ear and whispered, "Maybe we all do." Devil's Kin turned and carried them back down the hill.

"If kisses were the water, I'd give you the sea.
If hugs were leaves, I'd give you the tree.
And if love was time, I'd give you eternity.
Anon

2168 – Ardrigan Quadrant

Lt. Commander Kat York strode down the barren hallway to her rooms. Button after button slipped out of its hole loosening the uniform she had worn for the last 26 hours. This had been a long shift and tested her meddle as a leader in more ways than one.

She smiled broadly, full of confidence and pride that she had proven her capabilities on this day. Her team reacted to her directions like the well-oiled entity they had become. No one questioned a single order nor shirked their duties. Even her curmudgeonly chief, who outdid her in age and experience but not rank, nodded at her as she left the command deck. High praise from such a surly old man.

She should be thinking of her bed and a hot shower, but her mind was filled with much more exciting thoughts. Her nightly trip to the holodeck was waiting. And that touch. His touch. She shivered in excitement. The door swept open as she reached her rooms. She stepped into her Spartan cabin staring into the holodeck portal on her wall. He wasn't here yet. She had time to prepare. She let the uniform drop unceremoniously to the shelf near the door, crossed the room and stepped into the clean room. After a brief wash off and blast from the air dryer, she walked into the dressing room and pulled out the emerald-colored diaphanous caftan. She watched the cool fabric drift down over her nude body in the mirror. She released the pins that had held back her thick red waves and let them tumble down her back. Another quick shudder of anticipation raced through her as she returned to the holodeck wall.

She pushed in her security codes and stepped back to enjoy the view. Moments later, the lights on the holodeck lit up in a golden sunset color. Before her stood a garden, rich, verdant and heavy with the smell of tropical flowers. In the center she saw a man with his back to her.

Broad of shoulder, slender of hip, the gold light glinted off his oddly silver hair. She could see his arms moving in front of him. She cleared her throat softly and the man turned his head. His brilliant blue eyes lit up at the sight of her. He turned and continued rolling his sleeves to the elbow just like he knew she loved.

She sighed deeply, enjoying the vision of her husband. There he was—man who made her feel complete. The instant they met, they'd had an immediate connection neither of them totally understood but hadn't even tried to fathom. Their friends made jokes that the rest of the world simply disappeared when they caught sight of each other. From that moment, they were in their own world – a small bubble of joy made just for them – whenever possible.

Now even though they were stationed hundreds of miles apart in different quadrants of space, thanks to the holodeck, they could meet every evening.

"Are you just going to stand there?" He asked, holding out his hand and waiting for her to step forward. "Come on Katherine. Its time."

She smiled and stepped into the glorious arms of the man she had been born to love.